D1563106

IN THE BACK OF MY HEAD

A NOVEL

I.Y. MASLOW

Dedicated to Shimi; never confuse love with *love*.

The Defeatist

The story I'm about to share with you has an awful message.

One I do not agree with.

One you might not agree with.

It's riddled with twists and turns, and will leave you guessing until the very end.

You may get irritated at certain points.

But you wouldn't be here if you weren't curious.

Curious for this story.

Curious for the truth.

Curious for what really happened that night.

I buried all the answers alongside your sister and my wife, long ago. Hoping they'd never resurface.

But they have.

Children are dead.

Finn is missing.

And sadly, Cole's at the center of it all.

You're not going to like what I have to say; but remember, no one is forcing this onto you.

You asked for this…

Part 1

I remained too much inside my head and ended up going insane.
-Edgar Allen Poe

The Existentialist

My vision is blurry, but I can make out a blurry figure standing in front of me. The rough concrete I sit on is cold, and the brick wall my back is propped up against is coarse. A soft, tender hand is wrapped around my wrist, lifting it. There's a certain familiarity to this hand, which eases my nerves. That ease fades when I feel a pinch in my forearm—a syringe. The pinch feels reminiscent of the flu shot the doctor gave me last September. Regardless, at eight years old, I know this shot won't help me fight the flu.

"I-I already got the flu shot," I whimper.

The blurred figure holding my wrist pats my head. "Everything is going to be okay." The honeyed voice is reassuring.

The figure removes the syringe and I feel as if it is 2:00 a.m., when I'm usually asleep. My head drops, but I swiftly raise it. I'm resisting the urge to sleep.

There's a disembodied voice mumbling to my right, or is it my left? I've always struggled differentiating between the two. As I tilt my head right, it feels like a sack of rocks and my neck can't support this change in weight. My head drops against my shoulder.

"Protect." The voice is brittle, not like the voice of the blurry figure. I want to ask her what she's saying, yet for some reason the words are unable to form in my mouth, almost as if my brain stopped sending signals to my lips. "Protect…"

Who? Who should I protect?

The familiar tender hand grabs my other wrist and ties something around the midsection of my arm, causing it to quiver. I feel another prick. He's injecting something in me.

Before my grandmother died, she was brain dead. I was in the room when they 'pulled the plug', and I wondered what she was feeling in those last moments. I imagine it feels something like I'm feeling now.

I hear the voice again. "Protect… protect her, protect…"

There's another person in the room—the blurry figure—yet I know she's talking to me. But why is she asking an eight-year-old to protect anyone?

On the verge of drifting off she says, "Protect Olivia."

I awaken from a resounding knock, and opening my eyes I see the sun beaming in through a window behind me. I scan my surroundings. I'm in my room. It's morning.

It was just a nightmare. The same annoyingly recurring one I've had since I was eight years old. Like a dog playing fetch, they come and go, never leaving me. They re-emerged months ago and my dad had to remind me, as real as they seem, they aren't.

Mrs. Freed, my psychologist, taught me how to differentiate between reality and imagination. She reminds me: *if something seems far-fetched, bizarre or scary, then it's not real.*

"Wake up, you're going to be late for your first day of 12th grade."

"I'm up, Dad!" I shout, like I do every morning. I rise from bed and yawn while stretching my arms outwards, shaping a *Y*. After getting dressed, I head downstairs, greeted by the fresh aroma of cinnamon. Sitting at the kitchen table, Dad places a fresh plate of French toast in front of me. My favorite.

"French toast? What's the catch?"

"Who says there has to be a catch?" Dad asks.

"You always talk to me about being open with you, trusting you. If you have something to ask me, ask."

"Okay. Okay." Dad throws his arms up like he's guilty of a crime. "You caught me." He drags the chair outwards from the table and sits across from me. "You're about to start school, 12th grade to be more specific. It's your last year of high school, you've made it so far and I am so proud of you."

"I sense a but coming."

"But towards the end of last year you stopped putting an effort into your school work. I know you struggle academically. You're street smart, not school smart. But I really want you to try."

"I don't see a point in trying. I either fail, or just pass."

"I know. And I don't care about your grades. It's about what trying means. It's better to have tried and failed than to have never tried at all."

"Isn't the saying 'it's better to have loved and lost than to have never loved at all'"?

"You know, you're probably right, but my point still stands." Dad laughs then continues, "Please Cole, for me."

"Okay Dad, I'll try … for you." I reach for the plate of French toast.

"I almost forgot; I got your favorite syrup."

"You should have started with that."

When we finish eating, I grab our plates along with the utensils, bringing them to the sink to wash. Once I finish, I head to the bus stop, ready for the first day of school.

I get off the bus and stare at the building, trying to gain the courage to walk in. I hate this place.

Despise. Hate is an extreme negative. Remember what Mrs. Freed said; negative thoughts lead to a negative being.

Okay. I despise this place.

It's difficult to focus with all the clamoring in the hallway. Everyone bad-mouths each other behind their backs. Mrs. Freed taught me that if you hear negative voices, they are a product of your imagination. That advice is great except that in high school every voice is negative.

I miss summer vacation. I know, how typical, but before you form preconceptions of me you should know why I miss summer. All summer I was isolated, only leaving my house to visit Green Point Lake. It was nice being alone. Easy. I find comfort in it. The only people I saw, I knew were real: Dad and Nate. I'm not inept at making friends, in fact I have quite a few. Even so, teenagers are mostly a homogeneous breed, which bothers me. Most people my age, well ... they act my age. I don't. They like video games, drama, partying. There were plenty of boisterous parties over the summer, none of which I went to, although I was invited.

School's going to start soon. You should get going, sweetie.

You're right.

Plodding toward the intimidating building, my legs wobble. The brown metal doors are wide open, and banners dangle from the ceiling; welcoming students back. There's a certain scent to this building and I don't know how to explain it. Honestly, I don't know where it's coming from but whenever I'm here I smell it. In fact, whenever I'm in any school, I smell it.

Lockers cover every inch of these walls. Breezing along them I stop by the only unlockered wall in this building. Signup sheets are posted here: chess club, tennis, debate team, etc. I run my hand through my hair, trying to relax myself. I can't think about extracurricular when I'm already struggling with regular curricular.

"Cole, what's up?"

Turning around, I spot Nate and shrug, "I think I need to find a tutor." I want better grades this year.

"Tutor?" Nate laughs. "We're seniors now. There's no time for studying. This year *we* run the school. I heard there's going to be a 'back to school' party," Nate winks, "at Sam's house. You should come."

"You know I don't like parties."

13

"Right, but I think it would be good for you to get out of your comfort zone."

I shove my hands in my pocket. Me being around this many people is out of my comfort zone.

"You know," Nate says, "you have broad shoulders, muscular arms, and though I've never seen you shirtless, I'm pretty sure you have abs. You could have any girl in this school. If I were you I'd be getting laid every day."

"I'd like to believe high school isn't that superficial," I say. "And, besides, you know that's not why I work out."

"I know," he says. "I just think you should enjoy this year. Come to the party. Don't spend all your time alone."

Maybe he's right.

"I can come over to your house after school, and we could study together."

I appreciate the sentiment. Nate's grades, while half decent, are better than mine. Nonetheless, when we are together, there's more talking than studying. Which isn't his fault. We both tend to get distracted.

"That's okay Nate. I think I'll study alone."

Nate places his hand on my shoulder. "Everything okay?"

"Yeah, it's just…"

"I know."

He hugs me and I realize we are getting too sentimental in a high school. "I'm going to head to class, I want to get there early."

While strolling to class, I notice Emily standing by the entryway to our classroom. When she spots me, her sky-blue eyes fixate on mine. I try maintaining eye contact but get distracted by her buoyant blonde hair. She enthusiastically waves at me the same way a toddler waves their parents hello.

I hope to get out of this conversation as soon as possible. She isn't an annoying person; actually, she's extremely nice, and outgoing, which is the problem. Every time I talk to her, I leave feeling like crap.

"Hi Cole, how was your summer?"

"Good, and you?"

"Amazing, my father flew me to Africa. I built huts for the villagers there. It was a challenge, but the smile on their faces made my summer."

"Oh, that's really nice." My eyes shift to the lustrous silver cross on her chest. I wonder if it is real silver, then I remember who I'm talking to and I know it is real silver.

Emily coughs.

I realize I've been gawking at her chest. She probably thinks I'm a pervert.

"It's real… the necklace, I mean."

In case there was any misunderstanding.

Despite what just happened, I'm not usually this awkward with girls. It's these dreams. Ever since they resurfaced, I haven't been myself. I'm hoping that changes soon.

I walk into the classroom, and Emily follows. I place my bag on one of the desks and on the desk closest to mine, Emily sits.

"Hey Emily, you're on the honor roll, right?"

"Yeah, I've been on it since eleventh grade. My parents are really proud. It's a challenge to stay on, but worth it."

I think everything is a challenge with her.

Cole, that's mean. Stop.

Ok fine.

"Do you think you could tutor me?" I ask.

"Oh Cole, I'd love to!" The smile on her face is more eager than her tone. Can a person really be this perky?

"Great."

"There's just one catch. You'd have to join my celibacy club."

I laugh, hysterically. She doesn't. She can't be serious.

"My dad is very strict with boys. Especially boys who don't go to church. He'd make an exception if you were in the celibacy club."

15

Jesus. I'm all for religion, just not when it's pressured onto people. Let them decide for themselves. I'm all for getting my grades up, but I'm not going to join a club I don't believe in.

Mr. Rodriguez enters and class begins.

When the weekend comes, I'm besieged with uncompleted school work. Every time I try completing it, my mind drifts off to the nightmare. I'm plagued with them every night, and they're always the same—*Protect Olivia.*

Sleep is a daunting chore. My bed feels like a prison, my mind a cell, and I keep locking myself there. Choosing to suffer. Each morning I wake more exhausted than before. At school, it's a fight to focus on what's being taught. I'm still trying, like my dad wanted. I'm going to get good grades this year.

My phone buzzes; it's a text from Nate.

"You coming to this party? Ashley's here."

I *despise* parties. The alcohol, the blaring music, people shouting. That's the worst place someone like me can be. Yet I'm still shrugging my jacket on, heading towards the party. While I may despise parties, it's better than what's waiting for me in my dreams.

This party will be good for you.

You don't need to tell me that. I've already decided on going.

I walk to Sam's house. He lives in my neighborhood so it's not far. His house is one of the newer modern ones. It's perfectly square shaped, like something a kid would draw. The siding is dark oak wood and the roof is a large, concrete slab.

Setting foot inside, a light flickers above me. The floors creak below me, and the walls vibrate beside me. If this house wasn't bristling with teenagers, I would assume it was haunted. I'm not sure which I prefer.

"Cole, you made it!" Nate extols. "Get over here." He gestures for me to come closer.

16

Walking to Nate, the pungent smell of alcohol grows, making me wince.

"Glad you could make it. Have a drink," Nate says, as he passes me a beer.

"You know I don't drink," I reply, not grabbing the beer from his hand.

He drinks the beer he offered me. "Eh, more for me. Anyways, there's a keg I can't get on the table. I figure with your strength; you'd be able to."

Before I could respond, Nate cajoles, "Everyone, Cole's here!"

The house begins to roar, like fans in a stadium when their team scores a touchdown. Nate takes another sip of his beer. Continuing to speak—something he shouldn't do when drunk— he says, "Cole, I heard a rumor that Ashley's into you. You should totally ask her out." He puts his arms around my shoulders. With a can of beer in hand, he points across the spacious living room. "She's there in the corner now."

I reluctantly look in the direction he's pointing. A petite blonde girl grinding against two guys stares straight into my eyes. Then she wets her lips.

"I think I'll pass," I say.

"You've been stressed out since school started. You need something to relieve your stress... Or maybe *someone* to relieve your stress."

"That's disgusting," I reply, despising Nate when he's drunk.

"Whatever, you know what I mean."

Nate continues talking, but I tune him out. I can't take it in here. The music is ear-piercing. The odor is foul. The people are awful. I glance at my watch, five minutes passed since I walked through that door. Impossible. I feel like I've been here long enough to have reached the legal drinking age. I head outside and sit on the staircase, gazing at the unlit sky. I made a mistake coming here. I would've been better off at home.

"Need a break from all the drunk people?"

I turn around. An emerald-eyed girl stands beside the door. Judging by lack of odor and her standing still, not slurring her words, I conclude she's sober.

"Yeah," I say, "I don't really enjoy drinking."

"Then you chose the wrong house to come to."

"Says the mysterious sober girl."

"Touché," she smirks. "You're not going to ask why I'm not drinking?"

"Nope."

"Why not?"

"That's not really any of my business."

The mysterious brunette sits beside me.

"You're not going to ask why I'm not drinking?" I ask.

"I wanted to, but now I'd sound like an asshole."

We laugh.

"It's alright, I can't drink while on medication." Crap. Why did I tell her that? I cover my eyes. The only two people who know I take medication are Nate and my father. I don't know if it's her amiable smile or her long chocolate brown hair, but something about her makes me trust her.

She places her hand on my lap. "I've seen the dark sides of alcohol abuse. When you're in high school you think it's all fun and games, but when you're older and the addiction forms, it's less fun."

I'm resisting the urge to hug her, seeing as I just met her. Instead, I say, "Well, I'm glad you're out here, not drinking."

Her emerald eyes fixate on my hazel eyes. This time I don't struggle maintaining eye contact. Actually, it's hard looking anywhere but her eyes.

"Oh, I didn't catch your name."

"It's Olivia."

The Cynic

The cozy scent of coffee infuses the gloomy teachers' lounge. There isn't a soul in sight—a rare occurrence. No one grading papers, chatting, or eating. It is just…silent. Everyone is outside relishing the cloudless skies and the clement weather before the seasons shift. I take a deep breath, cherishing the stillness while it lasts.

"Mr. Haynes!" Devin shouts, bursting through the door, the gateway between my safe haven and the outside world. Panting, he begins, "There's a fight down the hall."

Goddamn it. The day has yet to begin. "Go call a teacher."

"I just did."

I grunt, "I haven't punched in yet." Which is a lie.

"So, punch in now and come help."

I give him a stare that must say enough because he leaves me alone. I don't understand what's wrong with two kids fighting. How else should they relieve their frustrations? Who am I to tell them not to? And if someone gets hurt, that's life. What could I do? I'm off shift.

It scares me, what the world has come to. Fights are what these rodents need. Every direction I look I see safe space posters, anti-hate speech; if you ask me, I think the world needs a little hate to keep it running. There's no good guy or bad guy, no love and hate. I refuse to see the world through black and white lenses

The irritating bell rings, pressuring me to head to class.

I arrive at the classroom five minutes late, hoping to use the students' tardiness to my benefit. Nope. Just my luck. A full class of students are seated, gazing at me as I walk in.

So much for wishful thinking.

"Good morning Mr. Haynes," Emily says.

Emily: the cold sore of my life.

"Huh? Oh right, good morning, Emily." I drone.

The dark, shabby bag my ex-wife gave me thumps as I place it on my desk. It's seen better days. I use it every day. I guess that makes me a decent ex-husband. I unclasp it, searching for my chalk. It squeals against the blackboard as I write: *review*. With school having started this week, the students—more accurately me—should ease into the school work. I figure I'd let them review amongst themselves while I get some shut-eye.

"Class, open up your textbooks, brush over and review everything you've learned last year." The musty textbooks we use are grade 11 and 12; they could pass for antiques.

"Mr. Haynes," Emily inserts. "We've learned nearly 400 pages worth of material last year."

"Jesus, Emily, I'm the teacher."

The class laughs quietly. Emily's face starts mirroring her strawberry red nail polish. She slides down in her chair, tucking her body under her desk.

I loathe every rat in this school, but the one I truly abhor is Emily. With all her self-righteousness, holier than thou, Jesus-loving bullshit. She really shoves it in my face, always having something to say about my teaching style. "It may be easier to learn if you make the kids in the back be quiet."

Oh, would it Emily? You think that would make it easier?

Fuck off.

How could a person be both a snarky bitch and quintessential kiss-ass at the same time? She radiates so much passive aggressiveness it's palpable.

During lunch, my burger sputters in the microwave so I take it out. Looking like an inflated balloon, I use my fork to poke a hole in it. White steam hisses out.

Holding my Rubbermaid, I search for a place to eat in the teachers' lounge; there's a couple of black leather couches and a coffee table, and in the center, a long cream-colored table with twelve office chairs around it. I choose the table.

The teacher sitting across from me sighs, then rises; looking for somewhere else to sit. The sound of a dolphin's squeaking makes me cringe. I tilt my head to the left. Keera and Jessica, who are both married—not to each other—are sitting beside Frank on the couch, reacting to something stupid he must've said. Frank's the school's gym teacher.

Jessica notices I'm staring at her. "What the hell do you want?"

I stare at Jessica, not saying anything. The bell rings again, lunch break is over. Jessica returns to her office.

After going to the bar and adding six beers to my tab, I drive home. I live on Roosevelt Road; a street in the nicer part of town. All the upper middle-class folks live here. The accountants, lawyers, and realtors. And then there's me, a single dad working as a teacher in a public school.

Pulling into the driveway, fatigue makes me park partially on the lawn. I own the property so if I really wanted, I could park entirely on the lawn. I trudge to the door and try to unlock it. The keys aren't fitting in the keyhole. I swear I'm not that drunk, someone must've changed the locks. Finally, the key enters the keyhole. I go in, throwing my keys onto the entryway table. I think I missed the table but I won't find out until tomorrow morning when I'm late to work. I'd like to be optimistic and think I won't be late but I've made quite the routine for myself, after all, we humans are habitual creatures. All the same, I've been late often enough to incorporate it in to my routine

Finn walks past me and closes the door. I thought I did that already.

He returns to the kitchen as I collapse onto the couch. Finn leaves the kitchen holding a glass of water with ice cubes in it.

"I know how much you like cold water, Sir." His prepubescent voice irritates me more than his lack of eye contact.

I gulp down the entire cup, then slam it on the end table beside the couch. Finn gazes at me, waiting for something.

"What?!"

Looking everywhere but at me, he says, "It's just…it's 7 o'clock and I didn't eat dinner yet."

"Ok, what do you want to eat?"

"I like breaded chicken."

"I don't know how to make breaded chicken. I can make you some macaroni and you can throw some cheese on it."

Finn starts tearing up; something that happens more than it should.

"Christ. What did I do now?"

"Nothing. It's just Mom, she used to always make breaded chicken. I miss her."

Why did he have to bring her up? The world is a cruel place. We don't always get what we want. I thought I taught him that, but I guess he still hasn't learned.

I stand up, towering over his young nine-year-old body.

"It's fine I'll have mac—"

Before he could finish speaking, my fist meets his face. Blood gushes down his nose. The red reminds me of the stripes on the American flag. "I do this because I love you," I say. "This is me showing you that I love you."

Love is something I teach him often. Real *love* at least. Not the mushy stuff you see on TV. Real love is rough, and ugly, and not something you want, but something you need.

I plod to the kitchen to make macaroni, which I guess is also a way of conveying my love for him.

Gasping for air he mutters, "I know you love me."

The Existentialist

Why am I here? How did I get here? Why am I tied up? And why is my heart beating louder than the blaring cars outside?

The biting coldness along with my exasperating anxiety cause me to shiver. Peering at the girl in front of me, I see she's tied up, lying on the floor. Even in her sleep she's panting, with sweat dripping down her arms. Besides her blanched face, and her short brown hair, her appearance parallels that of Olivia's.

I'm anxious to talk to her, to ask her questions. Yet I can't. I don't want to wake her because whenever she's awake, she screams in agony.

Her eyes open, meeting mine. They're green, just like Olivia's.

"Cole."

I observe her. How does she know my name?

"Cole."

What?

"Cole!"

I open my eyes, deliriously. Mr. Rodrigues stands in front of me, his mouth set in a hard line.

"You fell asleep in my class, again." His voice as bland as the impassive expression on his face.

He hands me my test. I failed. Of course, I failed, I spent three hours studying, why would I expect anything more than an *F?*

I examine the students in the long, narrow classroom. Their facial expressions tend to indicate the grades they receive. Judging from the smiles and the light in their eyes I deduct they've passed.

There's also the fact they're saying things like "easy A" and "senior year's going to be a breeze". But their facial expressions are what really led me to believe they passed.

I bury my face in my desk. The bell rings, but I can't bring myself to stand up. If that's an easy exam, what's going to happen when I get a hard one? I want this day—no, this *year*—to be over.

It's okay sweetie. Everyone has different difficulties. You just need to work harder.

"The bell rang you know. Don't you have classes to be at?"

Lifting my head, I see Olivia standing beside me, her brown hair wrapped in a pony. At the party, after she told me her name, in a panic, I told her I had to go. It was a lie. One I know was transparent. Now I'm surprised she still wants to talk to me.

"What's wrong?" She asks.

I thought she was referring to why I was staring at her, then I realize she's referring to the glum look on my face.

"I just failed one of the easiest tests of the year. At this rate I don't think I'm going to graduate."

"Did you study?" She asks.

"I studied and failed. I almost always do."

"It could be the location you're studying in isn't good. My house is loud, so I study at the library. It really helps me focus."

I scratch the back of my head. "I don't see how a place could help me study better."

"Hey, don't knock it till you try it. And if you're always failing, you have nothing to lose."

She's cute. I like her.

I usually study in my room. I never thought of studying anywhere else, but I have a science test coming up and being that it's my hardest subject, I know I'm destined to fail. Considering I have nothing to lose, I figure I'll accept Olivia's advice.

After school, I go to Green Point Lake. It's peaceful and calm here like my room, but unlike my room, the nightmares don't follow me here.

I'm surprised Mom's here.

I search for a rock to pick up and skip in the lake. It could just be me, but I feel like you can't stand idly beside a lake and not toss rocks in it.

"I heard you started school."

"I did."

Pointing to a flat rock on the ground, she asks, *"How'd it go?"*

I pick up the rock and skip it in the lake. It flaps against the water twice. "Not so well. But I met this girl; she's actually the reason I'm here."

"I know. Do you like this girl?"

"Mom, she's just a friend, if that."

"Whatever you say."

I sit on a log, bordering the leafy lake and Mom joins me. I thump my school bag on the ground, glancing at it, confirming nothing fell out. I come here often and whenever I do, I tend to lose things.

"You know these woods are not so safe, you should really bring some form of protection out here."

"Protection? What like a gun?" I chuckle.

"Not like a gun. Ophelia and I used to carry those little Swiss army knives when we were younger. I think Robert has a pocket knife with all his hunting equipment. You could carry one of those when you come here."

"I'll think about it."

I reach for my bag, unzip it, and take out my textbook. I need to study. The chattering animals, along with the rustling leaves, create a divine white noise. I feel absorbent out here. All my problems seem to gust with the wind and the only thing on my mind, is what's in front of me: a science textbook.

I return there every day for the next week. Studying, focusing, learning. I feel great. I feel content. For the first time in a while, I feel bliss.

My bed creaks as I collapse onto it. Tomorrow is the test. I've learned not to get my hopes up, seeing as there have been plenty of times I've studied abundantly hard, only to fail. As I sink into my bed, intoxicated by drowsiness, I fall asleep.

Days later I'm sitting in Mr. Kenyan's class. He hands me my graded test. I'm incredulous, I didn't just pass, I got a *B* plus – the highest grade I've received in a *long* time. I search the school looking for Olivia, finding her by what I presume to be her locker. As I lock my arms around her, she takes a deep breath.

Her face reddens and unable to tell if that's a good thing, I unlock my arms.

"I passed," I blurt, joyously. "Because of you I passed."

Her eyes crinkle. "That's great Cole. I'm happy to hear that."

"I need you to tutor me from now on."

Olivia chuckles. "I'd love to but I need to focus on my own studies. My dad is pushing me to get into NYU. I can't have any distractions. I'm sorry." She rubs her arm.

"Tutoring me would look great on your application. Taking a student with "learning disability" and helping him get straight *A*'s."

"'A learning disability'," she uses air quotes, chuckling. "Extracurriculars are great, but so are good grades. It's hard for me to focus on both."

"So don't tutor me. Let's have a study group together."

"We study at different paces."

"True, but I'll learn more studying with you than without."

I know I was being too insistent. I'd like to lie to myself and say it's because I need better grades. But I'm horrible at self-deception, at least intentional self-deception. The reason I want to study with Olivia is because I've noticed since I met her, my nightmares have been less frequent.

"Graduating this year means a lot to me. It would mean a lot to my dad too. I'd really appreciate it if you help me."

After nibbling on her bottom lip, she concedes. "Okay. But just know that while I want to help you, my grades come first. I need to get into a college next year. If you start slowing me down, I'm going to have to stop our study sessions."

"No problem. And I won't slow you down."

Olivia laughs. I realize I love her laugh.

"Did anyone ever tell you how tenacious you are?" she asks.

"Nope, if you could believe it."

"I can't." She laughs again. "So…our 'study group' it's just you and I?"

"If you want, I could get more people."

"No!" She blushes, embarrassed for blurting that out. Twirling her hair, she clarifies, "I mean we could study more efficiently if it's just the two of us."

I nod and smile. "I'd like that."

We plan on meeting at the library to study and as I'm getting ready to head there, I receive a phone call. It's my neighbor. Reluctantly, I answer.

"Cole, hey. I need you to do me a big favor."

"Yeah?"

"I'm in the hospital now, I fell at work. I won't be back until later tonight and I don't have anyone to watch Timothy…"

I despise when people can't just rip the bandage off and say what they want to say. Don't beat around the bush.

"You want me to watch him."

"Could you?"

You need to watch him. Poor Timothy could get hurt being alone, or worse.

Could you not get involved right now? I watched him most of last year. This year I need to focus on grades. I finally found the person that could help get my grades up, that could get rid of these nightmares, and I'm not losing her.

What's more important, your grades or the life of a child?

You know you're really great at making me feel guilty.

What else are moms for?

Ugh.

"Cole? Are you there?"

"Yeah, I'll watch your son."

The next day, in school, I catch Olivia by her locker. Ill-tempered, she says, "I thought you were serious about learning."

"I was, I am. Something came up."

She reaches in her locker looking for something. I presume a book. "What, you realized studying actually requires work?"

"My neighbor was in the hospital. She needed me to watch her kid, okay? Why are you so mad at me? I called you to let you know I couldn't come."

She turns her face away from the locker and slowly exhales. "I'm sorry. Is your neighbor okay?"

Her voice is more placid now.

29

"Yeah, she's feeling a bit better now. I'm serious about getting my grades up. I'll do whatever I need to in order to do that."

"I believe you. I'm not mad at you. It's just," she pauses, "I'm dealing with a lot at home and I guess I was just taking it out on you." She rubs her arm, gazing off to the floor.

"What's going on?"

Crap. I'm being too intrusive. Back off, Cole. This is none of your business.

"You don't have to ans—"

"My parents have just been fighting a lot lately." Olivia's eyes widen. "I'm oversharing. You don't need to know what's going on with my family. I agreed to help you study, not for you to be my therapist."

"You're not oversharing, I'm just over asking."

The bell rings.

I continue, "And just so you know, you talking to me about your problems doesn't make me your therapist. Just makes me a friend."

Just then, a distant voice calls my name. I cock my head, searching for who's calling me. There's a scrawny, middle-aged man standing in the hallway. Mr. Haynes. "You coming to class?" he asks.

I think of myself as moderately tall, however when I'm beside him, I feel like one of the Oompa Loompas from Willy Wonka. There are only a few teachers in this school that genuinely care for their students, that don't just teach, but educate. Safe to say, Mr. Haynes isn't one of them. In fact, I think he despises all of us, except me. He has an off-putting fondness for me, which often makes my blood run cold. His sympathetic disposition toward me is unmatched. He makes sure I arrive to class on time, have a ride home, and am feeling *ok*.

I've caught him staring at me during lunch on multiple occasions. The steady wideness of his eyes, always indicates he's in disbelief. It's as if he knows something about me. I'm

IN THE BACK OF MY HEAD

probably overanalyzing, looking for irregularities. I can't help it, it's the paranoia instilled in me. I'm schizophrenic after all. But I often wonder, if my dreams are real...was he the person that took me?

The Cynic

I haven't always been intrigued by Cole Torsney. I used to think of him as no different than all the other rats in school, until I figured out who he really was. What he really went through. Now, I study him like a hawk, amazed he's still alive. I mean... nobody's ever survived what he went through. It's unheard of. I don't think he fathoms how lucky he is to be alive or how close he is to death, even now, years after being abducted. Regardless, I care for him more than I do my own son, which isn't saying a lot. I just know one of these days, Cole won't be returning to school.

Around twelve years ago, a psychopath the press tagged The Cauterizing Killer started killing and branding children. The killings ended almost ten years ago.

I googled Cole's name after learning the truth about him. A truth I'm not even sure he knows. What not only shocked me, but made my fascination grow, was the discovery that there isn't a single news article about him. It doesn't make sense. I mean there are news articles on every victim this killer has been in contact with. Except him.

It's almost as if it never occurred. Except it did, because I have proof.

The Existentialist

Weeks later, my grades have incremented, making my father proud of me. My high grades are a reflection of my and Olivia's study sessions.

Currently, I'm in the library; we've been meeting here a couple times every week. Walking to *our* table, I see Olivia sitting there, legs crossed, with no textbooks beside her.

"What's going on?" I ask. "I thought we were going to study."

"You've been acing most of your tests. I don't have any projects this week so I figured we could just relax, talk about school, problems, life."

In all our study sessions over the past few weeks, Olivia's never really wanted to talk, always staying reserved, keeping to herself. We say hello, study, then say goodbye. Whenever I've tried to talk about anything outside of school, she tries to shut down the conversation, answering with a simple yes or no. One time she outrightly said, "We are here to study, not talk." Now she wants to talk about life and her problems? I'm intrigued.

I sit on a chair opposite Olivia. "Problems? What's the going rate for therapists these days?"

Olivia facepalms and her laugh gets muffled out by her hand.

"Honestly, I could use a break from studying," I say. "What do you want to talk about?"

"There's a Halloween party at Sam's house next week. Are you going?" She uncrosses her legs.

"I haven't decided yet." I say, massaging my neck. "Halloween isn't my favorite holiday." I feel uncomfortable telling her that and I hope she doesn't dig deeper.

"I heard Jack is going to be there," she says. "Is he in your gym class?"

"Yeah. We have gym class and language arts together."

A smile rises on her face, but she tries to swallow it down. "Just out of curiosity, did he mention what type of girls he's into?"

She's asking because she likes him. Of course. No wonder she suddenly wanted to *talk*. I don't know Jack too well. The mature thing to do would be to tell her the truth, but where's the fun in that. Instead, I say, "Yeah he loves girls with brown hair who just moved from another town."

She can't contain her emotions anymore and a lustrous smile appears on her face.

"Oh, also, if you're planning on going to an Ivy League college next year, he's *really* into that."

"Very funny." She frowns, realizing I was messing with her. "I'm being serious."

"Is this why you wanted to take a break from studying? Listen, if you really want, I wouldn't mind asking him about you."

"No. I can deal with it myself. I just wanted to know a little bit about him. Now I feel kind of rude. So, you can ask me about girls you like."

"I'm not really into any of the girls at school."

"Not even Ashley?" Olivia scoffs.

Chuckling, I reply, "Not even Ashley."

"So, what's your deal then? Everyone our age is in a relationship. Are you into guys?"

"It's not that. It's just, most girls our age are very superficial, they don't care about a lot of things. And if a girl dated me, she'd eventually find out that I'm—" I almost slipped up.

It's difficult to talk to kids here about my struggles. Even harder for them to understand. Most of them complain about the phone or car their parent bought them, while I have to question my reality on a daily basis. I'm not saying I have a copyright on adversity or that it's some type of competition. I just want to talk to someone that could understand trauma.

My perception of Olivia is that she's reluctant to overshare. The way she talked about alcohol abuse that night I met her tells me she's akin to trauma. Whatever that trauma is or was, compels me to tell her everything.

Olivia looks confused. Needing to get out of this hole I buried myself in, I shift the conversation.

"Your parents must be so proud you get good grades all the time."

Nice job. That totally wasn't awkward.

"My mom is, but I'm not really close to my dad," her voice weakens and her chin lowers.

I got out of the hole I buried myself in, but inadvertently buried her there, too. Seeing her grief, I try to throw her a ladder.

"I get it. I'm not close with my dad either. My parents are… separated."

Her chin raises, looking me in the eye. We find some type of solace in each other's unspoken trauma. She's climbed the ladder successfully, getting herself out of the hole.

The next day, after gym class, Jack—along with his friends—are in the locker room. I've had a few conversations with Jack before but I usually refrain from talking to him seeing how he's one of those guys in school who enjoys talking behind other students' backs, spreading rumors, and badmouthing everyone.

35

I know. Judgmental, right? I'm just critical of everyone I talk to. If that's a crime, arrest me.

Olivia, wanting to handle this herself, asked me not to mention her to Jack. But she's helped me so much with my grades, I feel obligated to do something to repay her. Besides, this is the type of stuff friends do.

The locker room is next to the showers so it's slightly foggy. It reeks of body odor and axe body spray. It's ironic the dirtiest place in school is the place you go to become cleanest.

I overhear Jack, Tyler, and a few other guys laughing.

"Hey Jack, what type of girls do you find attractive at this school?" I ask.

Jack grimaces. "That's a random question. You know as long as she's got a nice body, I'm cool with her." He glances back at his friends, making sure they laugh. Of course, they do.

Disgust digs into me the same way my fingernails are digging into my palms. I shouldn't bring Olivia's name up to this guy. The way he talks, like he's hot shit, he'd hurt her, and while she'd never admit it, she's been hurt enough.

No. Olivia seemed interested in him. She's your friend, you need to help her.

Goddamn it. I'm going to regret this, but here goes nothing...

"What do you think about Olivia?"

A smirk rises on Jack's face making me feel instant regret, as predicted.

"Why are you asking? Did she say she likes me?"

Crap. This was a mistake. I should've worded my question better. "No–no it's not like that. She didn't say anything."

"So, what then, you're into me?" Jack and his friends laugh. "Listen, tell Olivia I'll see her at Sam's Halloween party." Jack slams his locker shut. His friends follow him to class.

School ends and I find Olivia outside heading to the buses.

"Olivia!" I call out.

She turns around. "Hey Cole, how'd that math test go?"

"What? Oh, the math test. It went well. It's just I—"

"See? I told you we didn't need to study. You know, soon you won't even need me as your tutor anymore."

God, I hope that day never comes.

"I need to talk to you about something. Remember the other day when you told me not to mention you to Jack? Well, I kind of mentioned you to him and I think he knows you like him now."

Olivia draws a deep breath, then lethargically drags herself away, not saying anything. No reaction. I can't get a read on her. She doesn't appear to be angry, or joyful.

I call and text her all night. Nothing. No response.

Olivia has been ignoring me for days. Glimpsing outside my bedroom window I see kids walking around the neighborhood, dressed like things that don't exist. Large synthetic spiderwebs on bushes, dummy skeletons half buried in lawns, pumpkins resting on front porches; it's Halloween. Needless to say, I hate this holiday. I usually stay in bed all night this time of year, but currently Halloween isn't my biggest concern, Olivia is.

I wish I could take back what I did. I wish I could've been a better friend to Olivia. I wish...

I wish she asked about me. And not about Jack.

God. I feel like a teenager.

You are a teenager.

I know. But now I feel like one.

Nate's here making sure I'm okay. "How are you doing? I know how hard this holiday can be for you."

"Honestly Nate, I couldn't care less for this holiday. Right now, Olivia's center stage in my mind."

"Well, she might be at that party tonight, though, I don't think you should go."

I chuckle. "If you didn't want me to go, you wouldn't have told me she might be there."

37

A smile slips from Nate's face.

"I'm going to that party and you're coming."

Walking into Sam's house, shattered glass crinkles under my feet. It's spread across the floor like sand at a beach. I don't recall the music being this ear-piercing last time I was here. That, along with the blinding lights, makes my head feel like a merry-go-round. I shift my foot from one to the other, struggling to balance. Unable to see clearly, I stick my hand out, searching for a wall. I need to lean against something before I stumble.

"Yo, check it out. Cole's, like, completely wasted."

I need to find a wall. I'm about to collapse. "H-h-help."

My knees buckle. Nate swings my arm over his shoulder, supporting me.

"He's not drunk you idiot. Can't you see he needs help?"

"Chill, dude, I didn't know."

"I don't give a shit. Go get him some water while I bring him to the couch."

After sitting me down, Nate says, "Didn't I tell you to wait outside while I find parking?"

Losing this rush of vertigo, I say, "I needed to find Olivia."

Some guy comes back and hands me a cup of water.

"Drink it." Nate demands.

Without thinking twice, I drink the lukewarm water.

"I'll find Olivia. You wait here."

Nate leaves the room and I wait a few minutes. Realization dawns on me; Nate's not searching for Olivia, he's getting drunk.

I start searching myself. Everyone I ask, too drunk to give me a simple yes or no answer, feels the need to tell me their life story, before offering me a beer. Time's being wasted.

Finally, I see a hammered girl holding a red solo cup with what I assume to be beer in it. Olivia drunk seemed like a dubious idea, yet looking at the hammered girl, I'm sure it's her.

38

She's dancing along to the rowdy music and I warily walk over to her.

"Olivia, I came to tell you I'm sorry for what I did."

Olivia continues dancing, untroubled.

"I can't hear you!" She grabs me, pulling me in. "Come dance with me!" She tries yelling over the intrusive music.

"Olivia, can we go someplace quieter?"

"You're no fun." She notices Jack dancing near her. "Jack come dance with me!"

Jack looming closer, starts dancing with her.

"Olivia, you're drunk right now. I need to get you home."

"She'll be fine. I'll take care of her tonight." Jack being brash, nods at the door. "Get lost."

I think back to the girl from my dreams. "Protect Olivia."

I want to, but she doesn't want me to. I head towards the door.

Don't turn your back on her. She needs you.

Maybe she needs me, but she doesn't want me. I can't force her to leave. If she wants to be with Jack, I'm not going to get in her way.

After finding Nate, surprisingly sober, we head outside.

"You're not drunk," I tell him.

"I know what tonight means to you. You're like a brother to me. I'd never get drunk when you need me."

Sometimes I forget how fraternal Nate could be.

"I found Olivia but she doesn't want to leave. She's with Jack and she's drunk."

"And you're going to leave her there drunk? With Jack of all people?" Nate's eyebrows lift.

"There's not much I can do," I give a weak plea. "She doesn't want to leave."

Nate bobs his head. "For the past couple days—since she started ignoring you—you've been beat up over her. Now, I know you like her," he says as he points to himself, then to me. "Do you know you like her?"

"I do."

"Then go back in there and stay until you know she's okay. Even if that means being there all night, and if you need me to, I'll stay with you because you're my friend."

Now that's a friend. I'm glad you have Nate.

Will you please shut up?

Needing to do this myself, I tell Nate to head home. I come back in and just as before, Olivia's missing. Only difference is, this time, Jack's missing too. I try asking people for their whereabouts but the only thing they are focusing on is the music and the alcohol. If they are still here there's only one place they could be: upstairs.

Everyone here knows what happens up there.

No, she wouldn't. She couldn't. She can't be up there. Gaping at the stairs I hear my heart beating louder than the music, or is that just my imagination? Doesn't matter, I'm getting distracted.

Lifting my leg, I trudge up the first stair.

Do I want to know what they are doing up there? Maybe this whole thing is stupid. I'm being hyperbolic. I'm sure she's fine. I turn to the door, ready to leave. But she told me she rarely drinks. I saw how drunk she was before. There is no way she's okay. Something's wrong.

I turn around, tediously sprinting upstairs. The stairs feel like quicksand against my ponderous feet.

I need to reach Olivia. I need to protect her.

Upon arriving upstairs, muffled yelling sets me off. Placing my ear against the door, I hear Olivia shouting, "Stop!"

I touch the knob. It's locked so I pound on the door. No one answers.

"Stop! Stop, please."

I continue pounding on the door, making it rattle, like it's going to break. The knob rotates and the door opens. Jacks stands there disoriented with his belt loose. I glance at him then behind him. Olivia's on the bed, crying.

I swing at his face. "What's wrong with you?"

I shove him, then run right into him, clinching his body, and plunging onto the floor. Then I start pummeling him.

Treading to Olivia, I see her shivering, arms around herself, teeth chattering. I take off my concrete grey hoodie and hand it to her. As if her shivering was on account of the climate.

"Did he...?" I ask.

"He-he tried but-but then y—" she can't finish her sentence. She isn't crying, and this might not make sense, but I think she's too scared to cry.

"Let's get you home," I say.

The Cynic

"Here's some money, go get breakfast from school."

"B-b-but they don't give out breakfast at school, j-j-just lunch."

"Oh my god." I blurt. "Then use it to buy some snacks from the vending machine and have that for breakfast. You are going into third grade now. You should start learning how to take care of yourself."

Finn's eyes drift to the floor. They remind me of the Hoover dam on account of the tons of water being held back.

Moving to the entry table, in search of my wallet, I find a few pieces of mail. FINAL NOTICE. My home mortgage. I already have enough bills to pay, between school tuition, my car, and student debt. I don't need a reminder that I need to pay my house off. The only reason I bought this house was because I thought it would be a great place for me and my wife—sorry, my ex-wife—to grow old in. Now I'm swimming in debts; no wife, no sex, and a child to take care of. It's a miracle I've survived as long as I have.

Gazing at my class, I realize I've been presumptuous. I thought I'd be happier when school started, seeing as I wouldn't have to deal with Finn as much. Now I realize I've just replaced him with twenty prepubescent teenage rats. And man, do I hate rats. They reek of gag-inducing body odor, their faces covered in splotchy acne, and they have aggregating voice cracks. They are undisciplined. Parents these days don't have the patience to discipline their kids. They think that's the school's job. It's not. Our job is to teach them Science, Math, and English, among other things. We aren't babysitters.

Emily coughs. I notice she has been raising her hand for a couple minutes now.

I let out a sigh. "Yes, Emily."

"The bell rang five minutes ago, you've just been…staring at us. We are here to learn. Could you please teach us?"

Bitch.

Last year there was more bootlicking and less cynicism. This year it seems she's switched things up. How convenient for me.

"Right. Class open up to page 23."

Jack shouts, "Who's the teacher Emily or Mr. Haynes?"

My eyebrow twitches while the class erupts into laughter. How dare she embarrass me like that. How dare she. I want to discipline her and Jack right now, the same way my mom did me. Then they will know who the teacher is.

The laughter fades and we move on with our lesson.

The bell for lunch rings and as always, the slothful class turns fervid, running out faster than they came in.

I make my way to the teachers' lounge, where there's a handful of teachers, all socializing. I'd prefer there be none.

I brought week-old macaroni and cheese. There is a bit of green fuzzy stuff on it. I scrape that part off and heat it up in the microwave. The timer beeps and I take it out seeing the cheese is still rubbery. I splash water atop it and mix it with a flabby fork. The musty smell is gone. I place it back in for another two minutes. Now the cheese is gooier and less rubber. Better, I guess.

A text interrupts my lunch. It is from Finn's school, informing me about the unpaid tuition.

Finn. Always causing me problems. I don't have money for tuition. There are too many bills. They all keep adding up. Sometimes I look back to when things were simpler. When I lived unruffled, with my dad on the farm. There was no stress. No burdens. Everything was plain-sailing. I need more overtime, more work, more shifts. I could cover for other teachers. Maybe I could get a raise, I have been working here for five years now. I deserve a raise.

Principal George Parsons enters the teachers' lounge, sauntering to one of the teachers, and starts whispering in his ear. I catch a whiff of his cheap cologne. I have to wonder how many times he's sprayed it on his cheap suit.

After finishing my lunch, I walk to the garbage and throw out my fork. Above the garbage there is a sign informing teachers of the school's lack of janitorial staff. I didn't like what the sign insinuated. As if one of us would ever become a janitor. I went to college. Along with all the other teachers here. Why would anyone of us ever think about becoming a janitor? I would never stoop so low.

George walks past me, opens the door, and leaves. Now's my chance. I need to ask him for more work. The door closes. I open it, sprinting after him.

In the hallway, I shout, "George!"

He freezes, almost like he has been shot. Then slowly turns around with tangible irritation. "Mr. Haynes, on school premises, you must refer to me as Principal Parsons. We've talked about this."

Someone is clearly on a power trip. "My mistake. *Mr. Parsons*," I say, suppressing an eye roll. "I wanted to talk to you regarding more work. Could we talk in your office?"

"I'm afraid I don't have much time. We'd have to talk here or at another time."

He wasn't busy. He's never busy. He just wanted to display his power in front of the students walking by. "Um okay." I scratch my ear, glancing at the corner of the floor, then back to him. "I've been working here for 5 years. And I rarely take a sick day or any vacation days. I was hoping I could get a raise."

"Everyone wants a raise these days. I'd like a raise, you'd like a raise, hell, I just heard the students want a raise." He laughs. He thinks he's funny. He thinks me asking for a raise is a laughing matter. He continues, "But sadly we don't have an infinite amount of money in our budget this year. And we are underpaid workers. This is a known thing. Teachers are underpaid. But we do this for the kids, not for the money. Otherwise, you would've chosen a different field of work, right?"

No. Not right. Definitely not right. "Well, it doesn't have to be a raise. Maybe I could get some more shifts, cover for some teachers, get some overtime?"

"You know what, I like you, *Blake*." Blake. Of course, he could use my first name but I can't use his. "I have a lot of teachers fighting for the detention shift, but I'll give it to you on the condition you pick up the janitorial work afterwards. You are okay with working as a janitor, right?"

"Yes, I'll work as a janitor if it means I could get the detention slot."

"We have ourselves a deal then," he says as he walks away.

At 5 o'clock, getting ready to leave, Principal Parsons shouts my name from across the hall. I turn, looking at him. He does an awkward half run, half walk towards me. I'd call it jogging, but that feels wrong, it's too arrhythmic.

"Glad I got a hold of you before you left."

When he reaches me, he's slouching, hands on his legs for body support. Catching his breath he says, "The janitor didn't come in for his shift today. I'll need you to start immediately."

"I can't."

He tsks. "Oh, I'm sure you could find time, after all you want more shifts. Then again, I could give that shift to a different teacher.

I stare at his throat. My hands lust to grab it. I want to feel the warmth of it fading against my palms. I want to feel him squirming as he sees it's me taking his life.

"You know where the janitorial closet is. Enjoy."

The Existentialist

The hasty wind whistling against my face makes me kind of wish I didn't give her my hoodie. No, she looked like she needed it more than me. "Where do you live?'

"Sev-seven blocks down." Her arms are crossed, hands gripping them.

"We're going to walk there so you can sober up."

"I can walk alone," she insists. "I've done it before."

I look into her solitary eyes. "I'm not leaving you. Not until I know you're safe."

I shouldn't have left her before. I should've stayed with her. If I had just stayed another minute, maybe I could have prevented them from going upstairs in the first place. If I had gone up a bit earlier, she would've never screamed stop. If I hadn't asked Jack about Olivia that day in the locker room, he never would've thought Olivia liked him, and he never would have started dancing with her. This was my fault. I'm supposed to be protecting her, yet here I am; the cause of her pain.

"You're awfully quiet."

"I'm sorry. This is all my fault. I shouldn't have told Jack you liked him. I should've stayed with you when you were drunk."

Olivia giggles. "Cole." She shakes her head. "This isn't your fault. None of it."

It is. I'm supposed to protect her, yet I'm the one putting her in danger. "I'm not going to let this happen to you again," I say.

"Nothing happened, thanks to you."

I notice she's stopped shivering. I wonder if I can get my hoodie back.

"This isn't your fault. I need you to know that. Tell me you know that."

She wouldn't like my answer so I don't respond.

She continues, "Last week I was avoiding you because I was scared."

"You? Scared? I remember one time when we were studying and there was a spider on your science book and you killed it with another book."

"Right, how could I have any fears?" She rolls her eyes. "My sister was my best friend, the person I relied on more than anyone, including myself. Sure, we fought a lot, most siblings do. But she always had my back. She was my partner in crime. We'd do everything together. Shopping, watching TV, pranks on Mom. When my parents fought, she'd hold me while I cried. I relied on her for a lot. Almost everything, really. Then she died. My parents were too distraught to take care of me. I went from having my entire family raising me to having no one. I had to raise myself. I had to rely on myself." She pauses. "No one's ever tried helping me the way you have in a long time. I know it sounds stupid, but I'm scared I might rely on you, that I might open up to you. And right when I feel safe with you, you'll leave me, just like she did…that's what scares me." She stops, and points to a big, blue house. "This is me."

Her house is painted white and has an ocean blue door, with an American flag hanging from the porch.

She opens the door. It's dark, but streetlights shining through the windows add just enough light to see a dog's head lifted. The dog—a Pit Bull Terrier—scurries towards me before repeatedly bouncing against me, trying to lick my face.

"Wow I've never seen her like that," Olivia says, amused.

I'm glad she's feeling brighter. "What's her name?" I ask.

"Mocha."

I rub between her ears. "Hi, Mocha, aren't you adorable?"

48

Olivia and I go upstairs, to her room.

"Could you stay a bit longer?" Olivia mumbles. "I just don't want to be alone, not right now."

I rest beside her, comforting her. We stare at the ceiling for a few minutes, relishing each other's presence.

"My parents are talking about getting divorced. I'm a bit scared."

"I'm so sorry to hear that."

"That's why I was drinking tonight."

I'm an idiot. Here I was thinking she was drinking to impress Jack.

"Your parents are divorced, right? What made them get divorced?"

Taken aback by her bluntness, I clear my throat. "They aren't divorced. They're...separated."

Olivia rests her head on my chest. "I can tell you're not telling me everything." Her voice is dry. "Maybe it's because you aren't comfortable with me, maybe it's because you don't trust me. You don't need to, but one of these days you will."

I believe her.

She wraps her arm around my waist and falls asleep. Not wanting to wake her by leaving, I text my dad, saying I'm staying with Nate and won't be home tonight.

The November sun glints through the window, awakening us. Olivia yawns. "I don't feel so good." She runs to the bathroom and I rush after her, finding her on her knees, throwing up in the toilet. I hold her hair up, ensuring it doesn't get wet.

Nauseated, she looks up at me. "I look horrible, don't I?"

Something must be wrong with me, because even as she's throwing up, I'm attracted to her. "I think you look genuine."

"Genuine." She chuckles.

49

Struggling to stand up, I extend my hand, trying to help her. She continues struggling, ignoring my assistance.

We go back to her room and she strips down to her tank top, revealing the outline of her ebony bra.

"Where are your parents?"

"Oh no, what time is it?' Olivia asks in distress. "I think they already left to work which means we're late for school. We need to go now."

"Relax, if you go to school hungover and hungry you won't last an hour. I'll quickly make coffee for us while you get started on French toast."

"I don't know how to make French toast."

I gasp, dumbfounded. "You don't know—what?"

"Don't you look at me like that. My mom usually makes it. Why is that so funny?"

"I don't care how late we are for school; I'm teaching you how to make French toast whether you want to or not."

After she changes, we go downstairs to the modern kitchen. She shows me where the eggs, cinnamon, sugar, and bread are.

"Crack some of the eggs in that bowl over there." I point to the bowl on the marble counter.

"I don't know how to crack an egg."

"No. You can't be serious."

She giggles. "I'm not, I just love messing with you." Olivia's enamoring bubbliness induces a smile on my face. "Although… maybe you can show me how to crack an egg?" She says, nibbling on her index finger, flirtatiously.

I've never been so turned on being asked to crack an egg.

Leaning in from behind, my palm grasps her hand. My heart's pulsating and my breath thickens. The immaculate kitchen begins feeling as steamy as a sauna.

Her sensual arm grazes mine, spreading goosebumps from my wrist to my shoulder. Peeking at her arm, I see she has them too. We slowly thrust forward reaching for the distant egg. Her smooth hips slide against my crotch. Grabbing the hard egg, we thwack it on the bowl. Our hands are wet and some of the egg drips from the side of the bowl.

I whisper in her ear, "We should wash up."

She turns around and I wrap my arms around her waist. Ogling at me, she purses her pouty lips. And then like something out of a tv show, my phone buzzes on the counter, ruining the moment. I retract my hands and reach for my phone.

What am I doing? I'm getting too close, too soon. I'm supposed to be protecting her, not doing…whatever this is.

I glance at my phone. Nate texted me.

What happened last night? People are saying Olivia tried to drug Jack and have sex with him. And that you came in and saw and beat him because of it. They are calling her a whore.

Jesus Christ. Unreal. High school.

"I think we should go to school soon," Olivia suggests.

Protect Olivia.

I can't bring her to school. Not right after what had just happened. Not with all these rumors spreading. "I was actually thinking we could go somewhere else today."

Olivia raises a single eyebrow. "Don't you have a science test today?"

Crap. I totally forgot about that. "Um, no. It got postponed."

She raises a single eyebrow "Your science test got postponed?"

"Yes." I take a loud gulp, swallowing my lies.

That's one of the worst lies I've ever heard.

Yeah, like you could come up with anything better.

"Ok. I guess we could skip one day of school. What do you have in mind?"

"I was thinking we could go to Green Point Lake, then maybe walk around the town square. There's a scenic bell tower there with a ladder in the back we could use to climb up."

51

"That sounds really nice."

"It is. In fact, if today was my last day, the last thing I'd want to see is the view from up there."

Olivia glances at her phone, then massages her neck. "Do you think we could just stay here, until my parents come back?" Her voice sounds desolate.

I scratch my head and peer at her.

"Cole, I have a phone. I know what everyone is saying about me."

Social media. This is why I stay off it.

"I kind of just want to lie with you on the couch all day, watching movies and relaxing."

"Are you ok?"

Sweetie, look at her, you know she's not okay.

I was asking to be sympathetic, not because I question her mental state. I know she's not ok. I just don't know how to make it better.

Boys, always so oblivious. She literally told you, she wants to cuddle with you.

She didn't say cuddle, she said lie with me.

Like there's a difference.

"I'm okay, I just want to cuddle with you."

See?!

I hate when you're right.

The Defeatist

I didn't enjoy doing it.

Taking your sister's life.

I did it out of obligation.

That's at least what I thought at the time.

Mrs. Dalton on the ground, beaten and bruised, by me.

Cole was tied up.

Grace was staring at me.

I could see the fear in her eyes. She thought I was a monster.

Maybe I was.

I mean I did let all of this happen.

I never knew how scared someone could be of another human. But I soon learned.

As I drew closer, I laid my finger on her cheek. Every muscle, every fiber, every vein in her body flinched.

She was petrified.

I knew when the cops came, she'd tell them who was behind this; me.

I couldn't let that happen.

I had just convinced myself I was going to change.

I was set on change.

She stood in my way…so I killed her.

The Existentialist

Sunlight streams through the only unboarded window, illuminating the dilapidated room. Olivia's short-haired doppelganger is awake, lying on the floor. Dazed, her eyes dart around the room. Realization dawns on her; this isn't a dream or a nightmare, this is our reality. I gaze at her as she attempts to sit upward. The unyielding rope knotted around her suppresses her.

She gives up. Lying flat on her back, she turns to me and asks, "What's your name?"

My parents warned me not to give my name out to strangers, but the predicament I'm in, is far worse than whatever they feared. Knowing that talking won't exacerbate my situation, I mutter "Cole. Cole Dalton." I say it so quietly I didn't think she heard.

"Hey Cole, I'm Grace." Her voice's affability is soothing.

"Dad said I'm supposed to shake hands whenever I introduce myself," I state.

She smiles. That was the first time I saw a smile on her face. "I think he'd make an exception in a situation like this."

An alarming car horn honks outside, frightening us. Her smile fades. "Where is your father?"

I shrug, doing probably the only body movement these frustrating ropes don't restrain.

"Do you remember how you got here?"

I shake my head, no. Seems I found another body gesture I can do while in these ropes.

"How old are you?"

I put out eight fingers, then realize my hands are tied behind my back. "Eight," I say.

"Do you know why we were taken?"

"No." I can't help her. A slow-moving tear rolls down my face.

She notices it and says, "Don't cry, we're going to get out of here."

She starts twisting and turning, trying to get loose, but ultimately fails. "The police are going to find us; they're going to arrest this psycho and we'll be free. Back with our family."

"I'm not scared, I'm strong like my father."

She frowns. "It's ok to be scared, I'm scared. Fear isn't a weakness, in fact surviving amidst it is a true testament of our strength."

In that case I'm very scared.

"Do you have any siblings?"

"No."

"I do, she's actually around your age. Her name's Olivia." Her eyes get teary. "We fought before I... before I was taken. If you get out of here Cole, I want you to warn my parents. Protect Olivia."

I don't understand. Why me? Why does she think I may escape?

"Could you do that for me Cole? Could you protect my sister?"

"Y-y-yes...I can."

I hear footsteps behind me. I see a shadow walking in the hallway. It's him, it's whoever took us.

I wake up, it's 3 a.m. Of course. My heart is racing too much to fall back asleep.

Good morning.

"It's never a good morning when I wake up this early."

55

Being the productive insomniac that I am; I work out, make myself breakfast, then study a little bit. Getting things done before the day even starts.

I look outside, the bare trees are creaking. The November wind looks strong enough to blow a toddler down. I wonder if I should warn Timothy's mother.

Before heading to school, I go to my father's room. While he is sleeping, I rummage through his messy dresser. I'm not going to end up in that decrepit room ever again. I finally find it. His tactical knife.

I arrive at school before it starts. It's as cold as my nightmares, but I want to be here when Olivia arrives.

Olivia.

Grace's sister.

How'd I not realize it sooner? They look identical.

But how is that even possible? If I was kidnapped, I'd know, wouldn't I? Could these nightmares really be distorted memories?

Olivia also told me her sister died. Could she have died in that room, when she was with me?

No, it's impossible. Remember what Mrs. Freed said, "If something seems far-fetched, bizarre or scary, then it's not real."

This is my mind playing tricks on me.

When in doubt... doubt.

My mind is trying to play games on me. It's not going to work. Not when things are finally going so well. I need to put this behind me, with all the other hallucinations.

My teeth are chattering and my eyes are welling up. I look at the entrance to the school. The heating must be nice in there. I could wait for her in there.

Cole, don't divert.

I'm not, I just can't worry about this right now. There's too much going on.

A rusty yellow bus with flakes of paint peeling off it stops outside. Please, if there is a God let Olivia be on that bus. I can't take it out here anymore. The flimsy bus doors open. There is a God after all. Olivia steps off and raises a hand, greeting me.

I might have to start going to church again.

"How long have you been outside? You look like you're freezing," Olivia asks.

"Not long. I just got here a couple minutes ago." I glance at my watch. 30 minutes? I could've sworn it's been hours.

She twists her face, raising an eyebrow.

I walk into the building, and snug heat envelops me; I've never been happier walking in here.

"If this is about the rumors, I can handle it myself."

Of course, you could, you wouldn't be you if you couldn't.

Distant voices mention my name and I'm unsure if it's in my head or if it's someone in the halls.

Before I can continue silently talking to myself, like any sane person would, I'm being shoved against a locker. I look to see who's shoving me. It's Chris and some of his friends.

"I heard you messed with my friend Jack while he was drugged by your psycho girlfriend."

"That's not what happened. He wasn't drugged, and she's not my girlfriend."

"Really? Because someone told me you and your whore have been going to the library a couple times a week." Chris looked back at his friends. "And we all know what the library's good for." Chris and his friends laugh.

I'm sensing a pattern here with affirmation and high-school douchebags.

"Watch your mouth," I caution him.

"Or what?" Chris smirks. "Are you going to do something?"

I tuck my hand in my pocket, grasping the knife.

Mr. Garcia intervenes. "Is there a problem here students?"

Chris starts sweating. "No problem at all. We were just having a friendly conversation."

"Well, Chris, you're late for my class, so how about I walk you there."

Of course, he shoves me against a locker and just gets escorted to class. Teachers, their motto is and always will be: passive-aggressiveness before passive paperwork.

At lunchtime I sit next to Olivia and Nate. Olivia has a salad and Nate has two trays of tacos. One must be for me.

"Thanks Nate, but I brought my own lunch."

Confused, he looks at his tacos then back at me. "Oh, this isn't for you, they're both for me."

I slap my head. Right. Of course, they are. "You know there are children in Africa starving."

"Oh, they wouldn't want any of this. Who knows what they put in this stuff? It's basically toxic for humans." He starts vacuuming the toxic tacos into his mouth.

Amused, I glance at Olivia to see what she thinks of this. She's not eating her salad, but instead picking at it with her fork.

"You know if you're next to me all the time, people might think the rumors are true." Olivia says.

"They can think whatever they want to think."

She continues frowning.

I look at her uneaten salad. "If you don't eat that salad I'm going to have to. And I hate salad."

"So why would you eat it?"

"For the principle. My mom taught me never to let good food go to waste."

"So, you'd eat something you don't like just so it doesn't go to waste?"

"Watch me." I pinch a piece of lettuce from her salad and toss it in my mouth. Then scrunch my face.

Nasty.

She laughs. "God, Cole."

While chomping on his food, Nate wiggles his finger at us. "So, are you guys dating or…?"

"We're just friends," Olivia says.

Nate swallows his food. "That's too bad. You guys would be a nice couple." He licks his fingers.

"Nate, you're my best friend, but do us all a favor; don't talk with food in your mouth."

Olivia cracks a smile.

When I get home, Dad is waiting beside the door, anxiously tapping his foot on the ground, arms crossed. I toss my bag on the floor. I think he knows I took his knife.

"Cole, what's going on?" he asks. "I got a call from Mr. Browning today. He told me you missed a day of school."

Thank God. He doesn't know.

"You also failed your science test because you didn't show up. He told me that if you fail another science test, you might not graduate this year. You've worked so hard to get to where you are. Why throw it all away?"

"Dad, someone did something bad to this girl and then started spreading rumors. I didn't want to take her to school with all that happening."

"That's very kind of you, but she's not your concern." He sighs. "If you don't start taking care of yourself, you won't be able to take care of her."

"Dad, I've been taking care of myself."

"No, you haven't. I've seen the medication bottles. They aren't meant to be as full as they are."

Oh, Cole.

"It's not my fault, I've been busy. And besides, forgetting to take them a couple times won't kill me."

"What's our number one rule? The only thing I ask from you."

"To be honest."

"After your mom left the way she did, I expected you not to lie to me, not to deceive me, but to be honest with me. So, tell me and don't you dare lie, did you spend the night at that girl's house?"

"Yeah...I did."

"Cole, I'm your father. I'm supposed to be watching you 24/7. You are more mature than most kids your age. That's why I give you so much freedom. You lied. You broke my trust. I'm sorry, but you're grounded for 2 weeks."

I don't bother arguing with him because I know he's right. Shocking, isn't it? A teenager letting his parent ground him, with no fuss. It's improbable. But I just know he's right.

I trust him, he trusts me, and we never break that trust. It sounds stupid because I'm a teenager and he's my dad. It shouldn't work, yet it does.

The next week, the rumor surrounding Olivia begins to fade, along with all the other high school rumors, and everyone moves onto the next piece of gossip. I've realized, adults tend to fret about how damaging teens' short attention spans are, but in situations like these, it's more beneficial than detrimental.

Olivia sits across from me in the library. We're supposed to be studying but I can't focus. She seems different today, less talkative. And when she does talk, her voice is tired.

Closing my textbook, I ask, "What's wrong?"

Her eyes lift from the table. "Who says anything's wrong?"

"Olivia..."

"Cole..." She says, smiling with glossy eyes.

I have never seen a smile more despondent than hers in this moment. "It's your parents, isn't it?"

She turns her head to the left. I can tell she's holding back tears.

"I know you're holding back from speaking because you don't want to cry. One thing I did when my parents split was cry. It helped a lot."

She wipes her eyes with her sleeve. "God. Why do you have to be so intuitive?"

She rests her hands on the table and I reach out to hold them.

Looking her in the eyes, I tell her, "It's going to be okay."

She slowly bobs her head. "I thought moving here...I thought it would make things different, better. Make my dad more loving, make my mom stronger." Sniffling she continues, "One of those things became true."

The Defeatist

Do you know why this psychopath is called The Cauterizing Killer?

Cauterization is the medical practice in which you destroy a tissue in order to minimize potential harm. You inflict a little pain, intending to prevent a lot of pain.

These kids are harmful tissues, and killing them prevents further harm to society, to their future children, and to themselves. See, the cycle of abuse doesn't end with the abuser, it ends with the victim.

After being injected with enough pentobarbital to kill a horse, they're branded. The branding serves as a reminder. A self-justification. This is for the better of the world. For a virtuous cause. And no letters act as a better paragon then O.M.

Now I assume the question on your mind is, if it's such a noble cause, how is Cole alive?

And the answer is, he's alive on accident. It was a mistake. A mistake I fear is about to be corrected.

I love Cole. But I can't protect him anymore. I don't want him to die, but I'm afraid... he's on borrowed time.

The Existentialist

A month and a half later, the nightmares have faded and thankfully, I've successfully put Grace behind me. I'm glad this frosty December is coming to an end. The affectionate heating in our school broke by the end of November, and the school being as negligent as they are, still hasn't gotten it fixed. Some days the coldness is more numbing in here than outside. I've seen students carry an extra jacket to put on in school.

Walking to my locker, I see the festive Christmas decorations being stripped from the halls, being replaced with signs enlightening students of the winter formal. In our school, we have a banal tradition: we put a "love letter" in the locker of the girl or guy we want to take to the dance. I know, very cliché and typical, but it's a high school, what do you expect?

Nate's wearing a thick protective winter coat and Olivia is wearing a long quilted one. She rubs her hands together, trying to warm up.

I take off my woolen mittens and hand them to her.

Her eyes light up. "Thanks."

Nate opens his locker, and jerks his head backwards. Dismayed he says, "What? Only 3 letters?"

"Is that not a lot?" Olivia asks.

"I don't know, did you guys get any letters in your lockers?"

"Nope," I answer.

"Me neither. I think every guy in the school is scared of me."

"Can't blame 'em," Nate says, unaware of his callousness.

I punch him in the arm. Sometimes I really wonder what goes on in his head.

Olivia's shoulders slump, and her eyes drop to the floor. "I think it's safe to say, I'm going to be single until I graduate."

Trying to redeem himself, Nate says, "Who needs a relationship anyways?"

"You apparently. You're in a different relationship every other week," she says with a mocking voice.

I laugh.

"Ok, I deserved that."

Before school ends, I put a letter in Olivia's locker. She doesn't deserve to be alone. She didn't do anything wrong.

The next day at school, Olivia's hopping my way, with springiness in each step she takes. I let out a grin when I see she's wearing my mittens.

With her chin raised, she looks into my eyes, beaming. "Something strange happened yesterday. I was talking to you about how no one gave me a letter. Then I got one."

I place my hand on my chin. "That is weird, especially considering I wrote one."

"Weird," she says playfully.

"Weird."

She giggles, then wraps her arms around me.

"So, should I take this as a yes?"

She laughs. "Of course, I'll go to the winter formal with you."

I wonder what people think when they see me. I know it's very self-conscious of me. I'd like to think I'm in shape, after all, I work out a couple times a week, and try to eat healthy. But I'm seventeen years old, and you see someone my age in shape, you'd think he's a jock, or someone else fairly popular. Fair to say I'm neither. Whether that be by choice or not, I'll never know.

I get second looks from girls walking in the halls, and in class. Emily once asked me out. However, the life I live is easier lived alone. At least I thought that, until I met Olivia. Still, I try not to be in large social functions. Or small social functions. Really, I try to steer clear of people all together. It's hard, differentiating fantasy and reality every day. My dreams follow me out into the open.

You may think I live an odd life for a teenager, but probably a normal one for a schizophrenic. I've joined forums, but no one's experienced schizophrenia like me. No one holds my doctrines.

I'm not even normal among the un-normal.

I'm a minority in the minority.

I'm a purple sheep among black sheep.

But tonight, none of that matters. Tonight, I'm going to be the man that takes Olivia to the dance. The man that she deserves.

I knock on her door and wait for someone to answer. I've only ever been here once before. Halloween. It looks different in broad daylight. The house isn't white, it's painted a warm yellow and the porch isn't black, it's dark brown. Also, the American flag that hung from the porch isn't here anymore. I assume it was her father's.

Her mom answers the door, with a smile, inviting me in. Her hair is a familiar brown, same as Olivia's and Grace's, but she's shorter than them. I follow her to a Georgian staircase where she calls Olivia down. I wait there while her mom goes to the kitchen.

When I see Olivia, my mouth goes agape and my heart starts racing, compensating for the stiffness in my body.

She's wearing a light sleeveless ballroom dress that ends by her knees. It tightens around her waist, accentuating her perfect figure. But I'm not focusing on her figure or her protruding, cherry lips. It's her eyes that always captivate me; whenever I look at them, I see Green Point Lake. They're serene.

"Stop staring at me," she blushes. "It's weird."

Her mom exits the kitchen. "Oh my god!" She shrieks. "Let me take a picture of you guys." She starts patting her skirt, looking for her phone.

Olivia looks at the flowers I'm holding. "Are those for me?"

Lord knows they're not for me.

"Er…Um…Yes."

She giggles. "That's so sweet, thank you."

"Olivia, do you know where my phone is?"

Ignoring her mom, she takes the flowers from my hand and puts them in a vase that sits on a credenza. Next to the vase are pictures of Olivia's family. One picture is of Olivia as a baby.

"Aw, you were so cute."

"Were? Am I not now?"

From the tone in her voice, I think she's teasing me, though I answer as best as I can. "Now you're beautiful."

"Smooth." She grins.

"Where is my phone?" her mom mumbles in the background. "I'm going to check the kitchen."

Olivia rolls her eyes, leading me to believe this happens often.

There's another picture that catches my eye. A girl with brown hair and verdant eyes just like Olivia, but this girl's hair is cut shorter. Anyone else might simply mistake her for Olivia, but I know better. That's not Olivia.

That's the girl from my dreams.

From my nightmares.

That's the girl that was tied up.

That's the girl that told me to protect Olivia.

Olivia noticed my gaze and says, "That's—"

"Grace."

The Defeatist

There were two sisters.
    That's what I failed to realize that night.
    Two seemingly indistinguishable sisters.
    One is now dead.
    The other is alive.
    One I killed.
    The other I could've killed.
    If only I had known.
    Cole has confused these sisters, too.
    It's understandable.
    Cole loves one of these sisters.
    The other sister, he's had a couple conversations with.
    He assumed she was a product of his imagination.
    She wasn't.

The Existentialist

She's real. Grace is Olivia's sister.

Olivia peers at me. "Yeah...how'd you know her name?"

I don't know how to answer that question. I don't even know how I know. She's from my dreams and Dad said she's a product of my imagination.

But you know that's not true.

It has to be. Dad wouldn't lie to me.

Sweetie, there's a picture in front of you confirming her existence.

I know. None of this makes sense. I'm having such conflicting thoughts. I know she's real, there's no doubt about that now. Then again, how could she be? How could I confuse something so monumental for a dream? How could I have forgotten what happened to her?

"Cole?"

Crap. She's waiting for an answer. "You told me before."

I know I shouldn't lie, especially to Olivia. But how exactly do you tell the girl you like that you've been having dreams of her dead sister since you were eight? Except they aren't exactly dreams, they're *distorted* memories.

Would she believe me?

Do I believe myself?

I believe in you, sweetie.

Great, the voice in my head believes in me. That's very reassuring.

Olivia's mom returns with her phone. "It was in my hand the whole time."

Olivia laughs. "Mom how does this manage to happen every other day?"

Her mom snaps a picture, then I drive her to the dance.

I need to get my head on straight, for Olivia's sake. I need to forget about what had just happened, just for tonight. This whole night's meant to be about her. I want to make her feel as special as I see her.

I need to put all this behind me.

I need to store it with all my other hallucinations, in the back of my head. Once I do, I'm onto my next struggle—trying to act normal around Olivia. Her beauty is staggering. It's hard to treat her like a queen when I can barely formulate two words.

When we arrive at the dance, Olivia and I walk to a round table. I pull her chair out and gesture for her to sit down. She smoothens down her dress.

I see Nate by the drink table. Hoping fluids and Nate will diminish my nerves, I tell Olivia I'll go get her some punch.

"I wouldn't drink that if I were you," Nate says. "Chris spiked it with vodka."

Alcohol doesn't sound too bad right about now.

Cole, you know how bad the hallucinations get when you're drunk.

Relax, I was only kidding.

"So, you finally locked down Olivia?" Nate asks while slurping the alcoholic punch.

God, I hate that term. It's obnoxious. You use that term to describe confining prisoners. I'd never want to use it romantically.

"I didn't 'lock her down', I asked her to the prom."

"Potato, *potato*."

I feel like I'm dripping buckets of sweat. I lift up my arm and sniff my armpit. It doesn't smell.

Thank God.

Something I've been doing a lot of lately.

"Jeez, you really are nervous," Nate says.

"I don't know how to act around her." I gape at Olivia, sitting alone. Just looking at her makes me think the world is a better place, simply because she's in it.

I continue, "Her beauty isn't just from head to toe, it's her mind, her soul, the way she talks and what she talks about. She is the prettiest girl in here Nate. I mean no one even comes close, yet she doesn't even realize it."

"Well, you realize it, so stop chatting with me and go back to her."

"Okay, you're right." I know I need to go back there, but my legs refuse to move. I fear I'm going to mess this night up.

Nate pats my back. "Cole, if you don't start moving, I'm going to push you there."

I walk back to the table, holding a plastic cup of water. I hand Olivia the cup. "The punch has alcohol in it, so I got you water. I hope that's okay."

We both sit there in silence, neither of us saying a word. We have hung out many times in the past. It shouldn't be as weird as it is, except it was different this time. Though we didn't say it, we knew. We knew how we felt about each other.

After minutes of unbearable silence, Olivia rises from her seat. She holds her hand out, in my direction. "Do you want to dance?"

"Last time we danced you told me I was no fun."

"Last time we danced I was an idiot."

She grabs my hand leading me to the dance floor, chin raised, eyes sparkling with bliss.

Lean On by Major Lazer is playing. Olivia's dancing carefree, with an infectious sense of euphoria. I don't know if people are staring at us or not, and I honestly don't care. I'm having fun, and judging by the grin on Olivia's face, I get the feeling she is too.

The upbeat music abruptly stops and a slow song comes on. I pull Olivia closer and wrap my arms around her waist. She places her soothing hands around my neck, interlacing her fingers, then lies her head against my chest as we sway to the music.

"Thank you."

"For what?" I ask.

"For everything."

With her head on my chest and my arms around her. I want to stop time, remaining in this tranquil moment forever. There are no voices. No nightmares. Just me, and Olivia.

The song ends, and with it the moment. We return to our table. Nate taps my shoulder. Surreptitiously, he signals toward the other side of the gymnasium. Jack is sitting by a table, arm wrapped around a visibly intoxicated girl.

"It's getting kind of boring," I say. "What do you say we head home?"

"Already?" Olivia chuckles. "We just got here." Her eyes dart around the room until narrowing in on Jack. "Is he seriously here with another drunk girl?!"

Olivia rises from her seat and paces to the crystal punch bowl, high heels click, clacking against the gymnasium floor. I follow her, carefully. She carries the bowl to Jack and…

"Olivia, what are you…"

Holding the bowl above her head, she splashes it on him.

Christ.

Jack's face turns crimson, though I'm unsure if that's the punch dripping down his forehead. "You whore," he barks.

Olivia drops the bowl and gives him the finger, making the drunk girl laugh hysterically. She cups the drunk girl's arm. "Do yourself a favor, and go home. He'll take advantage of you otherwise."

71

I.YMASLOW

I glance around the gymnasium, everyone's eyes are on Jack, smirking with hands over their mouths.

A few of Jack's friends stand up and with rage filled eyes, stride towards us.

"We need to leave now," I say.

Olivia spots them and nods pointedly at the emergency exit which leads to the parking lot outside. She twists off her high heels and tosses them to me, running barefoot. I try not to slip on the punch while bolting behind her.

She pushes the steel door open and still holding her heels, I slip through.

The parking lot is vast and brimming with parked cars. It's a challenge for us to find ours, but once we do, we know we're safe. I unlatch the car door for her. Before she hops in, she stops and looks at me with a smile that makes my lips yearn for hers. I think she wants me to kiss her.

"My feet are cold," she says.

I burst out, laughing. "You're crazy, you know that?"

"Yeah," she tosses her hair over her shoulder. "And you love it."

I can't deny that.

The gymnasium door slam shut, and angry murmurs in the distance alarm me.

After getting in my car, I slam the gas pedal, and zoom away.

"The night's young," Olivia says. "Could we grab a bite?"

I glance out the window, spotting a diner. I pull over and after she puts her heels on, we walk in.

A neon sign mounted on the window reads **OPEN 24 HOURS**. The black and white checkered floor is glossy. I notice there's a wet floor sign beside the counter.

Without looking at the menu, Olivia orders a milkshake, a double cheeseburger, and fries.

I wonder if she's been here before or if she's just that sure of herself.

She looks back at me.

"Um, I'll just have a coke and a burger," I say.

An elderly man that looks like a stereotypical grandpa, types in our orders. I eyeball his name tag: Doug.

He hands us our food on trays. We sit in one of the red booths.

Olivia gobbles her burger like a lion eating its prey.

After finishing the double burger, she pats her stomach. "That was good."

"The hamburger or what you did to Jack?"

"Both." She scoffs.

She moves onto the fries, dipping them into her milkshake. When she takes a bite, she shuts her eyes and releases a moan.

Grinning I say, "You look like you enjoyed pouring that punch on him almost as much as you like those milkshake-dipped fries."

"Shut up." Olivia giggles. "And a milkshake with fries is the perfect combo."

She dips another fry into the milkshake and hands it to me. "Here, try it."

"It's tempting, but I won't succumb to peer pressure," I tease.

She rolls her eyes. "Oh, come on."

"I'll try it—"

"Yesss."

"*If* I sit in the same side of the booth as you."

"I fail to see what one has to do with the other."

"You want me to try it, no?"

"Ok, fine."

I slide into her side of the booth, grasp the fry, and stare at it. What am I getting myself into? A French fry mixed with ice cream. If schizophrenia doesn't take me, diabetes will.

That's not funny, Cole.

"Jesus, Cole, you're acting like it's a plan B pill. Just eat it."

I toss it in my mouth.

A moment passes before I say, "Whoa…"

"Right?"

"Okay, that was actually a really good combination."

I gaze at her and she gazes back at me. We don't speak for a moment.

"You didn't think sitting beside me would result in a kiss, did you?"

"What? No—"

She presses her lips against mine. After she pulls away, she says, "Well, I did."

I press my lips back against hers.

"So did I."

Doug interrupts. "I'm sorry to bother you guys." He looks at me. "But you're Mrs. Haynes' son, right?"

I glance at Olivia, and her head is pointed in his direction; he's not a hallucination. "I think you're confusing me for someone else."

"You may be right. It's a side effect of old age." He chuckles. His chuckle reminds me of Santa Claus.

"That was odd," Olivia says.

"Yeah, it was…"

I lean in, pushing my lips against hers.

The Defeatist

I'm not happy I had to kill Grace.

Looking back, there were a bunch of things I could've done different.

But at the time I only saw one option.

I didn't even know what these kids were going through behind closed doors.

It's a horrible thing.

Naiveness.

Thinking the world is better than it actually is.

Because if we aren't exposed to certain things, we believe they don't exist. That they can't exist.

And if they do exist, it isn't as bad as it seems.

Some of us create self-justifications. We tell ourselves *what could we possibly do to help?* Or that *someone else will take care of it.*

We need these self-justifications because without them, we'd be forced to make a difference. And that would require real work.

Something none of us want.

I remember reading a news article about a woman who was killed in her own apartment.

A deranged psychopath would repeatedly break in and attack her.

It was loud and vile.
All her neighbors admitted to hearing these heinous attacks.
When asked why no one called the police, their answers were all the same;
I assumed someone else would.
No one ever did.
The woman was killed in her apartment while her neighbors listened.
Could you imagine what that's like?
No?
Of course not. You've never experienced anything like that.
And if you did, just like the neighbors, you'd say *it's safer to let someone else handle it.*
Because if it's not happening to us, why worry?
We live in a society saturated with neighbors.
You can disagree with me, but as I stated prior, you've never experienced being in this situation.
I have.
See, I'm not speaking from a place of contempt.
I'm a neighbor. Or at least I was.
Until I took Grace's life…

The Cynic

The truth about Cole Torsney is one that often confuses me. It's a complex truth. One I'm not sure even he understands. One I barely understand myself.

It was a surreal moment, realizing a student's sister here at the school was also murdered by The Cauterizing Killer. I see them in the halls. Love fills their arrogant eyes. They seem so normal. They act so normal. But they are far from that. Both of them are in for a world-shattering surprise.

It's not a coincidence she's just moved here. Someone is planning something. Something so elaborately destructive it will destroy everyone involved. Like a burning building, no rooms will survive. And even after the fire's out, the smoke will be in the air, polluting everyone else.

But I've put it behind me. I've realized the match has already been lit. The safest thing for me to do is get as far away from the burning building as possible. And with all the stressful work I've been doing, that won't be a challenge.

See, Cole's a puzzle to me, one I'm not going to solve. But after watching him with Olivia walking home that night at the party, I know someone else is about to.

It's starting to get dark early. Here at night, the low-lit school is depressing. I'm hoping to get all the work done quickly so I can go home as soon as possible. I've mopped most of the ground floor. I may have forgotten a couple rooms, but I doubt anyone will notice.

I enter the joyless detention room. I recognize some of the students. Shame washes over me. This is what I've come to. The students that fear and respect me are watching me mop the floors.

Mr. Hurd is sleeping while a Vietnam War documentary plays. Tyler's here drinking a cup of soda. He notices me and plasters a smug smirk onto his face. Then, he splashes his cup onto the floor.

"Oops," he says. "Mr. Haynes, I spilled my soda... clean it."

That kid. The world wouldn't miss him if he was gone. His father needs to beat some respect into him.

Clasping my mop, I walk over to him and wipe the floors.

He whispers, "That's for giving me a D, Blake."

My name being uttered by a student sends chills down my spine. I want to use his body to clean the floors. No that's too easy, I want him to lick the floors clean, not stopping until it's spotless.

One day, this kid will get what he deserves.

After the janitorial shift, I go home. As I walk in, Finn's waiting beside the door, eager to show me something.

"You're going to have to wait a minute," I say. "I have papers to grade." I sit by the table, taking the papers out. Then, I dig in my bag, searching for my red pen.

"A minute passed." Finn says.

Where is this stupid red pen? Its incongruous color should stick out. I turn the flashlight on in my phone, point it in the bag, and start shuffling things around.

"Sir, a minute passed. I want to show you what I made you."

"Ok, Finn." I turn my bag upside-down over the table; everything rustles out.

"You said in a minute you'll look at what I drew. It's been a minute."

"Jesus Christ, Finn, will you ever shut the fuck up?!" I smack him, making him plop onto the hardwood. He's crying now. I need to make it better, so I could work. If I could, I'd hit him until he's silent, but I've learned that doesn't work. "You know I love you Finn," I say. "This all comes from a place of love. You understand that don't you?"

He wipes his tears from his face. There's revolting snot running down his nose.

"I know," he says.

"Good. Now get some tissues and wipe your nose. You're a man. Act like it."

He runs to the bathroom, dropping a drawing of a lake he was holding.

I know I seem abusive. I'm not. Not really. You see I'm a realist and as a teacher I know, the greatest way to teach a child isn't verbally or through a book, it's hands-on learning, where the student is actively engaged. It helps them retain information better. Me hitting Finn is the best way to teach him. And if it mitigates my stress, then that's just an additional benefit of being a benevolent parent.

The next day, during my much-needed lunch break, my phone rings—unknown number. I answer it, and it's Finn's school. Apparently, he doesn't have lunch. One of his teachers is asking me to pick something up and bring it to him.

Finn. I want him gone. He's a burden in my life, straining my soul. Foster care isn't a choice. His mom went there and she turned out to be a bitch. I wouldn't subject him to that form of abuse.

I do so much for him. I don't understand why he can't do something as simple as making his own lunch. He's nine years old. How hard is it to spread peanut butter on two slices of bread? An infant could do it. Regardless, I'm going to have to pick something up and bring it down.

Great.

Finn's public school is consolidated; each classroom crammed with as many students as the state permits. It makes me question the ethics of our local government. Carrying a bag of lunch, I walk along the narrow halls. I see Finn sitting, shoulders hunched, outside the teacher's office.

I'm going to give him hell. He knows it. I could practically see the butterflies fluttering in his stomach. I don't know what's more tortuous for him; Anticipating my affliction, or the affliction itself. I'm savoring all of this.

"Finn!"

He twitches at the agitation in my voice.

A red-haired teacher steps in my way. She's wearing a pastel blouse and tailored pants, holding her hand out in my direction. "You must be Finn's father. I'm Ms. Bailey," she says with perkiness. "But you can call me Katherine."

I stare at her inviting hand. I realize I'm supposed to shake it. I've been devoid of a woman's touch for so long. I shake it, graciously, though I don't show it. Her hand is smooth and delicate. I don't want to let go, yet I do. I don't want to mess this up.

She tilts her seductive head and points to the bag I'm holding. "Is that Finn's lunch?"

"Is that Finn's lunch? I mean, yes, it is. It's his lunch." Oh no. I messed up before I even started. This always happens to me. Eh. Fuck that. Who cares? I don't need her.

She giggles, and all the humiliation I feel dissipates. "Finn told me you're funny."

Wow, she's still talking to me. I might actually have a chance.

She turns to Finn. "Go, get your lunch buddy."

He trudges, stopping in front of me. "Can I have my lunch sir?" He stands still as a soldier. Katherine looks at Finn then to me, confused. I need to salvage this before she jumps to conclusions.

"Yes, you may cadet." I throw him a salute, then hand him the lunch. He grabs it and runs to class. I want to yell at him for grabbing it the way he did but I don't. Not in front of Katherine.

"The way you play army with him is so cute," she says. "I don't see many dads doing that."

"Yeah, well, I care about Finn."

"That's really attractive. I know how hard it can be for a single dad to raise children." She thrusts her chest forward. "You know, if you ever need someone to cook a meal for you and Finn, or to help around the house, you could call me."

I'm getting laid tonight.

"I have to get back to class, but it was nice meeting you, Blake."

Or maybe not.

She smiles and I smile back. It's been a while since I smiled.

I return to my car, incredulously replaying what just happened.

The Defeatist

What is a life worth to you?

Scratch that. That's a very ambiguous question.

What I meant to ask is this:

Would you ever murder someone?

Again, scratch that. Stupid question. Most people would impulsively answer no.

But if someone held a gun to your loved one's head, and they gave you a choice, kill me or I kill them, then your answer to my question would change.

So, for a third time, let me reword my question.

Under what conditions would you feel it necessary to take a person's life?

Well, don't just stare at me blankly.

I know it's a difficult question.

One you probably haven't given too much thought to.

One you would rather not give too much thought to.

One you're fortunate enough not to give too much thought to.

You may be optimistic and say, *let's hope that day never comes.*

You may even be a delusional optimist and say, *that day never will come.*

But have you ever heard of Murphy's First Law?

It states, that anything that can go wrong, will go wrong.

What you fail to grasp is that I was like you.
An optimist.
Until I was required to answer that demoralizing question.
What is a life worth to you?

The Stoic

Weeks after the winter formal, I ask Cole to come over. Mom's been pestering me to visit Dad. I don't want to see him, seeing as he belittles every little thing I do, and he's degraded Mom repeatedly.

I can't fathom why she of all people is pushing me to see him. I know people say "family is family." But with some people that's not the case. With some people *toxic is toxic.* And if he's toxic, I should be allowed to walk away from him.

Sitting on the couch, I hear someone tapping the door.

Cole.

I dash to the entrance, but Mom whooshes past me, wanting to talk to him before I could. She opens the door and whips a smile onto her face. "Hey Cole, maybe you could convince Olivia to visit her dad."

Cole tilts his head, looking at Mom then back at me.

"Mom leave him alone. We're going upstairs." I grab his hand leading him to my room, hoping Mom won't embarrass me anymore then she already has.

"Don't forget to leave your door open, honey." Mom announces.

We sit on my bed and I dig my palms into my face, almost like a Korean face massage. "Ugh."

"What's wrong?" Cole asks.

"My mom wants me to visit my dad." My eyes drift to the floor. "She says I haven't seen him in weeks."

"I'm sure it's hard to be around him," Cole says. "But I think you should visit him."

"Why?" I ask. "Because family is family?" I roll my eyes, then gaze at the corner of my room.

"No." Cole put his hand on my chin twisting my focus to him. "Because everyone deserves a second chance."

Silently, we stare into each other's eyes.

"You guys better not be making out up there!" Mom shouts.

I facepalm. "Mom!"

Cole chuckles. "I'll go with you. If anything bad happens, I'll be there."

"You don't have—"

"I want to."

Standing in front of Dad's studio apartment, on the other side of town, I knock on his rickety door. Dad opens it wearing joggers and a yellowed undershirt. I get a whiff of something sour, though I can't place its origin.

Dad hugs me and I locate the source of the odor.

"Come in, come in." He motions with his hands.

We sit on his blanketed futon. The coffee table in front of us is littered with beer cans.

Dad unlatches a folding chair and with the backrest between his legs, sits across from us. He initiates the conversation with a very generic question. "So, how's school?"

"It's—"

"I assume you're getting decent grades," he says.

I don't bother speaking. I know my father. He's just going to cut me off or respond with something crude.

"You better not be getting too distracted; you need to get into NYU next year."

I.YMASLOW

Tugging at my earlobe, I say, "I was actually thinking of going to a college more local."

"Ha-ha."

"I'm serious."

He points his stubby finger at me. "You're not going to any of these loser colleges unless you want to end up living on the streets."

I soften my tone, "Local colleges have a lot to offer and I think with my grades I could get a scholarship. That saves Mom lots of money."

Dad chuckles and rolls his eyes. "Susan's a lawyer. She doesn't need to be saving any more money. You're going to NYU!" My dad yells. Then he rises from his chair and my shoulders slump. "You know this is why you don't have friends. You're always looking to argue. Just like your mom."

Cole stands up. "That's enough."

Dad squints while inclining his head. "Who the hell do you think you are? Just because you're fuckin my daughter you think you get a say in her future? This is a family matter. You're. Not. Family."

I tug at Cole's hand. He turns to me and I shake my head. It's not worth it.

Cole and I walk to the door.

"Are you serious?" Dad asks. "We have a small argument and you leave? Just like that. You're more like your mom than I thought."

It's not a small argument. This is how we converse. How he converses. If I stay here longer it's going to perpetuate. I came here out of respect for my mom, and I'm leaving here out of respect for myself.

Outside Cole says, "I'm sorry you had to go through that."

I giggle. "I'm the one that should be apologizing to you."

He opens the car door for me. Once we're both seated inside, I say, "There's always something depressing on the news."

Cole looks at me. "What?"

"I remember when I was younger, my parents were sitting on the couch watching TV. The news anchors were talking about a local killer. One that kills and brands children. They thought he was a pedophile." I pick at my nail. "You know when the typical response to hearing about a child dying is *I don't know what I'd do if that was my child.* But my father, he's not typical. He said that *the pedophile would get more pleasure out of our daughters than we ever would.*" Looking out the window, I continue, "I'll never forget those chilling, therapy inducing words."

Cole doesn't respond. I don't know how he could. I wouldn't know what to say. I shouldn't have opened up. I should've kept my problems to myself. Like normal people do.

"Olivia." Cole says, while maintaining focus on the road.

"What?"

"I'm not going ask if you're okay," he says. "You know why?"

"Why?"

"Because even if you weren't okay, you wouldn't tell me."

"I guess I'm so weak I can't open up to the one person I love." Crap. Did I just say that out loud?

"No," he says. "You're so strong you'd never let anyone know they saddened you." He continues, "If anyone hurt you, you'd never let them see you cry. If anyone managed to knock you down, you'd never let them see you limp. And if anyone broke you, you'd never let them see you as anything but whole. A moment passes before he says, "And I love you too."

The Defeatist

Euthanasia.

The word's origin is Greek.

It means good death.

Most people today associate the word with the killing of animals.

It's been a common practice passed on for centuries.

The most innocent of God's creatures, suffer. And when that happens… we kill them.

Dogs, for example. Their only sin is the undying trust of man.

When they get hurt, it's man that kills them.

When they get sick, it's man that kills them.

When they are too violent, it's man that kills them.

Dogs, like children with their parents, have a misplaced trust.

I'm not going to question the ethics of euthanization.

We kill them to end their affliction. It's painless. That is when they die through injection of sodium pentobarbital. However, some states are permitted to use gas chambers.

I can't vouch for how painless those are.

Now you may be surprised to learn, here in the U.S., human euthanasia and medical assisted suicide is legal in ten states.

Besides that, in every state it is legal to pull the plug. You may say, *well that's with the patient, or family's consent.*

Now at the risk of sounding pedantic, you'll once again be surprised to learn that this is not always the case.

A hospital can ask a provincial board to overrule the wishes of a patient or decision maker.

They can decide to end a man's life without the man or his family's consent.

Earlier I asked you, would you ever end a man's life?

Now, you probably thought you'd kill the person holding your mom's life at stake.

What if she was the one putting her life at stake?

What if she was suffering?

What if she was brain-dead?

What if she was bound to die a tedious and painful death, and you killing her would be a mercy?

What if she was going to kill herself anyways?

These are profound questions that require heavy contemplation. Not the type seventeen-year-olds usually think about. I'm sure you'd rather abstain from thinking about this stuff.

But if you want to know why your sister had to die, you have to ask yourself these questions.

The Cynic

Tonight, Katherine's coming over for dinner. Things need to go well. This is the first dinner I've had with a woman, or anyone for that matter, in a very long time. She's bringing homemade eggplant parmesan and a salad. The table is all set; with a white table cloth, matte black dinner plates, and stainless-steel silverware. I even went as far as buying rolls. I've seen families do that on TV. I assume that's normal.

I hear a chair squeal. I rush to the kitchen adjacent dining room. "Jesus Christ! Are you fucking stupid?"

Finn gapes at me, shocked, with a roll in his mouth. His face turns ashen as he grips onto the chair, prepared for what I'm about do.

"That was for Katherine you idiot."

I yank him off the chair, once again resulting in him slamming onto the hardwood floor.

Grabbing the half-eaten roll, I go to the kitchen and drop it in the garbage. When I return to the dining room, there are crimson puddles on the floor. It's blood coming from Finn's nose.

Oh God.

How can this much blood come from something so small? Then again, he has always been a bit of a hemophiliac.

I glance at my watch. Katherine's going to be here any minute now. Finn's sniveling. There's blood running down his nose onto the floor. I'll kill him if he ruins this for me. I need to call her and cancel.

No. I can't do that. I don't want to mess this up. I'll tell her to come later.

The doorbell chimes.

Crap. She's here.

"Finn, go to the upstairs bathroom and wash up."

He throws me a helpless look.

"Don't look at me like that, you did this to yourself and you know it."

His shirt and pants are now stained with blood. He drags himself upstairs.

I snatch a bunch of paper towels and wipe the blood off the floors. The doorbell chimes again.

"Hello?" Katherine calls out. "Anyone home?"

I toss the paper towels into the trash and flutter to the door.

"Hey, sorry about that. Finn got himself into a little mess. I was just helping him clean up."

She smiles. "That's so sweet of you."

That's me... *sweet.*

There's a wooden bowl on top of the ruby red roaster she's clutching. I invite her in and we walk to the table. I realize there's a splash of blood still on the floor. I wipe it with my shoe, hoping she didn't notice.

Katherine exhales as the roaster thumps onto the table. It sounded heavy. Was I supposed to take it from her when she walked in? Whatever, doesn't matter now.

She blushes. "Ok, so I'm going to apologize in advance for offending your taste buds, but I left the eggplant parmesan in for too long, and it got a little... 'well-done.'" She takes the foil off the pan.

The food is a little burnt, but honestly, it looks tastier than any-thing I've had in months.

She pulls the side chair out for herself. "So, where's Finn?"

I forgot about him. He should've been back by now. His nose better be all dried up. I don't want to see a drop of red on him.

"Let me go get him."

I walk upstairs, to his room. When I see him, I slam my fist against the wall. Bloodstained tissues scatter across the floor. The new outfit he put on, just like the old one, is now drenched in blood. He's standing, holding a sock up to his nose.

"Jesus, Finn. You had one job. One. Job."

He always does this. Ruins things for me.

"Everything okay up there?" Katherine asks.

"Yeah. I'll be down in a minute," I shout. I place my hands on Finn's shoulders and sit him on the rickety bed. I clench my jaw, trying not to scream at him. After a moment passes, I plaster a smile on my face. Biting my tongue, I say, "Listen, you are going to stay up here the rest of the night. You're not to come down no matter what. If you wanted to come down you wouldn't have made this mess. You're going to close the door and stay quiet until Katherine leaves."

Coughing on his blood he asks, "What about dinner?"

"I'm sure that bite from the roll filled you up plenty."

Leaving the room, Finn says, "The blood…it's not stopping."

"Don't be stupid. It always stops." I slam the door behind me.

The Defeatist

People avoid talking about trauma.

We like to act like we live this perfect life.

Like nothing bad has ever happened to us.

Like nothing bad is happening to us.

Like nothing bad could happen to us.

Yet, we all know life isn't perfect.

The world is more often than not, a cruel place.

As much as we like to believe we don't, we all suffer from the same disease.

Life.

However, some suffer more than others.

Some suffer from the force that's meant to be protecting them.

From the force that's meant to be nurturing them.

Teaching them.

Loving them.

When the thing keeping you breathing is the thing suffocating you, then you are no longer alive.

You are a walking corpse.

At least that's what I thought. Until someone taught me that these people are alive.

They live a life worse than a walking corpse.

A walking corpse isn't sentient. It doesn't feel torment or agony.

That's all these people feel.

Each step they take is like walking on needles. The further they walk, the sharper and longer the needles grow.

They are damned before death.

They are damned from conception.

With their souls in anguish, they're detrimental to themselves.

These people are alive, but they don't live life.

They suffer from it.

The Stoic

The school cafeteria is swarming with babbling students. As I enter, the smell of mop water makes me grimace. Directly to my left, the janitor is mopping soda someone spilled.

He takes note of my grimace and says, "If you hate the smell so much, tell your friends not to be so clumsy."

I think he believes all teenagers here are friends.

I usually sit with Cole at lunch, but he hasn't been in school for the last two days. He also hasn't answered my text messages or phone calls. I don't know what's going on with him. He's never ignored me before.

I find Nate by a lunch table with a few unfamiliar guys. I knew he had other friends, but I've never seen him hang out with anyone besides Cole and I. He's deep in conversation and doesn't notice me standing beside him. I tap his shoulder.

He turns to me, bewildered. "Oh hey, Olivia."

"Have you seen Cole?" I ask. "I don't think he came today."

Nate's expression dulls. "Yeah…" His mouth hangs slightly ajar, yet he doesn't speak. He looks like he's carefully choosing his words. Scratching his nose he says, "he's uh…not feeling too well. Best to leave him alone today."

"What does he have? A cold? The flu?" I ask. "I could bring over some soup after school."

Nate's buddies now look at him like they want to know what's going on just as bad as I do. He rises and walks to the side of the cafeteria, beckoning me to follow.

He glances left then right, almost like he's making sure we are alone. We aren't, there are people all over. This is a school cafeteria and it's lunchtime. Regardless they all seem distracted.

With a soft undertone he says, "Cole gets…unwell, at times."

"What's going on?" I ask. "What do you mean unwell?"

"Just trust me, you don't want to see him like this. I know him. This stuff passes. He's best left alone at times like these."

Left alone?

"Nate, I love him. I want to make sure he's okay and until I know that, I won't leave him *left alone*."

Nate pinches his temple. "That's not what I meant. It's just, when he's alone, it's easier for him to distinguish reality from—" his mouth shuts. Then he inhales. "Cole's my best friend. It's not my place to tell you what he's dealing with unless he wants me to."

"Does he want you to?"

Nate doesn't respond, which is response enough.

This is futile. Nate's not going to tell me what's going on with Cole, and I can't say I'm angry at that. He's a good friend. I just wish I knew what was going on.

When school is over, I head to the bus, wanting to get off at Cole's stop to make sure he's okay. As I'm about to step onto the bus, Nate swiftly puts his hand in front of the entryway, blocking me.

I'm exasperated. "Nate, what are you doing?"

"I know what you're thinking of doing and trust me, don't."

Cole's been with me through my worst. Whatever he's dealing with, I need to help him get through. "I'm going to see Cole."

"Olivia, if you see Cole like this... you're not going to want to see him anymore."

"You don't know that," I say. How can Nate even say something like that? "I love him."

"No, you think you do. You don't know him. Not really."

I don't know what Nate is talking about, nor do I care.

There's a line of people now waiting to get on the bus, some groaning. Nate realizing this, rubs his shoulder. "Okay, if I can't stop you, the least I can do is get this thing over with faster. Rip the bandage off." Nate nods at the parking lot. "I'll drive."

Nate's car is a large Jeep Wrangler. It looks expensive, with the barricade on the front bumper and a LED light bar on the front roof. Nate's parents must've bought him this car considering he doesn't have a job. Cole told me Nate's parents used to struggle with money until they found their latest job. Nice to see they're doing okay now.

"Nice car, right? My parents bought it for me."

Thought so, though, I act surprised.

"You must think I'm some spoiled rich kid now. I used to babysit my younger siblings every night. Actually, Cole babysat them too, some nights. Once my parents got hired at this big firm, they started making a lot of money. They got me this car as a way to thank me for giving up all those nights to babysit my siblings."

Now I feel like a jerk. "That must've been hard," I say. "Juggling schoolwork and babysitting your siblings."

"Eh, everyone has their fair share of hardships in life. There are worse things than cooking my sibling's dinner, bathing them, and reading them bedtime stories." Nate makes a sharp right turn. "Sorry about that."

Gripping onto the handle for dear life, I say "It's alright, barely noticed."

He continues, "You know, I guess in a way I am spoiled. The only thing I have to worry about are finals. There are people, some of whom are in our school, that have to deal with a lot more." He nods to a house. "We're here."

I've never seen Cole's house in person. The house is a two story, traditional house with a smoke-stained roof. I notice the first-floor windows are barred.

Nate parallel parks in a tight spot. I don't think his car will fit. He tells me to go outside and while he backs up, inform him on how much space he has.

I hold out my hand. "Ok, ok. Stop there's no more room." He must not hear me because he continues backing up.

After Nate exits the car, we walk to the door, and I see at least six different security cameras attached to the house. The front door appears to be wooden but when Nate knocks, it clangs. It's metal.

No one answers.

He knocks again.

A clean-shaven, middle-aged man opens the door. He's wearing a maroon henley and retro black glasses. That must be Cole's dad. I just realize I have never seen his dad before. How have I never seen his dad before? What if Nate is right? What if I don't know enough about Cole?

And if I don't know enough about him, how could I love him?

We walk in. "Cole still in his room?" Nate asks

"Same as when you left this morning," Cole's father responds.

"Has he eaten anything?"

"Nope. Nothing all day. I'm worried for him. It's never been this bad."

Nate eyes drift to the floor. "We'll talk to him."

We walk up the beige carpeted stairs. Nate knocks on the door. Without waiting for a response, he twists the knob, slowly opening the door. "Hey Cole, It's me and Olivia. We wanted to check on you. See how you're doing."

Cole doesn't reply.

Nate walks in with gentle, measured steps. I imitate him. A tray of uneaten French toast and a glass of milk sits on his nightstand. I assume it's been there since the morning.

It is frigidly dim in here. The lights are off and the shades are closed; blocking off all sunlight. Cole's resting on his bed with a white blanket covering him, head facing the side, eyes mindlessly fixated on the wall. He looks like he is thinking of so much and so little at the same time.

"I think it's best if I leave you two alone. Cole, I'm going to be right outside if you need me." Nate exits the room.

I sit upright on the side of his bed, leering downward at him. He looks devoid of life, his disposition echoing that of a traumatized soldier. I don't know what to say. I don't know what is going on.

"Cole, I missed you at school today."

No response.

I grab his tepid hand. "Cole, you can talk to me. Whatever this is, whatever is going on with you, know you can talk to me about it."

His eyes are still fixated on the wall. I let go of his hand, reaching out to open the curtains, but he grabs my hand stopping me.

"No." He mutters under his breath. He looks barely conscious, though his eyes are off the wall, focused on me.

"Cole, I need you to come downstairs, eat something. Anything." I plead.

"Leave," he croaks.

I pretend not to hear that.

His face scrunches up and he groans, "Leave."

"I'm not leaving you. Not until I know you're okay."

His eyes narrow. "Leave!" His capricious gravelly voice makes my heart fluster.

I have never heard him talk like this. I don't recognize him.

He goes ballistic, pointing to the door, he yells, "Get out!"

99

I spring off his bed, shuffling backwards, not stopping until my back is against the door.

"I don't want you here." Glaring directly in my eyes, he rises from his bed and flings the tray of food against the wall. He stomps towards me until his face meets mine, then he barks, "Get out!"

Nate knocks on the door. "Is everything okay in there?"

Feeling ambivalent, I tell him, "You can go now, Nate. I'm staying the night."

"Are you su—"

"Yes." I look into Cole's fiery eyes and shake my head. "Cole, I don't know what's wrong with you. This isn't you. You're not acting like yourself."

Cole turns around, sluggishly walking toward his bed. He mumbles, "You don't know me. You don't know anything about me."

You don't know anything about me. Those chilling words reverberate in my head, making my neck stiffen.

"Maybe I don't know you. But you know me. I've never opened up to anyone and I opened up to you. I'm not leaving, I promise you that."

The fire burning inside him inexplicably vanishes and he returns to bed, covering himself with the blanket. Scared to be next to him, I stay seated on the floor, against the door.

What have I witnessed? Who is this person? What happened to the Cole I knew? Or the one I thought I knew. I opened up to him. Told him things I never told anyone.

I awaken on Cole's bedroom floor. I knead my back; it's sore. My head is throbbing and I don't want to know what my hair looks like. Opening my phone, expecting ten missed calls from Mom, I'm surprised, there are none. I'm incredulous.

I call her immediately to let her know I'm okay, and honestly, to see if she is okay. "Mom, before you get mad, I want you to know I was going to text you and let you know—"

"Honey, I'm not mad. Cole's beefy dad let me know what was going on and I totally understand. In fact, I'm coming over later to drop off some clothing. He explained that he gets like this sometimes. I figured you might want to stay the week at his house."

Whoa. I don't know what's weirder, the fact she described Mr. Torsney as beefy or that she's letting me sleep over at Cole's house.

For a week.

Mom over-sexualizes everything. In kindergarten I got invited to David Wilson's house for a playdate. Mom didn't let me go. She said he was too mature. Unbeknownst to her, he came out as gay in the 5th grade. In a way she was right. He came out earlier than most so maybe he was too mature.

"This isn't a vacation or a slumber party," she says. "You still have to go to school on Monday."

"I will, Mom."

"How's Cole doing now?"

I glance at his bed. "He's still asleep. Did Cole's father mention anything to you?"

"Oh," she says, sounding shocked. "I thought you knew."

"Knew what?"

"Honey, it's not for me to discuss. When Cole's ready to talk, he will. Don't pressure him. He's battling his own demons right now."

It seems like everyone knows what's going on with him except me. I thought I was close to him. In a way I guess I was. He just wasn't close to *me*. At least not close enough to tell me what he's going through.

I want to help but it's just so difficult.

It's hard to stop someone's pain when they don't want your help. It's even harder when you don't know what's causing it.

How do you heal a scar when you don't know where it is? It's like blindly stitching an open head wound. Except the person causing the blindness is the one that needs the stitches.

Cole starts yawning, then stretches his arms and legs out, keeping them stretched for a full minute.

"How are you feeling, Cole? Do you want to go downstairs and eat some breakfast?"

His frown is so depressingly animated it could kill a Disney character.

"I don't want to do anything," he says.

"You know I was thinking, with it being Saturday, maybe we could go to Green Point Lake together. I know how much you love that place."

"It's raining."

The dismal weather matches his disposition.

"Well, maybe we could watch Netflix together," I say.

Cole slightly opens the shades. Glimpsing outside, he lets out an extended sigh. "Why are you still here?"

I'm here because I care about you. I want to help you get through this. Whatever this is. I want to fight whatever you're fighting beside you. You can open up to me. You don't need to keep secrets from me. You can trust me. That's what I want to say. Instead, I remain silent.

Days later, I'm in science class failing to comprehend what a nucleus does to a cell. My hand prevents my head from falling onto the desk. For the last couple of days, I've been sleeping on Cole's living room couch. It's one of those contemporary sofas that looks really nice but are extremely uncomfortable.

When another mindless day of school finishes, Nate drops me off at Cole's house.

"Good luck," he wishes me.

I knock on the triple bolted door. Mr. Torsney unlocks it.

As I walk in, the smell of oregano fills my nostrils. Glancing to my right I see that Mr. Torsney ordered a pizza. To my surprise, Cole is in the roomy, bright kitchen.

Out of his room.

Eating.

Mr. Torsney now stands behind Cole, with his index finger pressed against his lips. I get the message: don't make this a big deal. Which it is.

In a deliberate nonchalant manner, I drop my school bag at the door, then join Cole at the kitchen table. I take a slice. Cole is eating his slice folded. I try not to watch him eating, but I'm astonished.

After taking a bite out of my slice, I say, "Mm, this pizza is delicious."

Cole finishes his slice and says, "Olivia, I wanted to know if I could talk with you."

Finally.

"Not here though," he says. "At Green Point Lake."

Despite how much Cole raves about it, I've never been to the illustrious Green Point Lake.

Cole looks toward his dad. "Is it okay if I drive there?"

Mr. Torsney's lips squeeze together for a moment before budging. "Okay, but I want updates every half an hour."

On the drive there, Cole plays country music with the windows down. The dirt road, along with the steady, but gentle breeze, is dreamlike and for a second, I actually believe I'm in the country.

Cole slams the breaks and the car drifts for a few seconds before coming to a halt. Stepping out of the car, my ankle twists on the rugged dirt road

Cole shuts his door. "Are you okay?"

I glance at my leg. "Yeah, just not used to this type of ground."

He points to the thick woods. "We need to walk along that path."

103

I scratch my head, perplexed. Not seeing a path, I wait for him to lead, then I follow.

After a long, tense twenty minutes, Cole stops, looks around, and draws a deep breath. I think this is the breathtaking place he told me about, yet, I don't see anything special. These are just ordinary trees. Regardless, if he likes it, I'll play along.

"Wow," I say. "This is really... *astonishing.*"

"Really?" he asks. "All I see are trees."

I try not to facepalm.

"Green Point Lake is further down," he says.

We continue walking along the taxing, obscured path. My aching feet are giving out. I don't know how much more of this I can take.

I gaze at Cole, who's not the least bit exhausted. He actually looks like he's enjoying himself.

How?

This is a wakeup call. I'm going to start jogging. Every other morning. No. Every morning.

Panting, I say, "maybe we could stop and sit. Just for a few minutes."

"Don't worry it's right there," he says, trying to put my mind to rest.

An immense lake emerges.

"This is it," Cole says.

I slowly embrace the panoramic view. "I'm speechless."

Cole sits on a moss-covered log, gesturing for me to join him. I sit beside him and he stares off into the distance.

"Remember that guy that spoke at the December school assembly?" he asks.

"Kinda," I lie.

"Do you remember what he was talking about?"

"You know as well as I do that nobody pays attention at those assemblies."

Cole smirks and nods. "He was talking about mental health. How anybody can be struggling with it."

Cole faces me, waiting for a response.

Confused, I say, "I don't understand."

"Olivia…I have schizophrenia. I hallucinate people that aren't there. I see things that aren't real. I hear voices and have scattered thoughts." He exhales. "There are periods of my life… kind of like right now, where I experience mood swings."

I don't know what to say. What do you say when someone tells you something like this? How should I react?

Not knowing what to do, I settle on hugging him.

A moment passes before I ask, "What do you hallucinate?"

"I hear these voices…I see this woman. My mom. Except, she's not my mom. My therapist said she's an auditory hallucination. Something I created."

"That must be hard," I say. "Living with your mom in your head."

"It's worse than you think. My mom, she… died. Killed herself when I was eight. Around the same time, I developed insomnia and was prescribed pentobarbital." His eyes drift to the ground. "I was the one that found her body. Her wrists were slit. My psychiatrist says because of that traumatic experience, and the lack of a mother, I created her as some fucked up compensation."

"I'm sorry you had to see that Cole," I tell him, not having the faintest idea of what else to say.

He continues, "I hear her a lot, most days. It's the most vivid whenever I come here."

"Then why do you like coming here?"

"It sounds screwed up, but I miss her. This curse I have is also a gift. Being able to communicate with my dead mother, seeing her, sometimes…is all I need."

I can't imagine having to find your mother dead, then having to live with her in your head. Having to mourn her, while she's right in front of you. How would you stay sane?

The sun fades and darkness rises. A wintry breeze sends chills down my spine. I wrap my shivering arms around myself.

"We should leave," Cole says.

In a rush to get back to the heated car, we pass a large tent. "People camp here?"

"Not really," Cole says. "This tent has been here for a year or two now, always in the same place."

I trip on an obscured branch and Cole catches me.

"Thanks," I say.

"Yeah, I think someone lives there."

The following day at lunch, Nate finds me before I could find him. The dreadful look on his face ties my stomach in knots, like a mother tightly lacing the shoes of her kid.

Nate begins, "Mr. Torsney doesn't know where Cole is." Nate's voice is trembling more than his body.

Doesn't know where Cole is. My heart doesn't just unwind from the knot it was in, it falls apart. Those words painfully remind me of something similar Mom said. *The police don't know where Grace is.*

I can feel a tear trying to escape but I won't let it. This is not the same. Cole has no connection to that psychopath that took Grace.

I swallow a gulp of air, trying to ease my intrusive thoughts.

"Did his father check Green Point Lake?" I ask.

"That was the first place he checked." Nate kneads the nape of his neck. "Mr. Torsney is panicking. This isn't like Cole. He thinks something happened to him."

I can gather what Nate's insinuating, and I swear he's trying to give me a heart attack. "You think someone took him?" Terror courses through my veins as I utter those nightmarish words. This seems so unreal I almost pinch myself.

"I know it's crazy," Nate answers. "His dad has always been paranoid. But he's a second away from calling the police."

"Did you check the bell tower by the town square?" I ask.

"No. What's there?"

"I'll explain on the way," I say.

Nate and I leave before lunch is over. He texts Mr. Torsney to meet us there. The double-arched bell tower is four stories tall. There's an adjoining Jewish café bustling with hungry individuals. Something tells me their food is about to become less than kosher.

Mr. Torsney is pacing back and forth, in the front of the building, when we arrive.

"The doors are locked," he says. "They're closed for some holiday."

"What holiday takes place in the middle of January?" Nate asks. "What happens if there's an emergency and someone..." Nate looks up at the green, weather-beaten bell, "needs to ring the bell?"

I hope he realizes the denseness of that statement.

Mr. Torsney looks at Nate and asks, "Are you sure he's here?"

Nate ponders at me.

No. In fact I'm extremely unsure of myself. What I really think is that somehow The Cauterizing Killer got to him. I don't say that though. Even in my head, I'm aware of how irrational it sounds.

What I do know, for a fact, is that Cole's been depressed. He's not the type to kill himself, but no one ever is. He once told me that if today was his last day, he'd want to spend it by the bell-tower.

"I'm going to check the back," I say. "You guys wait here, maybe someone will come and help."

The wind sweeps my hair behind me as I rush to the back.

"Olivia, wait!" Nate shouts, but I'm already gone.

There's a rusted ladder standing tall behind a few repugnant dumpsters. Not wanting to dawdle, I climb over them. The smell alone almost puts me in a coma, but I fight through it. For Cole.

107

I climb the treacherous ladder until reaching the roof. Cole stands across from me on the distant ledge, only a few feet separating us. He seems unfazed by the height, though, I can't say I am. The strong blowing winds up here could topple me.

"You're always there at the right moment," he says.

"No," I say. "I think you were waiting for me." I draw a heedful step closer.

"Don't." Cole holds his hand up. "I'm supposed to kill myself."

I shake my head in confusion. I feel the tears I locked away earlier attempting to escape once more and this time I can't keep them at bay. They rush from my eyes blurring my vision and I'm too shocked to wipe them aside.

"Cole, please," I plead, "step away from the ledge."

"You don't understand. I can't live with what I know. It's torture."

I can't focus on anything he is saying because of how close he is to that ledge. My eyes fixate on his foot; he's one step away from dying.

"I made French toast this morning," he says.

"That's great Cole, come down and we can make French toast every morning."

"It burned," he says.

He turns around and I sprint at him.

I blink and one foot's off the ledge.

The Defeatist

Could you manage to kill a person without ever laying your hands on them?

Could you take away his life before he stops breathing?

Before he hits the ground.

How could you convince a person to take his life so you won't have to?

I will admit, it's more than difficult. But not impossible.

That's just how conniving a killer could be.

Cole didn't need to be kidnapped. Not like Grace.

I wouldn't say he needed a shove. Just a gentle nudge.

He was already branded. Nobody needed to know who was really behind this.

But obviously I knew.

I also knew he wasn't going to be the last victim. Far from it.

A lot more people were going to die...

Thanks to me.

The Stoic

The night Grace was taken was a slow, rainy April night. My mom cooked mouthwatering meatloaf and mashed potatoes for dinner. She always cooked it just right, never too tough, and never dried out. She added the right amount of salt, pepper, garlic, and dried parsley. She hasn't cooked meatloaf since that night.

My sister and I had gotten into an argument after dinner. She was mad I kept stealing her hairbrush. I had my own, but her hair was always so pretty. I thought if I used her hairbrush, I'd have pretty hair like hers. I know, it sounds stupid and silly, but I was eight.

I idolized her. She was prom queen. She had the boyfriend, the popularity, the perfect grades, everything.

After our argument, Dad said she couldn't watch TV. She was watching reruns of Seinfeld, which was as odd then as it is now. I never understood her obsession with that show. As she stormed to her room, she grunted, "I hate you."

Those were the last words I ever heard her utter.

I hate you.

In the middle of the night, fast-approaching police sirens woke me up.

Peeking outside, I saw two policemen walking to the front door. One of them saw me and flapped his hand, mouthing hello.

I wasn't scared because I didn't know I should have been. At the time, the severity of the situation didn't dawn on me. I was confused. I soundlessly crawled to Grace's room, not wanting to let my parents know I was awake.

Grace wasn't there, but Mocha was. That's when fear consumed me. Something was wrong. Mocha wasn't moving. She was panting hard, but her eyes were closed. Wanting to wake her up, I poked her a few times.

"Mocha," I whispered. I needed something to hold, to hug. To make me feel safe.

She wouldn't wake up. My eyes narrowed in on the blood dripping from her fangs, onto the carpet.

I held her in my arms. "Mocha, please." My voice started breaking. "Wake up."

Tears fell on her limp, unconscious body. I realized I was crying. I didn't know if it was from fear or sadness.

I then trailed to the top of the staircase.

Downstairs, someone was weeping. No, that's not right, someone was bawling. It was Mom.

My heart fluttered and every hair on my arm stood up. There is not a single sound on this planet more disturbing, traumatizing, and appalling, than hearing your mother cry.

It wasn't the last time I heard those gut-wrenching tears either.

After trudging down the carpeted stairs, I spotted Mom standing by the doorway, taking quick heavy breaths, fighting back sobs as she talked to the stout police officer. I thought hearing her cry was atrocious, but seeing the redness in her eyes was a form of torture I wasn't prepared for at eight-years-old.

There was another police officer in the house, holding a Ziploc bag with a branding iron in it. I'd later learn his name was Johnny.

The iron had the letters *O.M.*

He tilted his head as he noticed me on the stairs.

"Where's my sister?"

His face turned ashen. "Let's sit on the couch."

We had two leather green couches in our simple living room. They shaped an L facing our TV, which hung on the wall. Johnny slumped on the couch, then patted the cushion next to him, gesturing for me to join him.

"How old are you?" he asked.

I held out eight fingers.

Johnny smiled a sympathetic smile. "Wow, you are a big girl."

"Yup. My sister is taking me to a big girl salon when I turn nine."

His eyes along with his smile, drifted to the floor.

I glanced to the doorway, where Mom was talking to the police officer.

"Where is my sister?"

"Oh my god!" Mom shouted. "Olivia."

I blink and before I know it, her arms are around me. With her face beside mine, I felt tears drizzling down my neck. When I realized they were hers, they burnt like acid.

"Mom, you're scaring me."

She took a long sniff, then said, "everything is going to be okay."

Years later when everything couldn't be further from okay, I realized… she was lying.

She never told me what happened to my sister or where my dad was that night. I think she was trying to shelter me from the truth and what had happened that night. Specifically, from how cruel and unjust the world was.

Johnny checked up on us numerous times in the following months. My mom forced me go to my room every time he came. They never explicitly told me what happened, but from the branding iron and the news articles I figured it out.

A psychotic serial killer, ridiculously dubbed: The Cauterizing Killer, broke into our house and took Grace, presumably killing her.

From what I read, he brands, then murders his victims. I don't know why Grace, and neither do the police. These killings are seemingly random. The only common denominator here is the fact that all his victims were minors.

They never found Grace's body. I used to think she was still alive. So did Mom. But this serial killer never leaves any survivors.

Except me.

He didn't take me that night.

The Defeatist

We live in world riddled with deceit and manipulation.

I lie.

You lie.

Cole lies to himself, though he fails to realize it.

That's how deceptive this world is.

That's how deceptive this world could be.

If we ever are telling the truth, being genuinely honest, people won't believe us.

It's only when we voice the truth that people claim deception and manipulation.

My wife lied to me.

For months.

At least I thought she did.

It was only after I killed her, that I realized...

She wasn't lying.

The Stoic

When I was younger, walking Mocha was like trying to tame a bull. My strength was feeble in comparison to hers and when she'd see a squirrel, she would tug at the leash, resulting in me letting go. The worst part was catching her, which was harder than holding her back. I'm neither strong nor fast. How I managed to grab Cole and pull him to me was nothing short of a miracle.

The look on his face didn't say he had nothing left to live for, it said he didn't know what he had to live for. His confusion confuses me. After tugging him we both fell over onto the flat roof.

"I don't know what's real and what isn't," he cried.

I told him, "I am."

He wrapped his arms around me and I think I heard him whisper, "Then so is she."

Now I'm in his kitchen, whipping up some French toast for him. He's in the living room with his father, who wanted to talk to him alone.

I generously sprinkle cinnamon on the slightly charred slices of French toast. Being that it's my first time making this, I know something's wrong with it. Either it's burnt or there's too much cinnamon. In any case, I screwed up. Tears re-emerge. Cole has done so much for me and I've done little to reciprocate.

And now he's tried to kill himself.

I'm still going to serve him the unpalatable plate of French toast because Cole's the type of guy that genuinely believes it's the thought that counts.

His dad is still talking. Not wanting to interrupt their conversation, I listen in, waiting for the right moment to enter the room.

"This can't be real, the things I'm dreaming." Cole's bawling.

"They aren't, Cole," his dad says.

"I googled it, though. She's dead."

"She is, but that has nothing to do with you Cole, trust me." He repeats himself in a sympathetic tone, "It has nothing to do with you."

"Then why do I keep seeing her?"

"We went through this. Mrs. Freed told you. These are fabricated memories. You must've heard about her somewhere and created them."

"Why would I create something like this?"

"Not intentionally. You're schizophrenic, Cole. This is all in your mind."

"I can't live like this. I keep trying to put it behind me." He sniffles. "For Olivia's sake." He stops bawling. "But how did I escape that night?"

The room goes silent.

I'm beyond confused. Have you ever left a show running while you went to the bathroom, thinking you won't miss much, then you come back not knowing what the hell is going on?

That's exactly how I'm feeling right now.

Is this what schizophrenia does to a person? It must be. I can't imagine what he's going through right now. What he thinks he's seeing.

I want to hug him. Let him know how much I care.

"Ahem." Entering the living room, plate of French toast in hand, I walk to Cole. He's wiping his eyes.

His dad glances at me and exits the room. I place the plate on the end table next to the couch. Cole cuts a piece and eats it.

"What do you think?"

"It's really good," he says with a disingenuous smile.

"There's too much cinnamon, isn't there?"

"Yes." The disingenuous smile fades. "But I appreciate you making it."

"One day my French toast will be better than yours."

Cole giggles. "When that day comes, I might have to marry you." He finishes the mediocre French toast. I realize he wasn't lying when he said he won't let food go to waste. Or maybe he ate it just to make me feel better.

Cole leads me upstairs to his dark, still room. The streetlights shimmer with enough light for us to see the bed. He's hush and so am I. The only audible noise, are the drums playing in my heart. He shuts the door, then locks it.

"What are you doing?" I ask softly.

"Shh. Can I kiss you?"

I grin, then nod. Even in the darkness his lips find mine, almost magnetically. And like magnets, I have trouble separating my lips from his, but once I do, he removes his T-shirt. I ogle at his dusky abs. I know where this is leading and I don't care. I slowly take off my crew neck and shimmy out of my skinny jeans. I glance at Cole who's kicking off his pants.

He looms closer until his hardbody touches mine. His stimulating fingers carry chills as he brushes them up my cheek. The feeling of his steamy breath against my neck makes me salivate.

"I've never…" I exhale.

"We don't have to."

Cole pulls away. I shake my head. Before I know it, my lips press against his, and our tongues flow against each other like waves in the ocean.

He throws me onto his bed, peering at me like I'm a sucking candy. Then he pulls off my scarlet underwear. The pain and pleasure coincide into one as I dig my fingernails into Cole, taking all of him in. Once we finish, he falls asleep beside me.

The birds are chirping, and I open my eyes. Beams of sunlight shine through the shades, making all the dust slowly floating in the air visible. I turn to Cole, who is still asleep with his mouth slightly ajar against a pillow. I kiss his forehead, then gaze at his hair which is still as spiky as yesterday. I'll always envy men for the lack of effort required to look good.

I should head downstairs before Mr. Torsney realizes I slept here last night. After rising from Cole's bed and dressing myself, I walk to the door. I turn back to look at Cole's chiseled jaw, caring hands, and lean abs. That's the man I made love to last night.

While giving him a once-over, I notice something odd on his abs. Not being able to clearly see it last night, I assumed it was a deformity. Possibly some type of accidental burn. Yet looking at it now, I fear this was no accident. This was as deliberate as the taking of Grace. Inching closer to him, I swallow a gulp of air.

My heart stops and blood rushes to my head when I see it: the letters O.M. seared on his skin.

The room feels like it's rotating, making me struggle to stand upright. Cole's query from yesterday pops into my head.

How did I escape?

Was he referring to being taken by The Cauterizing Killer?

Unable to breathe, I storm down the stairs, skipping a few.

Once outside, I try to understand what I just saw.

Questions jump in my head untamed, like kids in an overcrowded bouncy house.

It doesn't make sense. That marking on his skin. It's from the iron-branding The Cauterizing Killer uses.

If he was kidnapped, how is he not dead? How did he escape him? Did he know about Grace? Was he lying to me this whole time?

And most of all, did I meet him by chance, or was this all intentional?

Part 2

Which is worse, to be a sadist or to be a pessimist?

The Defeatist

I'm going to tell you a short story about a sadist and a pessimist.

The sadist loves to torture. In fact, he lives for it. It gets him out of bed each morning. Without it, he wouldn't know what to do.

One day he stumbles across an innocent soul.

The innocent soul wants nothing more than love from the sadist. But the sadist wants nothing more than pain from the innocent soul.

The sadist takes him in. The innocent soul is grateful for that, but as the door closes and the light fades, so does his gratitude.

The sadist inflicts unspeakable pain onto the innocent soul.

Years go by and the sadist is still torturing the innocent soul, always stopping when the innocent soul is on the verge of death, allowing him to heal just enough for the sadist to repeat the cycle.

This is where the pessimist comes into the story. He learns of the innocent soul's pain and he manages to free him.

However, the innocent soul no longer wants to leave.

He doesn't know life without torture anymore.

He doesn't want life without torture anymore.

Because life without torture is life without the sadist.

He wants—no, he needs—pain in his heart, like he needs oxygen in his lungs.

The innocent soul is now a tainted soul.

The pessimist knows the tainted soul is hopeless and irredeemable.

He ends the tainted soul's life.

Now, who is worse?

The sadist that started the suffering, or the pessimist that ended it?

The Existentialist

Why do I keep drifting off? I open my eyes, faintly. I want to rub off the crust but my hands are still tied behind my back. They are growing numb, though, I'm unsure if that's from the rope or something else. Grace's hands are tied up, too. She's not shivering or crying anymore which makes my bones chill. I look into her unblinking eyes. They are transfixed on the floor. She's dead. Grace is dead, I know it. And I'm next.

But why is she still tied up?

I'm startled out of my skin when her eyes shift to mine.

"Hope," she mutters, "there's none of that here."

She's not dead yet, however her optimism, her saving Grace, it's been taken.

"You're not getting out of here," she says with a gruff voice. "None of us are."

I shake my head. She doesn't know the gravity of our situation and neither do I. The police could come bursting through the door any minute now.

I notice there are syringes on the floor. I wonder if that's what we've been injected with. If that's what we're going to be injected with.

"We're all damned," she says.

"Stop," I mutter.

I can see my shaky breath in the bare room. The brick wall I'm leaning against feels denser. Like it's digging into my back. And the tightness of these ropes lead me to believe, even if I get untied, they'll be glued to me.

I need to get out. I twist and turn to no avail. Airy footsteps draw nearer. He's coming. I want to call out for my mom or dad, but I know they won't come to save me. I wonder if they even know I'm gone.

This is it. I know it.

I close my eyes. A strong breeze rushes against me and my whole body feels like it's been hit by a truck. I open my eyes and scan my surroundings.

Where the hell am I?

I'm in my room. On the floor. I fell off my bed. I squint at the alarm clock on my nightstand. 2:06 a.m.

You know that saying the early bird gets the worm?

Yeah.

I have enough worms to feed a flock of eagles.

At school, Tyler and Jack are parading around the wide halls like sharks swimming along timid fish. You never know when or who they are going to bite.

I *despise* it.

Students bat their frightened eyes, trying to avoid eye contact, as Tyler and Jack swim by. One student turns their body facing a closed locker, not moving a muscle. Jack gestures at the still student and gives a bitter laugh.

"Whoa, check this fag out," Tyler says.

Trepidation overtakes the still student's face.

"Look at me, weirdo!" Jack demands.

In a stereotypical bully manner, Tyler smacks the student's books out of his hands onto the hard floor.

"Leave him alone, Tyler," I say.

125

Tyler cackles, then stomps toward me. "Fuck off, Cole."
Don't do it. Leave it to the teachers.
"I said, *leave him alone.*"

He looms closer, until his bestial face is right in front of me. He glances back at Jack and I catch a whiff of his bitter breath— that alone is reason to *fuck off.* A timorous crowd is watching now.

He shoves me against the close-packed lockers, which clang against my back. "You messed up, Cole," Tyler says. "Now you and that dork are gonna get beat."

Jack chuckles.

Tyler turns around, striding to the student, whom is still, well... still.

My mind and body don't correspond. I know I shouldn't fight him, but every fiber in my body is telling me to attack. My vision is sporadic. All I see are my fists in his face, then him on the floor, me kicking, then teachers pulling me off.

Tyler's on the hard, tiled floor covered in blood, holding one of his rotten teeth in his hand. It's a blissful feeling, seeing him in pain. I don't think anyone in this school has ever fought him. Most people are scared. This was justice for all the students that he's victimized.

I glance at the crowd. There is a discernible face standing there. Olivia. Her hands cover her mouth. I haven't seen her since we...since she slept over. Before I can walk over to her, she's hurrying away.

The following morning, next to the bamboo plant on the kitchen island, there's an orange bottle; medication. Not exactly what I had in mind for breakfast but...

Dad emerges behind me. "It's a higher dosage."

"Dad, I don't need it."

"Cole, this isn't about you anymore. You're hurting people."

He's referring to Tyler. "He's a bully," I plea. "He deserved it."

Dad pinches his temple. "You sound just like—" he pauses. "You're taking this medication, Cole. I'm not asking."

I want to hurl the medication bottle at the wall, but I don't. I know all that will do is validate his belief.

Dad sits on one of the high-legged stools beside the island. "Listen, it's not for us to determine who deserves to be punished. You can't go inflicting pain on another because you think it's just. To inflict pain in the name of righteousness is a false virtue."

I grab the medication bottle, examining it. "I can't believe I'm being chastised for defending someone."

"You're not, Cole," he says. "I'm proud of what you did. But we all have our biases and I just want you to be aware of them."

My phone buzzes. It's Olivia.

Could we meet by the library after school?

The Stoic

I've never noticed the people in this dust-filled library. I've always felt it was just Cole and me here. I guess I'm usually too immersed in studying to realize my surroundings.

Peeking at Cole from behind a bookshelf, I see him sitting by our table, tapping his foot and checking his watch. I might be making a mistake talking to him about this, however I need answers. Not only for myself, but for Grace and Mom. And right now, he's the closest thing I have to answers.

"Excuse me," someone says, pointing to a book behind me. I've been standing here too long. Reluctantly I walk over to our table and pull out a chair. After sitting down, neither of us speak. I don't know how to initiate this conversation. How do you casually talk about murder, dead sisters, kidnappings, and human brandings? Especially when the person you are talking to is somehow involved.

Not wasting any time, I blurt, "Why do you have that marking on your stomach?"

Cole's head recoils and he raises his eyebrows. His mouth opens but no words come out.

"Did The Cauterizing Killer try killing you?" I ask.

Cole rubs his left shoulder. "I...don't know."

"What do you mean you don't know?"

"It's complicated," he says.

Exasperated, I say, "I'm sick of these lies, Cole, these secrets, hiding things from each other. Haven't we grown past that?"

"I'm not lying."

"You're hiding something from me."

"I'm not," he says.

"Yes, you are," I say, firmly.

"Ok, I am, you're right."

"Don't tell me I'm right just because you think that's what I want to hear."

"I'm not."

"You totally are."

"I am, but only because I love you."

I giggle, then he chuckles. And for a brief moment his charming facetiousness causes me to forget about everything. "Cole, what happened to you?"

"You wouldn't believe me if I told you."

"Try me."

Cole's chest fills and empties with a long breath. "Okay…" He looks away for a moment, thinking about what to say. He proceeds, "When I was eight, I went on a trip with my family. I forgot where. When I returned from the trip, my mom wasn't with us. And I had a throbbing scar on my stomach. I saw the two letters O.M."

"You don't remember how you got it?"

"My dad told me a psychopath staying by our hotel broke in while I was asleep and branded me."

"Is that what you remember?" I ask.

"Not really. I have these nightmares of me tied up in a decrepit building, being injected with something. These nightmares are the cause of my insomnia. I used to have to take pentobarbital to sleep."

"And you think these nightmares are real?"

"I don't know. What I saw was hazy and it felt like a dream. I kept drifting off and eventually woke up in our hotel room."

"Did you tell your dad about these nightmares?"

129

"Yeah. He said it was my schizophrenia."

"And you just listened to your dad? You never thought to google it? To google those letters?"

"I didn't need to. Why is that so shocking? I trust my father." My lips tighten.

He continues, "I know the average person would conduct his own research. People only believe what they see. *Your truth lies in your eyes.* But my truth? It doesn't lie in my eyes. It lies in other people's eyes. In what other people tell me. Because I can't trust what I see, what I hear, or what I remember. I saw something bizarre. So, when my father told me it was a hallucination, I believed him."

"But this guy was all over the news," I say. "How have you never heard of him?"

"He hasn't been on the news since I was eight years old. I only found out about him recently, when I googled it."

"And what made you finally google it?" I ask.

"My hallucinations were becoming more vivid. Especially after realizing Grace was real...and your sister."

"You knew Grace?"

"She was tied up in that building with me. She told me to protect you."

"She told you my name?"

"Just your first name. I wasn't certain she was your sister until prom night."

That's why he was acting so weird when he saw the picture of her.

"She made me feel safe."

"Then what?"

"I don't remember."

"Try."

"That's not how this works," he says. "If I could force myself to remember, I would. Don't you understand that?"

"Okay. I'm sorry."

Cole rubs his eyes.

"You must be the only person that was branded and survived," I say. "Why are there no news articles about you?"

"You know my father. He can be quite paranoid. He feared reporting this to the police would result in whoever did this," he gestures to his stomach, "coming back to finish the job."

"The police could've lingered outside your home, sheltering you."

"For how long? A week? A month? A year? They wouldn't have been able to follow us to school, or to the grocery store. And even if they did, it wouldn't have lasted forever."

He was right. When Grace was taken, the cops remained outside our house for a month. Even then, my dad didn't want them following him to his bar, and my mom was more than uncomfortable with a cop escorting her to yoga.

"I've wanted to tell you about this since I first met you," he says, "but it's not like they sell cards for this type of stuff."

Cole's eyes gleam at the floor. I reach for his hand across the cream-colored table.

"You moved here about ten years ago, right?" I ask.

He nods.

"Was that because of what happened?"

"My father doesn't talk about it," he says. "But I think so. He transformed into a whole different person after that trip." Cole's eyes focus on mine. "Are you going to tell your mom?"

"No, I can't."

"Why is that?"

"We're not sure if this dream is even real, and if it is, it doesn't change anything, she's still missing."

"I thought she was dead."

"Yeah, that's what I meant."

After our meeting at the library, I invite Cole to come over for a late dinner tonight.

The scent of the chicken and veggie roast Mom cooked is mouthwatering. Mom insisted on cooking something elegant. It's been a while since we had any guests over, and I think she was waiting for an excuse to cook. I'm placing the silverware on the bleached table and Mom's sweeping our already spotless floor. The table stands behind the comfy couches in the large open living room.

"What do you think of Cole?" I ask.

"He seems like a really sweet boy."

"And his father?"

"Robert?"

Her reference to my boyfriend's dad by his first name is slightly disconcerting.

She continues, "What is there to say? He's polite, muscular, and handsome."

Apparently, there's a lot to say.

"Mom, that's disgusting."

"Hey, you asked."

And now I regret asking.

A knock-knock makes Mocha spring off the couch, with enthusiasm in her eyes, and scurry towards the door.

"Cole's here," Mom shouts.

I shuffle to the door, where I find Cole kneeling and scratching the back of Mocha's ears. Her tongue is out and she's huffing. When he notices me, his eyes light up. He rises and wraps his arms around me.

Mom forces a cough, acting like we are having sex in front of her. "That's all the touching you two will be doing tonight."

"Mom!"

Cole chuckles.

"I have to run a few errands, but Cole, I hope you enjoy the food."

"What about me?" I ask.

"I'm your mother. You enjoy my food or you starve." She winks.

Mom leaves and we move to the dining room table. As I eat the savory chicken, Mocha whimpers beside me.

"Why is she crying?" Cole asks.

"She thinks if she cries, I'll give her my food."

"Aw," Cole says.

"Mocha you have your own food." I say in a soft tone.

Cole cuts a strip of chicken and tosses it on the floor. Mocha doesn't think twice, her nails screech against the hardwood floor as she runs in place, almost like a cartoon character. Note to self; cut her nails.

"You know if you keep feeding her, she'll always come back to you," I caution him.

"Thanks for the tip."

"It wasn't a tip, more of a warning."

"Why would I have a problem with her coming back to me? I love her." Cole tosses her another strip of chicken.

"Is it really love if you have to buy it?" I ask.

"You don't need to buy dogs' love. They give you that unconditionally. I'm buying her attention."

When we finish dinner, Cole grasps his plate and asks, "Are you done?"

"Yeah."

Cole takes my grimy plate and carries it to the kitchen. Mocha follows him. I hear the faucet handle squeak and the running water hiss. I make my way to the kitchen and see him scrubbing the dishes.

"Cole, you really don't have to do that. My mom will do them when she gets back."

"Please," he insists, "your mom cooked this amazing meal. This is the least I could do."

"My mom would be shocked if she saw this."

"Why is that?"

"She's old school, you know, where the woman does the kitchen work."

"So does that make me new school?"

Mocha barks.

We both glance at her and laugh.

"That answers your question," I say.

He grabs me, resting his lips on mine. His cool hands are wrapped around my waist. I realize they are wet. I don't care. He pulls away to switch off the running water.

We walk to the couch, wanting to relax. After sitting down, Cole says, "Wow, yours is way comfier than mine."

"I know! I have no idea why new couches are so uncomfortable."

"It's one of life's many mysteries."

Cole sets his arm over my shoulder, making me feel safe. Mocha does something she never does; jumps on the couch. She licks Cole's hand, grooming him, then rests beside him.

"You never saw my sister actually die, did you?" I ask.

"That was…"

"Blunt?"

"Yeah." Cole looks off to the left. "It's all a blur. I forgot most of what happened that night, but over the last few months it's all been coming back."

"But you don't remember seeing her die?"

"Olivia…"

"I'm not saying she's alive somewhere, I'm just curious."

"Ok. In that case, I don't remember seeing her die."

After Cole leaves, I sit by my tidy desk, opening my laptop to re-examine all the articles related to The Cauterizing Killer. God, I hate that name. It sounds like a comic book villain. It's unfathomable how society settled on labeling him that.

I used to study these articles religiously, playing detective, thinking I could find something the police missed. Stupid, I know, but I was depressed and I needed to believe there was something I could do. I know most of these articles by heart. I could recite them better than I could the National Anthem. But I'm hoping new findings have popped up.

There's nothing but one new article. Though it's not really new.

Anniversary of Oakley Child's Death.

The child's name is Jason. The article re-exhibits all the evidence surrounding his death. I already know of Jason, nonetheless I continue reading.

Something irregular catches my eye.

Jason died through pentobarbital injection before being branded. The medical examiner found matured bruises on Jason's body along with bite marks.

There are two things worth taking note of in this article.

One: The Cauterizing Killer uses pentobarbital to kill his victims. That's the same drug Cole's used to treat his insomnia.

Two: The Cauterizing Killer, while deranged, never bit a kid. He'd choke him, tie him up, subdue him, but never bit.

This is all too strange.

On my phone, I launch Google maps and type in "Oakley." It's 45 minutes away. I want to go there, talk to the parents. But I don't want to go alone. I need Cole with me. He survived an encounter with this killer. He may see something I might miss.

The Defeatist

I know I've been dragging this story out.

These metaphorical stories and epigrams are becoming redundant.

I'll stop, I promise. I just wanted to convey a point before getting to the real story.

So, let's start over.

I killed Elizabeth.

I killed Grace.

My actions caused Cole irrevocable damage. If I had done one thing different, we wouldn't be here.

But we are.

I'm not claiming innocence because I'm not innocent. I'm to blame for all these killings.

You're probably wondering how someone like me, could commit such vile actions.

Well, it wasn't my upbringing. I didn't have abusive parents, my dad wasn't an alcoholic, and my mom wasn't a narcissist.

They didn't possess any of the traits that I carry.

My upbringing was quite normal, at least compared to Elizabeth.

Which is how this all started.

One of the women I killed. Elizabeth…

The Cynic

The savory smell of fried bacon is refreshing, especially in the morning. The sound of the sizzling strips reminds me of my childhood on the farm. This one time my dad bought two new cows. He let me brand them for him. The fumes of their burning flesh were savory. Them crying in pain was a bonus. Though I've branded few things since then, not much else compares.

The peanut butter smells good, too. It's been a while since I've made a normal lunch for Finn. Katherine's been encouraging me to prepare him lunch instead of buying him those pre-made lunch packets. She's been encouraging me to do a lot of things actually.

Yesterday, she took a picture of me and Finn. I couldn't care less about that, but Finn seemed happy. And when he's happy, it helps me score points with Katherine. I haven't fucked her yet, but I'm working my way there. I have jerked off to pictures of her though. She's one hell of a tease.

Finn walks in the kitchen, and notices me making a sandwich. He knows better to ask if it's for him. He just stares at it.

"It's for you."

A smile flushes over his face.

"Can I hug you, sir?"

"We don't hug."

He frowns. I could never win with him.

"On second thought, I don't think this sandwich is for you."
He turns around, spine bent, face looking down
"I'm only kidding," I say. "Let this be a lesson; I can take things away just as easy as I can give them. Here you go." I hand him the sandwich and leave the room.

Walking down the school halls, I drink a satisfying cup of coffee. It feels good to be giving back. To be doing good. More good than I already do, I mean. Today when I dropped Finn off at school, I walked him to his class. I might've been hoping to see Katherine there, but a good deed is a good deed.

Someone bumps into me, and I turn around to see it was Tyler.

"Fuckin' janitor," he says.

What a lowlife. Him and his lowlife dad. Certain things in life you just know. They are a given. And Tyler ending up just like his dad is one of those givens. It's the cycle of abuse. His dad beats him, so he's going to beat his son, and his son will beat his son. It goes on and on. A loop of affliction. Tyler has no contribution to society except to make it worse. The world would not miss him if he was dead. The antagonized students wouldn't miss him, the teachers that turn the other cheek wouldn't miss him, and I honestly wonder if his abusive dad would miss him.

The Stoic

It's Saturday; Cole and I have no school today. We're on the road now, heading to the Ackerman's address. I found it online, through a public police report. It wasn't in any news article out of respect for Jason's parents. They're lucky.

After Grace was taken, journalists weren't as altruistic with my family. They leaked my address. Every now and then crime junkies would come, aggravating us with intrusive questions.

They'd insinuate that Grace was raped, because The Cauterizing Killer only targeted children. Disregarding that all the autopsies indicated the victims were virgins.

In Cole's crossover, the country music is blasting and he has one hand on the wheel, driving with leisure. He twists the small knob on the stereo, lowering the music.

"Did you hear about what happened to Tyler?" he asks.

"No," I say. "What happened?"

Cole monitors his side-view mirror. "He's been missing for over 48 hours. His father filed a missing person's report."

I chuckle. "He goes 'missing' all the time. I'm sure he's on a bender, wasted in a park somewhere."

He smiles. "Yeah, I just thought it was interesting."

The blinding sun causes Cole to squint his eyes. I pry open the sun visors. Better.

A few cars overtake us and I realize Cole's driving extremely slow.

"You know, you're a very… safe driver."

Cole glances at me. "Well, I have precious cargo."

"That's so sweet Cole, but I'm growing impatient. I wouldn't mind you speeding it up."

Cole looks at the dashboard, "I'm going 50 in a 45. I'm already breaking the law."

"The cameras won't catch you unless you're going 60."

"And what about the hidden highway patrol?"

"They won't catch you if you're driving faster than them."

Cole chuckles. "That's a good one, but I'm not speeding it up."

Worth a shot.

I don't know what I hope to accomplish by talking to Jason's parents. I just want answers. Clues. Something that might not have been in the news articles or police reports. Something that can link us together. That can link us to The Cauterizing Killer. I guess I do know what I hope to accomplish.

My eyes drift out the window. "How many kids do you want?"

"That's a random question."

"That's not an answer."

"I don't want any children."

"What? You babysit kids all the time. I thought you loved children."

"Let me rephrase that, I can't have children."

"Why is that?"

"Schizophrenia is a hard disease. I wouldn't want to pass this gene onto anyone. It takes lives, ruins them. If I love my kid, I'd never want him to go through this."

"You don't know that he'd get schizophrenia."

"I don't know that he wouldn't. I'm not willing to take that chance."

"I'm sorry to hear that."

"Don't be, it's not your fault."

The car accelerates. Cole cuts to the left-most lane.

I tug at my earlobe. "You told me you used to take pentobarbital for your insomnia."

"Yeah, only for a bit," he says. "It worked like a charm."

"Then why'd you stop?"

"My dad didn't feel comfortable with me using it."

"Why is that?"

He scratches his nose. "They use it for euthanizing animals, which definitely alarms him. It's also only suggested for short term use."

Being blunt I say, "They also use it for human euthanasia."

Cole's eyes widen.

"I didn't.... you don't think... you don't think that's what I was being injected with, in my nightmares—I mean memories."

Yes. "No, I mean there's no possible way of knowing."

Cole tenses up.

"We're safe now," I say.

I regret bringing this topic up. I see how scarring it is for Cole.

"Olivia."

"What?"

"Olivia, it's me."

I glance at the left. Cole's not driving the car.

"Grace?"

"Olivia, stop."

"Stop what?"

"Stop looking for me."

"Why?"

"I'm dead, Olivia. You remember what that Johnny said, 76 percent of children abducted are killed within three hours. 88 percent of kids are dead after 24 hours."

"That doesn't mean anything," I say.

"It's been a decade..."

"I know. I'm doing this for closure."

"No," she says. "You think I'm alive. I'm not. I'm dead."

The car comes to an abrupt stop. My body jerks forward, the seatbelt slices into my chest, and I close my eyes.

"Olivia, we're here," Cole says.

I was dreaming.

Cole steps out of the car.

Am I wrong for doing this? Should I leave the past buried in the past? We've all moved forward. Bringing this back reinvigorates everything we fought so hard to overcome.

I flinch from the ruffling knock on the car window. It's Cole. "Are you coming?" he asks.

He opens the door and extends a hand. I grab it and step out of the car.

We're in a typical residential neighborhood. Most of the houses are somewhat identical. They're all single, two-story houses, with a garage and green grass.

My shoe feels damp, and I realize there's a stream of water along the curb. My eyes track it back to a single lawn with its sprinklers on. A few smiley kids bolt past us. I think they are playing tag.

I let go of Cole's securing hand and walk up to the house, before knocking on the door.

I think I knocked too light. I don't think anyone heard. I turn to Cole. "Maybe they aren't home. We should g—"

The door opens. A small middle-aged man is standing timidly beside it.

"Can I help you?" he asks with an irritable tone, as if he's a petulant child and answering the door was one of his chores.

Cole starts, "We're doing a school paper on The Cauterizing Killer. We were hoping we could talk to you about what happened to your son."

He squints his eyes. "I'm sorry but I don't feel comfortable talking about this with a couple of *teenagers*."

He titles us teenagers like an accusation, as if it's something disgraceful.

Cole continues, "It would really mean a lot to us if you could. We understand it's a difficult topic to talk about, but we really want to bring awareness to the dangers of our society."

"That's really nice but I'm busy." He begins closing the door.

"The Cauterizing Killer murdered my sister," I blurt out.

The door stops midswing.

"Who did you guys say you were?"

He guides us to the low-ceiling living room as the grubby floor creaks below our feet. There's a grimy coffee table in between the parallel-facing couches.

I dust the ratty couch with my hand, before sitting on it. Cole doesn't. Neither does Mr. Ackerman.

A blonde-haired woman, wearing a silk blouse enters the living room, seeming incongruous in a place like this. With her long legs tucked in blue, skinny jeans she walks toward her husband, plastering on a smile.

"Darling, you didn't tell me we had company."

His shoulder slumps. "Er...I...they..."

"It's okay, just be a gentleman, serve them some coffee."

This must be Mrs. Ackerman.

"That's okay," Cole shakes his hands. "We don't drink coffee."

"Oh please, I insist." She looks at her husband and nods at the kitchen. "It's only polite." She sits down, her arm resting along the backrest of the couch. "So, what is it you guys are here for?"

"My sister was killed by The Cauterizing Killer. I was hoping you could tell me a little bit about what happened that night. Maybe we could find some similarities between our...situations."

I know I'm being remarkably candid. I'm just hoping that if I'm open with Mr. and Mrs. Ackerman, they'll be open with me.

143

Naive I know, but what other options do I have? I'm not a detective, I'm a high school student.

"I'm sorry to hear your sister was killed by that sociopath."

Mr. Ackerman returns, his hands trembling as he places the coffee on the coffee table. He used disposable cups and not mugs for the coffee which I find a little odd. Then again everything about this home is odd.

"Could you tell us what happened the night he was killed?"

Mr. Ackerman opens his mouth but Mrs. Ackerman gently places her hand on his wrist. He flinches, slightly, then shuts his mouth.

That flinch. It was almost imperceptible. I bet Cole didn't even notice it. But I did. He's scared of her.

"It was just like any other night." Mrs. Ackerman looks up to the corner of the room. Like a TV character giving a flashback.

Whatever she's about to say next I know will be a lie. I've met people like her before. The master manipulators, the narcissists, the abusers. Deception oozes from her pores.

"Our little Jason was upstairs. We were in bed, sleeping. I heard a window break. I ignored it. Then I heard footsteps. I opened my eyes. There was a dark figure above me. Before I could move, he smashed my knee caps with a crowbar. I couldn't walk. He tied my husband up then brought my son to my bedroom. He branded him in front of me, then killed him…" She covers her eyes and starts sniffling, emphatically. "M-my Jason." She bursts out, wailing, with her eyes still covered.

Mr. Ackerman doesn't cuddle her or offer any type of comfort. His eyes awkwardly dart around the room, avoiding any form of eye contact.

There's a tissue box on the coffee table, and I hand it over to Mrs. Ackerman, trying to comfort her. When she removes her hands from her eyes, I see they aren't wet, they don't even glisten. They look completely dry.

She wasn't crying. She hardly shed a tear.

"I mean what type of sicko not only kills a child, but does so in front of their parents?"

We sit there not speaking for a couple of minutes to let the Mrs. Ackerman 'recover.'

What I'm about to ask is audacious, and I'm not even sure if I should. I think I already found the answers I was looking for.

No.

I need to be certain.

"What about the bruises?" I ask.

Mr. Ackerman's head recoils, as if I said something profound.

The color drains from Mrs. Ackerman's face. She massages the back of her neck.

Mr. Ackerman's foot starts swiftly tapping. Mrs. Ackerman tightens her grip on his wrist making the tapping stop.

"There were bruises found on Jason's body. Prior to his death."

She scratches her head, almost deliberately. "I think that was from a school fight." She stands up. "I think you guys should go now," she says in an authoritative tone.

Cole glances at me with a confused look on his face. I expected this type of reaction from her. We tentatively rise and walk to the decayed door. Cole's head hangs low. Once outside he turns around, presumably to apologize, but Mrs. Ackerman slams the door before he could speak.

Instead, he turns to me. "Olivia, I want to help you get closure, but that was way too abrasive."

"There's something they're not telling us. You saw how weird they were acting."

"How exactly is one meant to act when discussing their dead son?"

"Not like that."

We stroll along the ragged, uneven walkway.

"They're hiding something. His wife isn't letting him speak."

When we reach the sidewalk, a car breezes past us. On the trunk, there is a bumper sticker that reads;

Proud Parent of Oakley Elementary Honor Roll.
"Oakley Elementary."
"What?"
"Oakley Elementary is the same school Jason went to."
"Olivia…"
The car pulls into a straight, short driveway, five houses from the Ackermans. I dash over there.
Cole follows behind me.
A wide-hipped woman steps out of the car, walking to her grocery filled trunk.
"Excuse me, I noticed you have an Oakley Elementary bumper sticker. Does your son go there?"
The wide-hipped woman whips her auburn hair over her shoulder "I'm sorry, do I know you?"
"Um…"
Cole speaks up, salvaging this conversation, "My little brother is being bullied in his current school, and my parents are thinking about switching to Oakley."
The woman lets out an amicable smile. "If your brother is being bullied, then I'd definitely recommend sending him to Oakley. They have an amazing zero-tolerance policy. So much as a weird stare gets a kid in trouble."
Sounds like an infomercial.
"That's a bit extreme, don't you think?" Cole asks.
"Maybe, but it creates a safe environment."
"So, if there was a school fight, what would happen to the students?" I ask.
"That would never happen." She corrects herself, "That *has* never happened."
Cole and I glance at each other, then back at her. "Mr. and Mrs. Ackerman told us a kid fought with Jason days before he was killed."
"Ha! Those people are as trustworthy as politicians. I can assure you that's not what happened. In fact, my son was in the

146

grade above Jason. He always told me how Jason would come to school with bruises. That poor boy."

"Do you think his mom was the one giving him bruises?"

"Think?" She chuckles, "I *know* it was her." She gazes at all the other houses on this street. "This whole block knows it was her. She tries to put on a front like she's a nice mother, but everyone sees the signs."

"If it was such a known thing, why didn't child services take him away?"

"Many of us called child services. But that poor boy, Jason. He really loved his mom. And whenever they'd stop by, Mrs. Ackerman would put on her greatest performance."

The kids from earlier are still outside, now across the street. We all glance at them.

"The worst part was, I don't think he knew. I think Jason thought that his suffering was normal. Like the more his mom hurt him, the more he loved her. It was horrible. Twisted. At least he's in a better place now."

The drive home is quiet. I think both Cole and I are trying to absorb the intensity of what we discovered.

I break the silence, saying, "You didn't need to do that for me back there."

Cole glances at me. "What?"

"When that woman asked us who we were...I could've handled it myself. The same goes with when Mr. Ackerman answered the door."

Cole chuckles. "I know you could've."

"So, why'd you speak up?"

His securing hand makes its way back to mine.

"Because you don't have to."

147

He continues driving at a steady pace, then says, "I'm sorry, Olivia. I know you were hoping to find something more substantial here."

"I think we did."

"What do you mean?"

"I think The Cauterizing Killer is targeting children of abuse."

I'm aware titling someone abusive is a treacherous allegation. With horrid implications. It could destroy a man's life. However, what's more damaging are the implications of never calling out an abuser. My dad was verbally abusive. Mrs. Ackerman's mannerisms were strikingly similar to my father's.

Child services never came to my house. No one ever called them, but I remember dinner parties and barbeques. He'd put up a front, acting like father of the year. Subtle things he would do that to the naked eye, seem innocent, that I knew weren't. I call it pseudo-politeness. A form of insincerity anyone aware of can perceive blindfolded.

Cole asks, "Do you really think there's a method to the killings?"

Maybe I'm wrong. Maybe his killings were random. If I could just talk to Mr. Ackerman alone, I know he'd tell me something useful. Something she's coercing him to conceal. I look down at the coffee cup he handed me. It's still full. I fail to comprehend why he put it in disposable cups.

Opening the window, I smell the fresh scent of damp wood along the highway. It's sunny today but it rained yesterday. Beams of sunlight scatter through the trees, causing leaves to glisten.

I turn my cup, bottoms up, spilling out the coffee. There's something written on the bottom. A phone number.

Did Mr. Ackerman write this?

I share this information with Cole, who suggests calling the number.

After dialing the phone number to no one answering, I leave a message saying to call me back. Then I add the number to my contacts.

Cole's phone rings on the car stereo. The screen reads: **Dad**

He taps: **answer**.

"Cole, where are you?"

"I'm driving home with Olivia."

"From where?"

He sounds frantic.

"Oakley," Cole answers.

"Oakley? Ok. After you drop her off, I want you to come home right away."

"Dad, what's wrong?"

"It's Tyler."

My heart flutters.

"He was murdered."

It can't be.

"A couple of campers in the woods near Green Point Lake found him..."

I squeeze Cole's hand, tight.

"They thought he was sleeping and turned him over. That's when they saw his lifeless eyes...looking down at his stomach they saw..."

"Don't say it."

"He had the marking. The branding, initials *O.M.*"

The Cauterizing Killer is back.

The Defeatist

I don't believe in love at first sight.

Shocking, isn't it?

How could a cynic like myself not believe in love at first sight?

Well, I don't.

Although, I do believe in attraction, intrigue, and curiosity at first sight.

I first met Elizabeth at a bar I used to frequent. I know it's one hell of a cliché, but I was an alcoholic; the bar was more of my home than my actual home.

That being said, I forgot the name of the bar. I do know it was something slavish like *beer garden* or *the love shack.*

Elizabeth was drinking all alone. It didn't seem right to me.

Not because she was sitting alone, but because she seemed sad. Someone as beautiful as her, sad. It wasn't right.

Now, I've used all kinds of pickup lines on women in this bar. I'd say anything to get them to sleep with me. But with her...I didn't just want to sleep with her, I wanted to know what her favorite drink was, where she grew up, how many siblings she had, and most of all, what her name was.

When I approached her, I didn't use any pickup lines. I just sat next to her and ordered myself a Coors banquet.

"It's been a shitty ass day," I told her.

She laughed. "If you're drinking a Coors banquet, it's about to get a whole lot shittier."

I glanced at her drink. "Says the woman drinking a Bud light."

She looks at her drink like she's never seen it before. "This drink is horrible, isn't it?"

I take a sip of my beer. "So why are you drinking it?"

"My therapist says I need to stop cutting myself so I've found a new way to self-harm."

I know right? She was implausibly forward. That should've been a sign to stay away. I didn't need additional problems in my life. If I had just stopped and walked away, I wouldn't be here today.

Honesty like that should scare any sane person away.

But that's what drew me to her: honesty.

I had just found out my girlfriend had been cheating on me for months. Lying to my face 24/7.

I was searching for an honest woman and there she was. Alone at a bar, drinking her sorrows away, just like me.

Another thing that drew me to her was our similarities.

So, I continued the conversation, saying, "Your therapist sounds like a dick."

She scoffed. "I love Mrs. Miller but she can be a dick sometimes."

"So, what are you doing here all alone?"

I know how that sounds—creepy as hell. But I was drunk and so was she.

"Once most guys get to know me, they run."

"I'm not most guys."

She chuckled, took another sip of her beer, then said, "That's what most guys say."

"Try me."

She took a long gulp of her beer, tilting her head backwards. Then slammed it on the bar. Everyone in here stared at her. Keep in mind, there were only four people in here, but still she didn't care, and I loved it.

"I'm an orphan, had abusive parents, my sister died when I was thirteen, and I suffer from bipolar disorder."

I take a sip of my beer. "That it?"

Her eyes widened before standing up. "I'm also 5'9".

Another one of our similarities. We were the same height.

I laughed. "If that scares most guys away, then most guys are pussies."

I stood up and kissed her. Then we fucked in the bathroom like animals.

It's funny, because later that's what we became...animals.

The Existentialist

I used to love Sundays. It was a break from school. Sundays were my Sabbath. Ever since I was a small kid, I remember waking up, eating French toast, and watching Disney channel on the TV. It sounds stupid because I had Saturdays off from school, but there was something about Sunday. It wasn't just the break from school. Sundays were magical for me. It was bliss.

Today, Sunday doesn't feel blissful. With everything going on, the only magical thing I feel is cursed.

I'm repulsed, gazing at the plate of French toast in front of me. What usually looks like heaven to me, looks just like bread-soaked eggs. I pick up my plate, walk to the garbage, and throw it out.

You can't waste food like that, I don't care if you are as full as a goat. You never throw out perfectly good food.

Sorry, Mom.

I trudge to the living room, then collapse onto the couch. Where's the remote? My eyes scan the couch along with the end-tables. I don't see it. I'm not in the mood to set out on an exploration, searching for it. My body feels like it's being pulled back as I rise. I walk to the tv, turn it on, then return to the couch. I move a throw pillow and spot the remote under it.

You hardly looked for it.

Mom. Not today.

I turn to Disney channel, hoping reruns of older shows are playing. Shows from when I was younger, before the schizophrenia. Nostalgia tends to sooth the soul. My luck, they aren't. Instead, a show about two Internet personalities is playing. I shut off the TV.

I close my eyes, resting back against the couch. A harsh whirling sound stemming from the entryway makes my heart skip a beat. I spring off the couch and examine the door.

"Dad? What the hell?"

He's kneeling by the door, clutching a drill. "Language," he says.

I glance at my watch. "It's 9 a.m."

"Yes, it is."

"What are you doing?" I ask.

"I don't want to alarm you."

Too late.

He places the drill on the floor. "The school notified all parents to be more precautious. I'm adding another lock to the door so no one can break in."

"Dad, we already have three locks on the door, plus multiple security cameras. If someone was going to break into a house, it wouldn't be ours."

"You can never be too safe," he replies.

He's not wrong.

My dad isn't schizophrenic, but I often think I acquired my paranoia from him. Not Mom.

Years ago, we briefly visited Greenville, determined to visit Mom and her sister's grave. We stayed in some rundown, dingy motel. He paid in cash. We avoided all our old neighbors and family friends. And he wouldn't just lock the door, he'd set a chair against the knob. The worst part was, we didn't spend more than a couple minutes at her grave.

Sometimes I think I know my dad, other times he's a complete stranger.

Tyler's funeral is today. I doubt many students will be present. Hatred is a horrible thing, and so is harassment. I'm not saying you need to forget about what he did. Or act like he was a good person. He wasn't. But he didn't deserve to die. The levelheaded response would be to acknowledge he was bad and still show up. But that requires maturity. Something not yet taught in my school. Not in vocabulary class, not in Drivers-Ed, not in Sex-Ed.

Students have been reeling. Not over his death. Over his actions. And I have to wonder if that's why he was killed. Was he killed because of how he treated students? Did a parent do this? Or was this just another life taken by The Cauterizing Killer?

A disturbing thought would be that the answer is all of the above. Could a child of a serial killer really attend our school?

"Are you going to Tyler's funeral service today?" Dad asks.

"I think so."

I text Olivia, wanting to see if she's going. Tyler was at the forefront of Olivia's rumors a few months ago. I wouldn't be surprised if she doesn't want to.

I wonder if Olivia's father knew about the rumors. Could he have killed Tyler? No, as temperamental and volatile as he is, I doubt he could kill a teenager. Right?

Are you asking me?

No.

Ok, well, anyways. I'm just a spectator, but in the murder mysteries I read, the guy least suspected is usually the murderer.

Thanks, but I wasn't really asking.

My phone vibrates. It's Olivia.

IDK Yet

"Dad?" I ask.

"Yeah."

"You think you could drive me to the funeral?"

"Of course."

I should change out of my concrete joggers and fitted undershirt. I glance at the stairs, there are so many of them. I let out a sigh. I'm sure what I'm wearing is socially acceptable.

In the car, I wait for Dad. Grasping a cup of coffee, he enters the car. Mm. Hazelnut. He throws me a look I don't have enough energy to interpret.

"What?"

He gives me a once-over. "It's a funeral, not a brunch," he says. "At the least, change out of your slippers."

I'm not wearing slippers. I glance downward. Oh wait. I am. Ugh. Okay. Brushing my laziness aside, I dash inside, throw on a white button-down, black pants, and dress shoes. Then I lock the door and while lacing a single shoe, hop to the car.

Dad bites his lip. "You made sure to lock the door, right?"

"Yes, Dad."

"Are you sure?"

I roll my eyes. "Yes."

"It's just you left the house really quickly—"

"Dad. Can we please go?!"

The crisp sun lessens the chilled temperature. The service is outside. The newly mown grass is unnaturally green. There are seven people here including me, and few are wearing winter coats. The wooden casket is small and flat. A balding man holding a can of beer with a sweat-soaked face is bawling. I assume he's Tyler's father. His stained T-shirt reads Harley Davidson. If this is how his father dressed, I think it would've been fine for me to show up in joggers.

Dad lightly elbows me, whispering in my ear, "I know what you are thinking and no. It wouldn't have been okay for you to show up in joggers."

"That's not what I was thinking."

He glares at me.

"Ok, it was," I submit.

I find it hard to swallow that most teachers didn't show up. I guess it goes back to what I was saying about maturity earlier.

A teal-colored car pulls into the distant lot. Olivia emerges wearing an oyster gray puffer jacket and black leggings. Her head turns left, then right, until finally spotting me. She waves, and starts walking toward me.

I hug her. "You came."

"I did."

"Why?"

"I may have not liked Tyler. In fact, I loathed his guts, but he didn't deserve to die. He's a victim of this killer. Just like you. Just like me."

"Shhh," the pastor insists. All eight of us go hush and the eulogy starts.

Olivia's phone rings. She gazes at her screen the same way everyone is gazing at us; confused.

"What are you doing?" I murmur.

"It's Mr. Ackerman."

The Defeatist

Being the gentleman I was, I didn't use a condom that day in the bar. Elizabeth was pregnant. She didn't want to get rid of the baby. She told me she could raise him alone. I didn't want her to. I wanted to be a dad. At least I thought I did. Up until my kid started hearing voices.

Elizabeth and I got married. Elizabeth Monroe was now Elizabeth Dalton. I bought her a huge ring, then we had a huge wedding, then I bought us a huge house.

I used to work for a big real estate firm, finding investors. The pay was high. We moved to an upscale part of Greenville. Big houses, fancy cars, everyone was so proper. At least in public. Behind closed doors, some of these people were the worst of the worst. And that's coming from me.

You'd never assume the woman you go to Zumba with puts hot sauce in her kid's mouth, or that your accountant locks his son in the attic, or even your neighborly priest touches his kid.

I mean, that teacher at your school abused his son for who knows how long, and nobody knew.

It's hard to know who is abusive and who isn't. And even when we do, how many of us bat an eye? How many of us turn the other cheek?

Social services doesn't want to rip kids away from their families; their job is to keep families together. That's great for the kids that aren't abused, but what about the ones that are? The ones who can't show the abuse. How harmful is it for them? What about for the ones that don't realize they are being abused? Not just the ones that develop a deranged form of Stockholm syndrome, but the ones that love their parents after all the abuse they've put them through.

Should we be giving abusers second chances? Or is that just giving them a second try to hurt us?

Then again, what constitutes abuse? I mean in extreme cases it's easy to determine, but sometimes the lines blur.

I mean teachers, many of which whom are still alive today, used to lash kids. Back then that was considered okay. Now it's considered abuse.

If your son curses and you put an excessive amount of toothpaste in his mouth, is that abuse?

What about verbal abuse? When do mean comments turn to abuse? Or are all mean comments abusive?

And why should a person that hit his kid once be put in jail, while a mother who constantly rips away at their kid's ego, tearing him to shreds day by day, gets to roam free and be a part of our society? How is that just?

I'm not expecting you to answer any of these questions, you're only seventeen. I just want you to understand better.

I'm not saying all these killings are right. I've learned there is no right, only wrong, and how you choose to depict it. See, innocence is a term society fabricated to feel better about themselves. It has no meaning nor value outside of what we give it.

We live in a world where people do good actions to self-rationalize the bad ones. A pseudo-ethical world, where every move is subconsciously calculated. Being good is an abnormality.

No one is innocent; we're all just different levels of guilty. And to think you are more innocent than someone, simply because they are behind bars, is obtuse. It's illogical. A fallible ideology. We have a false definition of justice. True justice is a hallucination. It doesn't exist in our world, in our society. If it did, people wouldn't feel the need to take it into their own hands.

You see, I've done a lot of research since Elizabeth died, but I'm still learning. I don't have all the answers and I know it's extremely pessimistic, yet that doesn't make it any less accurate. Anyways, I'm getting ahead of myself.

I just know that we live in an unjust world. Where abusers prosper and victims...

The Stoic

In the middle of the eulogy, with my phone against my lap, Cole and I stand up and walk to the distant parking lot. Everyone's eyes focus on us, like lasers.

When we reach the lot, with the phone on speaker, I ask, "is this Mr. Ackerman?"

"Yes. I can't talk for long. My wife's in the other room watching TV. If she hears me telling you this, she'll hurt me."

"Telling me what?"

"The truth."

"What exactly happened that night?"

"My wife doesn't like to believe she's a liar. The things she says may be partially true, but never entirely. That's just how she functions. It's her moral code. Her rationalization. The night Jason was taken started normal, well normal for us, but something tells me you've figured out our normal is anything but normal."

A car exits the parking lot. I didn't even realize a person entered it.

"My wife returned from work and... hurt me."

"Hurt you how?" I ask.

"Doesn't matter. But she did it in front of Jason. She showed him," he chokes up, "she showed him she is the one in charge. Not me."

Cole and I don't respond. I doubt either of us know how.

"It was Jason's birthday and I convinced her to take him out. At the restaurant, Jason was given a cake. His face lit up, and looking back, it makes me happy that even for a moment, on the day he died he was happy." He sniffs. "The moment faded once he dug right into the cake with his fork. He was a kid, and looking back, I don't think he'd ever seen a cake before. Which I know, is a crazy thought. All the same, he was a kid, acting like a kid."

"Then what happened?" I ask.

"She slapped him. Hard. She yelled 'You don't just dig in!' I thought the whole restaurant was looking at us. They weren't, they were looking at her. We left instantly, on her command. I mean we didn't even pay and the staff seemed too frightened to hand us the bill."

"Jesus," I say under my breath.

"Outside, by our car, she blasted Jason. I should've stood up for him. I just," he pauses, "I was scared."

"It's okay," I say, trying to comfort him. "What happened next?

"There was someone else there, on the sidewalk. A figure. The darkness prevented me from making out any distinct details, and I could hardly tell if it was a man or a woman. I hoped the figure would intervene. That he'd do something…anything. How could you just stand there and watch this? Then again, that's exactly what I was doing. The drive home was quiet, disturbingly so. And a car was shadowing us. My wife didn't realize, though I did." He continues, "That same car parked outside our house. I thought whoever was in that car was the same person from the restaurant. I thought…I thought he was going to kill my wife. No, that's not quite right. I hoped he'd kill my wife. It's a sickening thought. A sickening wish. One I never admitted aloud."

I have to wonder why he's saying it aloud now, not that I'm not grateful. But his wife tried manipulating us. I need some way to confirm his story.

"I left the door unlocked..." Mr. Ackerman is now clutching for air.

Cole intervenes, "Mr. Ackerman, you don't need to continue. I think we know what happens next."

He draws a deep breath. "No, you don't," he says. "The person did tie me up and did smash my wife's kneecaps. But he didn't kill Jason in front of us. He killed Jason in his room, leaving a note behind. A note I read to myself every day. It looked like it was—"

"Ripped from a notebook," I say.

"Yes."

And there's my confirmation. A link between us I didn't know we had.

Cole gazes at me. I'm sure he's wondering how I knew that.

Mr. Ackerman continues, "The paper said he took our son from us to free him from this world. Free him from our torture. Our abuse. That it was our fault he's gone. That he might have ended his life, but we were the ones who took it away from him. He freed him from life of torture and abuse. This was true justice. And he marked him to let us know."

"And you never told the police about that person from the parking lot? The unlocked doors? The note? Anything?"

"No."

"Why not?"

"She...she threatened me...she hurt me. Making sure I wouldn't tell anyone a thing except the story she made up."

"After all this time, you still don't want to go to the police?"

"I can't... she'll hurt me."

"Then leave her."

"I can't."

"Why?"

Cole grabs my shoulder, but doesn't say anything. He doesn't have to. His look says enough. I'm projecting the emotions I felt towards my mom onto Mr. Ackerman.

"I'm sorry," I say.

"It's okay. I deserve it."

"You don't," I say. "Why are you telling me this now?"

"Your boyfriend."

"Cole? What about him?"

"He… he reminded me of Jason."

Mrs. Ackerman is in the background saying something. Then the phone gets disconnected.

I turn to Cole, who's gaping at me, eyebrows raised.

Everything I just heard is so unbelievable and at the same time it all makes perfect sense. It's a like a truth I didn't know existed. This killer must have a false savior complex. He could have been abused as a kid. But why hurt the children? Why not the parents?

"How'd you know about the paper being ripped from the notebook?" Cole asks.

"I've seen it before, at my dad's house. Starting after Grace's death, he would always stare at it while drinking."

Needing to see that paper and what's written on it, I dial Dad's number.

No answer.

Of course. I glance at my watch. It's 11:42 in the morning. He's probably drinking right now.

Something occurs to me. A frightening thought.

"Olivia. Are you okay?"

Cole must see it on my face.

"If The Cauterizing Killer is murdering abused children, what if he's here looking for me, trying to finish the job?"

"That's not going to happen. I won't let it." The conviction in his tone almost makes me believe him.

"And what if he comes for you?" I ask.

164

Later, at night, I'm unable to sleep. My thoughts are running rampant. I look at the clock: 3 a.m. Insomnia's a bitch. Is this what Cole has to deal with regularly? I wonder if I caught insomnia from him.

No. That's stupid. Insomnia isn't contagious. Is it? I'm sure it's not.

But just to be safe, I'm going to google it. I rise from bed, walk to my desk, and open up my laptop.

Articles from The Cauterizing Killer pop up.

I'm reminded that he's out there searching for us. He knows our identity. How long until he finds us? He's going to kill me, kill Cole, and anyone else in this town that he deems…'abused.'

Are you still there?

Or have you just started tuning out? I do that, when I'm reading sometimes, just scroll through ten pages before realizing I didn't absorb anything I just read. I know you expected a thrilling story, not whatever *this* is. Listen, I'm a forty-year-old man. My patience is shorter than yours. I know you have no reason to trust me. I'm a liar after all, but all these seemingly normal details are anything but.

I know this story can be boring at times, and you may have even questioned why I mentioned certain things. We're almost done, just bear with me a little longer.

On second thought, you look a little thirsty. We could take a break if you want. I'll still be here when you get back. It's not like I can go anywhere else.

The Existentialist

It's mind-boggling that I got away from this sociopath. After reading all the articles, I realized surviving an encounter with him is like walking on fire and not getting burnt. What's more mind-boggling is how he found me again. That is, if he did.

Though I evaded him for almost ten years, I never escaped him. I never escaped that room.

At times I think I have. Then I go to sleep and there I am, in that unnerving room with Grace.

People say sleep is a break from reality. As if that's a good thing. I detest sleep. What lies for me there is hopelessness, misery, and disparity. All because of that psycho.

Now he's here, in Fairview.

He's going to find me. He's going to kill me. Surviving him was a fluke. A stroke of luck. It's only a matter of time before my reality becomes worse than my nightmares.

It could happen in a week.

It could happen in a day.

He may even be outside, lurking, right now.

In my room, I peek through the blinders. Dad's outside with earphones on, mowing the lawn. He waves at me.

I know I'm safe in my house. When we first moved here, Dad set up 24-hour surveillance cameras. All the doors, including the ones inside, have multiple locks. And the windows on the first floor are all barred.

It's outside where I feel more apprehensive.

I have no form of protection out there. I lost Dad's knife. The one I stole a while back. Outside, I'm exposed.

Cole you shouldn't think like that. You need to distract yourself.

My phone vibrates: Unknown number. I swipe answer. "Hello?"

"Hey Cole, it's Mr. Haynes."

"Oh." I try not to act startled by a teacher calling a student. How did he get my number?

"I heard you babysit."

"Yeah…"

"My son, he's nine years old. I usually leave him home alone but he's sick. Would you be able to watch him after school tomorrow?"

"I'm sorry Mr. Haynes, I have a lot going on right now."

Cole, come on.

Mom, please for the love of God, stay out of this.

"I know, it's just…" he pauses. "There's no one else I could ask."

Cole, if you don't watch him, I'm going to ground you.

What?

I'm serious.

How would you be able to ground me?

You'll see.

You are weird.

"Cole?"

"I'll watch him."

Mr. Haynes' house is in a nicer neighborhood than I expected. The houses are moderately ritzy, with double garages, large lawns, and a plethora of them have double doors. It also seems sunnier here, which I know doesn't make sense.

I park in the driveway of Mr. Haynes' two-story house. Mr. Haynes handed me a key today in school. Not wanting to alarm Finn, I knock on the door before unlocking it.

"Finn?"

The house is hush. The only sound I hear is a leaky faucet.

I walk up the shallow oaken staircase. Finn's in his room lying under his covers. He gapes at me, unnerved by the presence of a stranger. His dad must've told him I was coming.

"Hey Finn. I'm Cole. Your dad sent me to look after you."

"He did?"

"Yes."

"Okay."

Besides for the bed he's lying on, his bedroom looks abandoned. There's blue wallpaper peeling off the fissured walls. His single dresser is splintered and washed out.

I notice that his eyes are still fixed on me.

"Um. Why didn't you answer when I called your name?"

"I'm not allowed to raise my voice inside," Finn says. "It's disrespectful."

Disrespectful?

"Okay...well, I'm going to make you some pasta downstairs. Will you be able to come down when it's ready?"

"Yes."

I feel perturbed walking along the narrow, white-walled hallway. Something's off. I realized it when I first walked in. I shift my eyes to the right. Then the left.

There are no pictures of anyone. Anywhere.

No family portrait, no birthday pictures, no pictures of Finn's mom. Nothing. I don't know why that is. I guess Mr. Haynes just isn't the sentimental type.

In the warm kitchen there are pots on the dish rack. I grab one, pour water into it, and throw pasta in. Then I ignite the fire.

People say you should wait to add the pasta until the water boils, but I've tried both and hardly tasted a difference.

While the pasta's being boiled, I search for plates and silverware. There is a stack of paper plates on the kitchen table. I could use those.

No. Find real plates. The boy deserves a real meal.

I can't find plates anywhere; I'm just going to serve him on paper plates.

No, check downstairs. Maybe he put them away in boxes.

I don't understand why it matters.

Cole.

"Ugh. Ok fine."

I really should not be snooping around. I'll check the basement quickly. If they are not there, we are using disposable.

The steep stairs leading downstairs are so dusty I fear sneezing will cause an avalanche. Gripping the wobbly railing, I cautiously descend.

Be careful.

What do you think I'm doing?

There's a splintered white door framed on the landing. It reminds me of the basement door in my house. However, that one is solid steel.

When I touch the knob the door creaks open. A draft of sultry air whisks at me. With my hand, I screen my face. A vent must be open. The darkness causes my palms to sweat and my forearms to stiffen. I trail my hands along the walls, blindly searching for the light switch. The walls are flecked and cold, leading me to believe it's concrete.

I don't think there's any light switch.

How else would Mr. Haynes turn on the light?

There may be a cord suspended to a fixture.

Doubt it, but I'll check.

I plod with one hand raised above me, trying not to stumble on the jagged ground. I feel a ball chain and yank it. The room illuminates.

Whoa...
There's a tower of boxes touching the ceiling.
There must be one hundred.
There's not one hundred, though there's definitely a lot. Trying to find anything in there would be like trying to find a specific word in an un-alphabetically ordered dictionary.

I draw a box out from the center, hoping it doesn't cause the rest to topple over. It doesn't.

Unfolding the flaps, I find plates, bowls, silverware and...

I'm confused.

There's a mug here. And it's mine. Why does he have a mug I made when I was six years old?

I storm upstairs, forgetting to close the boxes behind me, then head to the kitchen.

JESUS!

Startled, I almost drop what I'm holding. "What are you doing in the kitchen?"

"I was hungry and wanted to see when dinner would be ready."

"Okay." I almost had a heart attack.

"What are doing with that mug?" Finn asks.

Disoriented, I don't process his question. Instead, I throw one back at him. "Where did your dad get this mug from?"

Finn shrugs. "I don't know."

Being the inquisitive 9-year-old that he is, he asks, "Whatcha doing with it?"

I shouldn't tell him. I should keep this to myself. Yet his face is so adorably innocent and sweet, I can't lie to him.

"I made this mug when I was a kid. Look, it even has my initials on the bottom." I turn the mug upside down, showing him the initials.

"Those are just two scribbles."

"My handwriting was sloppy back then and it also must have faded over the years. It's still mine. I made this mug in school."

Finn places his finger on his chin and tilts his head. "Oh yeah? Then how come it's in my house?"

That is a good question. Why is it in his house?

I made this mug back in kindergarten. My mom used it for her coffee every morning. My dad used it in the evenings. It kept his beer cold. That's what he would tell mom whenever they argued over it, which was a common occurrence.

I think it disappeared before that trip we all took together.

"If you want, you can take that home. I promise I won't tell my father."

"That's sweet of you, but he might realize it went missing."

"Nuh uh. He never goes in the basement. All those boxes down there are basically garbage."

I gaze at the ceramic mug. The mug fueled my parent's arguments. I'd cover my ears crying, not wanting to hear them fight.

I don't want it.

"Why don't you keep it?"

Finn's eyes light up. Bouncing on his feet he asks, "Really?"

"Yes, really."

He wraps his arm around me. Then he punches me in the gut.

I instinctively grab his arm and he flinches. I let go. "Finn...what...why'd you do that?"

His eyes dart around the room and his lips are trembling.

"Er...I just...I'm showing you love."

What the hell does that mean?

"Showing me love?"

"I was being affectionate towards you."

"Finn, that's not how you show love."

"I didn't... it's...I'm sorry." He squeezes his eyes shut.

"It's okay Finn." I want to hug him but I'm scared he's going to punch me again. "I'm going to hug you now, please do not punch me." A moment passes before I ask, "Why did you think it was okay to punch someone you love?"

"My dad," his voice breaks, "he loves me."

172

"I'm not sure I understand."

His sniffles, then wipes his nose. "He *loves* me."

"What does that mean?"

He doesn't speak, but looks vacantly at the floor, arms hanging low and slumping.

I think I get the picture. "Finn, it's okay to cry."

My heart contorts like a wet rag you wring to dry. I need to do something.

You can't.

Of course, I can. You can always do something. I'll go to the police.

Cole, Finn has no bruises on him. You don't have any proof.

My proof will be Finn's statement.

Look at Finn. Does he look emotionally stable enough to tell an officer that his father beats him?

"So, what do I do? Just go home and act like I didn't see this?"

"Who are you talking to?" Finn asks with a shaky voice.

Just be there for him. Be there until you can gather enough evidence.

"I can't just sit around while he's being hurt."

There's no other option.

"There's always another option."

"Cole, I'm scared."

I shake my head, trying to get a grip on reality. "I'm sorry. It's going to be okay."

When Mr. Haynes returns, late, the heavy stench of bleach follows him in. It's gag inducing. My finger twitches as I resist the urge to cover my nose.

"How was Finn?" Mr. Haynes asks. "I hope he didn't infuriate you too much." He winks.

I give him a tight-lipped smile. "Finn was fine. I actually wouldn't mind babysitting him more often."

Mr. Haynes chuckles. "Yeah, right." He tosses his keys on the entryway table. Then kicks his shoes off before glancing back at me. "You're serious?" His cynical tone indicates he's incredulous.

"Yeah, I am," I say. "He's a good kid."

Mr. Haynes raises an eyebrow. "Whatever you say."

As I walk to the door, I grow impatient for the day Mr. Haynes is behind bars. And one thing I know for certain; I'm the one that will put him there.

"Cole."

I turn around, seeing him hold the mug. My mug.

"Thanks," he says. "For tonight."

"Anytime."

The Stoic

I knock on Cole's door. Without asking *who's there*, he swings the door open. I wonder if he saw me outside through the cameras. Mocha attacks him with love. She jumps at him, trying to lick his face.

"Mocha, relax!" I say, trying to calm her.

"She hasn't seen me in a week," Cole says, sounding jovial. "Could you blame her?"

I'll never get used to how lively she is around him.

Cole's focus drifts from Mocha to me. With a smile, he says "I aced my math test."

"Of course, you did. You have an amazing tutor."

"Yeah, I do."

Cole wraps his muscular arms around my waist. He leans in and rests his sultry lips on mine. This feels amazing.

Mocha doesn't follow me as I walk to the couch. She waits for Cole to close the door, then follows him as he walks to the couch, joining me.

We decided every Sunday night we'd watch a movie or TV show together. Today's movie of choice: Rags. It's some 2010 Nickelodeon movie.

Cole picked this movie, but ten minutes in, his attention hasn't ascended from the floor.

"You picked this movie," I say. "If you want, we could watch something else."

His eyes dash to meet mine. "No, no, I'm just distracted."

Mocha walks over to the basement door and starts sniffing.

"I know. I am too. A lot's been going on…"

He reaches for the remote and pauses the TV. "Yeah."

I place my hands on his hands, firmly gripping them and say, "We're going to find out who this killer is."

He shakes his head. "It's not that."

"Then what is it?"

"Blake."

"Who?"

"Mr. Haynes."

"What does this have to do with our geography teacher?"

I hear Mocha obtrusively scraping the basement door.

Cole's tone lowers as he says, "I've been watching his son…"

I turn my head to the stairs, subconsciously tuning Cole out. Mocha is still scraping the door. "I'm sorry I can't pay attention with the noise. I think if you open the door, Mocha's curiosity will be put to rest."

Cole clenches his jaw. "Ok, we'll go down there. Quickly," he emphasizes.

We rise and he leads me to a white-paneled door. He unlocks it and Mocha runs down, skipping a few stairs.

At the bottom of the stairs, there's another door. This one's bigger. Mocha's reflection shines off the vault-like metal. Her mouth foams up as she barks at the door, acting like it's a hybrid of a squirrel and a mailman–her two worst enemies.

Hung on the door is a framed white piece of paper. Besides for the few numbers written on it, it's entirely blank.

The numbers read: **24.451 04/17/13**

I recognize those numbers. They mean something to me. I've seen them before somewhere.

Mocha's barking grows louder and more insistent, making it hard to focus.

"We really shouldn't be here," Cole says. "My dad may be back soon."

I snap a picture of the framed numbers.

"Mocha come on, let's go back upstairs." Cole grabs Mocha's collar, "Shit!"

She bit him.

Cole jerks his hand backward.

"Oh my god."

Palming one hand with the other, Cole says, "I think I'm bleeding."

"Mocha! Bad girl!" I scorn. She storms upstairs, knowing she's about to be punished.

Cole strides to the kitchen.

At home, whenever she acts out, I lock her in her cage. Seeing as there's no cage here, I do the next best thing and lock her in the bathroom.

I meet Cole in the kitchen. He's removing a bag of frozen green peas from the freezer and placing it on his hand.

Feeling guilty, I ask, "Are you okay?"

"No."

"I'm sorry she did that. You know she's not usually like that."

"It's fine. I know she's a good dog."

"Then what's bothering you?"

He draws a long breath. "I was trying to tell you before. Mr. Haynes, he beats his son."

Taken aback by his bluntness, I don't know how to respond. I wasn't expecting him to say that. "Um, okay."

Sitting down at the kitchen table, I ask, "How did you find out? Did you see bruises? Did he tell you?"

His eyes shift to the floor. "Kind of."

"Kind of?"

"I don't have enough proof yet, but I know he's abusing him." His cold eyes glare at me with certainty. "I'm going to expose him."

177

There's an engorged vein on Cole's neck pulsating. His neurotic behavior makes me scratch my head. Where is this all coming from? We were focused on discovering the identity of The Cauterizing Killer. Now he's fixated on our geography teacher.

He notices my silence and asks, "What is it?"

"Nothing, it's just that we're losing focus on what's important."

On what's important?" He snaps. "Like helping a child of abuse isn't?"

"That's not what I meant Cole and you know it."

"This kid is being abused. By a teacher of all people. This guy teaches us. He needs be locked up."

"I agree but there's a psychopath running rampant. He's been killing people for years. He took my sister—"

"Killed."

"That's what I meant," I say.

"I don't think it is. I think you believe she's alive, that you're hoping to find her. She's dead."

"Fuck you, Cole. You think I don't know she's dead? This has torn my family apart. It's ruined my mom's life, and it's ruining mine. I don't need you to remind me."

"I need to save this kid," he pleads. "I need to protect him. I need to put Blake away."

This conversation is getting too heated. Cole isn't like this. He's never been this bad-tempered. I feel like I didn't just step on a nerve, I stabbed one. Even so, Cole's always had a handle on expressing himself. He's never let anger cloud his judgment.

"Cole, what's going on with you?"

"What the hell is that supposed to mean?" There's a pause before a wrong form of realization hits him. "You think this is schizophrenia?"

"Cole."

"For your information, I started a higher dosage medication a few days ago. This isn't my schizophrenia. This kid's in danger. You of all people should understand what that's like."

"Me of all people? My dad never laid a hand on me Cole." I enunciate, "Ever."

"*Ookkayyy.*"

"This isn't you, Cole. I'm going home. Tell me when you're feeling better."

I hear rattling stemming from the kitchen. I think Mom is cooking. Mocha patiently sits under the dining room table, thinking I'm eating right now. I'm not. I'm pondering the perplexing picture on my phone.

What do the numbers mean? Why do they seem so familiar? Why was Mocha barking at that door? My head's burning up. I'm running on overtime. Mr. Torsney is hiding something down there. Something vital. I know it.

I look back at the numbers on my phone and write them on a piece of paper. **24.451 04/17/13**

Two sets of numbers. I can't stop staring at the second set of numbers. **04/17/13.**

It's a date. I know that date.

My sister was abducted the night before that. 04/16/13.

I'm reaching. It's a coincidence. There's no correlation.

Mom sets a plate in front of me. I'm in disbelief. The subtle garlic mixed with fresh fried parsley hatch a heady, flavorful fume.

"What's this?" I ask.

"Meatloaf."

"I know. It's just you haven't made meatloaf since..." I pause. "For a long time."

"I've been talking to Robert. He's been helping me progress."

"That's amazing," I say. "I'm proud of you."

I look at her for a minute before she says, "Stop staring at me."

She points to the food. "Eat up, before it gets cold."

Mom notices the paper with the numbers.

"Huh," she says.

"What?"

"Nothing. It's just, that's an address in Franklin."

"What?" I ask again.

"I was talking to my friend today. There's a high-rise that just opened up on 451 24th street in Franklin."

I look back at the paper with a newfound understanding. Two sets of numbers. One address. One date.

I know visiting that place alone is like crossing Main Street blindfolded. I can't go with Cole, not the way he's acting. I'll bring Mocha, she's seen this serial killer before. If he's there, she'll attack.

"Mom, you think I could go to Grandma's this weekend?"

"Oh dear, of course. She'd love to have you over."

The Existentialist

My mom was never maternal, which was understandable because of her being bipolar and the lack of parental figures in her youth. Still, her disregard for me…it always hurt. So, when she told me she wanted to take me to Green Point Lake, you could assume how elated I was.

I remember the feeling of Mom's hand gripping mine as she brought me there. She was never more motherly, and I never felt more secure. In that moment, I could be stuck in a burning building and she'd get me out. I could fall of a cliff and I knew she'd catch me. If I'd get lost, she would find me.

Like she always did.

She was my mom.

My *mom*.

It was fall time; I remember the leaves crinkling under my feet. I was sad they were all dead. Mom lifted my head and pointed up at the trees. Their colors were astonishing.

"Red, yellow, orange."

"And green." Mom chuckled.

"Yeah, but that's always there."

"Just because it's always there doesn't make it less special."

She was right.

She continued, "You see, Cole, it's not about the ones that die, it's about the ones that live."

Something about fall time always brought out the best in her. As a kid I'd track her mood swings. I don't know if she knew it, but she never had any mood swings in October. It was like a protective barrier, blocking all depression from coming in.

I remember seeing a salamander along the edge of the lake. I recoiled in fear.

"Don't be scared, Cole, he's friendly."

She dipped her hand onto the ground and the salamander climbed into her palm, making her smile. To say it was infectious would be an understatement.

Then my phone rang. I was ten. My dad gave me it in case anything happened to me. He was frantic and I couldn't latch onto a thing he was saying.

"Dad, I'm with Mommy."

"Cole!" He yelled so hard I almost dropped the phone. "Your mother…she's dead."

My heart sank to the bottom of the lake, under all the larvae, moss, and fish.

I glanced back to the person that I thought was my mom. "Who…who are you?"

She laughed, and what made me feel euphoric just a few moments prior now made me tremble.

What felt like a dream come true, became the cause of numerous nightmares.

She didn't stop laughing until my father came, finding me shivering in a fetal position. I was checked out by a few doctors, and assigned a psychiatrist: Mrs. Freed.

The voice talking to me, the person I thought I saw, the one that sounded like my mom; it was a hallucination.

Ever since then, everything I see, everything I experience, I cross examine. That advice Mrs. Freed gave me; if something seems farfetched, bizarre or scary, then it isn't real.

I clutch on to it for dear life.

That's my mantra, my ideology, my doctrine.

It keeps me in check.

But now there's Finn, and the dreams.

My intuition is being torn apart.

It's like my glasses are fogged up, yet I manage to see better this way.

The old me would think everything going on with Finn is just another horrid hallucination. I'd brush it aside. But now things are different.

Now…I'm not so sure my doctrine is as functional.

Finn's on the floor in front of me, sitting crisscross, drawing a vivid Green Point Lake. I lean forward from the low, plush couch I'm sitting on, trying to get a better glimpse. Few people know of that place. It's one of our town's hidden gems.

Finn tugs at my leg. "Excuse me, sir."

I let out a huff. "You don't need to call me sir."

"I'm sorry," he says.

"You don't have to apologize," I say. "What would you like?"

"I'm out of green crayon. Do you think you could bring some next time you come?"

"I'll bring a whole box of green crayons," I say. "Just. For. You."

After seeing the smile on his face, you'd think he won the lottery.

"Cole, I don't *love* you."

"We discussed this; your father's distorted definition of love isn't what love is. You don't hurt people you love. In fact, when you love someone, you go out of your way to make sure they don't get hurt. Even if that hurts you in the process."

Finn's face turns pale. He isn't computing.

This is too much for him to handle.

I should change the subject. I point to the drawings by his foot. "Have you ever been to Green Point Lake?"

Finn looks at me, confused.

183

"I. Don't. Know." He turns stiff.

Finn is one eccentric kid. I pat his back, then rise from the couch, heading to the basement stairs.

"My father knows you went to the basement last time you were here. He told me to tell you that you aren't allowed to go down there."

I put my index finger against my lip. "It'll be our little secret."

The steep stairs are no longer dust-filled. I can now see they are dark wood. Mr. Haynes must have swept.

I touch the knob, but the door doesn't open. Odd. I twist it, which does the trick. Once again, the vent whisks sultry air. I ignore it and beeline for the ball-chain, then pull it. Light floods the windowless basement. The box I left on the ground last time I was here has been returned.

Finn was right. He knows I was here.

Disregarding that tidbit of knowledge, I start rummaging through the boxes.

The first box I pull out is weighty. I unfold it, finding useless textbooks.

The second box feels filled to the brim, like it's about to burst open. When I unfold it, I find girls' baby clothing. I don't know what's more unnerving, thinking it belongs to Mr. Haynes or thinking it doesn't.

The third box feels airy and weightless. When I unfold it, there is a single stack of pictures, strapped together with a rubber band. I grasp it then unstrap it. I tilt my head and turn the pictures over, curious as to what's on them.

Oh my god.

I toss them across the room. They ruffle in the air, scattering around the floor.

I'm going to be sick.

A shiver crawls up my spine. My heart is beating out of my tight chest. I can't breathe. Why can't I breathe?

Count to ten, like Mrs. Freed recommended.

Ok. Ok.

One...two...three...four...five...six...seven...eight...nine... ten...

It didn't work. That didn't calm me down. My legs tense up. I glance downward at the other spine-chilling pictures. Each different. Each worse than the next.

One has a lifeless teenager, with a red burn, forming the letter O.M.

Another has a picture of a baby—I put a fist up to my mouth, resisting the urge to yack—a baby with a neck covered in dried blood.

My legs are now trembling, and I can hardly stand. I lean backward against the tower of boxes and some fall over me.

The vent blasts the door shut. At least I think it was the vent.

"Is...someone...there?" I say panting.

I walk to the door. What opened with ease days ago now won't budge.

Someone locked me in. Mr. Haynes.

I want to call out for help but that'll shorten my breath even more.

The basement walls now feel confining, like a straitjacket. The air feels dense. I scrutinize at the vent mounted on the wall. It's consuming more air than it is putting out.

I gaze at the door, thinking about how badly I need to get these pictures to Olivia. She needs to see this. She needs to know.

The knob twists and the door shakes. Someone is about to walk in. It must be Mr. Haynes.

My heart pulsates. Then, the door creaks open. The bullet train of panic I've been riding comes to a stop when I see Finn.

"The door often gets jammed," he says. "Are you okay?"

"Y-y-yeah."

"You sure, 'cause you don't look okay."

I grin. "I'm okay. Go back upstairs, I'll meet you there."

After putting everything back in its original place, I tug the ball-chain and dash upstairs.

The train of panic that just stopped starts again at full speed when I see Mr. Haynes.

"Where were you?" he asks.

He knows. What the hell do I say? Why can't I speak? I feel paralyzed.

"He was in the bathroom," Finn says. "S-s-sir."

Blake shoots a murderous stare Finn's way. The type of stare that could make the strongest of men shiver.

He looks back to me. "Cole, you should get going. I've missed Finn. I want to spend some quality father-son time."

Father-son time. Those words make me cringe. Heaven only knows what they mean.

"You know, I was thinking about taking Finn to a restaurant for dinner," I say.

"It's late," he says. "I'll cook him something with lots of *love.*"

I bite my tongue hard enough to taste blood. At least I think that's blood.

Blake squints at my hand and I glance downward, realizing I'm clenching a fist.

Blake reaches for my jacket from the coat rack behind him, then hands it to me. While tossing it on, I nod to the couch.

"Those are really nice drawings Finn drew."

He glances at the couch. "What drawings?"

I quickly analyze the living room. The drawings are gone.

That's odd.

"Finn drew a couple drawings of Green Point Lake," I say. "They were over there."

"Cole, I have no clue what you are talking about or what a Green Point Lake is," he says. Then throws me an *are you feeling okay* look.

"It's by that forest off of highway 59."

Heading outside, Blake accompanies me to the door.

"I've never taken Finn to any forests or any lakes. He detests the outdoors."

Blake shuts the door.

I ignore the oddness of what just happened, being more concerned about Finn.

Why did he have to cover for me? I shouldn't have asked him to keep that secret. That was wrong of me. What type of life is he living? Abused and tormented by his own father. Indoctrinated and brainwashed into this deranged idea of love. I don't understand why he covered for me.

Because you told him to.

What? No, I didn't.

When you love someone, you go out of your way to make sure they don't get hurt.

Crap. You're right. How could I be so ignorant? I'm not a teacher or a parent, I shouldn't pretend to be.

Cole, this isn't your fault. Some people are just irredeemable.

You're saying he's beyond saving?

Some situations in life, they are beyond fixing...

The Cynic

Finn's upstairs, with a busted lip. After Cole left, I didn't hold back. He knew Cole wasn't allowed down there. And he lied to me. *You never lie to your father.*

The look on their faces indicated secrecy. They were hiding something. Seeing them stand beside each other was a scary moment. In fact, I was so scared I almost confused them for each other. I thought he knew what I was hiding from him. What I was hiding from everyone. They are more alike than they know. And if he figured out the truth, he may never leave Finn's side. But like him and his father, I'm great at keeping secrets. Most people are.

It was risky having him babysit Finn. Especially with The Cauterizing Killer being related to him. But I was sick of watching Finn. And I didn't care if Cole babysitting him put his life at peril. However now it's putting my life at peril. When I went downstairs and found one of *the* pictures on the floor, I knew. Cole now thinks I'm The Cauterizing Killer. He has my key and I want him to keep it. I want him to come back here, thinking I'm not home. It's the only way I can end this, and once and for all, bury all his suspicions with his mom, in the grave. I tried to stay out of it, I'm still going to, but just this once, I'm going to have to do something.

The Existentialist

My father is obsessed with philosophy. Ever since we moved here, he's studied all types of things: Anti-natalism, Existentialism, Moral Idealism, Theodicy.

One of his favorites, which I find myself pondering, is Hard Determinism. It's the doctrine that the actions and choices we make are determined by forces and influences outside our control. All our actions are results of previous occurrences.

Say, someone broke into your house, and you killed them. You aren't morally responsible. If he didn't break into your house, if you didn't have a gun, if you didn't train at a shooting range, then you wouldn't have taken his life. All of your previous actions led to this.

Is that too confusing?

Yes.

Okay, Dad used to give me this example: If someone held a gun to your loved one's head and said kill me or I kill them. Being that I'm a loving, decisive person, I'd kill the person risking my loved one's life.

I'm sure it's still confusing. I may have even relayed it incorrectly. I didn't study this, my father did. But I don't agree with it. I believe in a world where everyone has a choice. A world where you hitting your son, is morally wrong. Where the only person to blame for your actions is yourself.

The ringing from my phone wakes me up. I look to the right, at my alarm clock: 5:32.

Who's calling me at 5:32 a.m.? I grab my phone from the nightstand. The brightness blinds me for a few seconds. Then a name fades in. Blake.

I pick up the phone. "Mr. Haynes?"

"You tell anybody about the pictures and you'll regret it."

The phone disconnects.

After blinking a few times trying to absorb what I just heard, I come to the conclusion that he's lying. I put all the pictures back, he can't know about them. This isn't real. I've imagined these last few minutes.

I return my phone to the nightstand, then rest back against my bed, staring at the ceiling.

But what if it is?

It's not.

Sweetie, if he did know, how do you think he'd react?

Definitely not by calling me. It's ill-conceived.

Unless he knows about your schizophrenia and is trying to play on that.

I shake my head.

He could come for you when you least expect it. By school. He'll abduct you like he did ten years ago.

That wasn't him.

How do you know?

I…I don't.

Check your call log.

I roll over and grab my phone. It's still open.

You should really change that in settings. It wastes battery.

Now's not the time.

Squinting at the call log, I see it there. The call was real. My breath quickens.

I call Nate. He answers on the fourth ring.

"Cole?" His voice is low.

My tone needs to sound rational because, I know, what I'm about to say is beyond irrational. "Our teacher is going to murder me," I say as casually as one can in a situation like this.

"What?" he asks.

I inhale some sanity, then slowly exhale insanity. "I know about his pictures. I'm close to putting him away and he doesn't like that."

"Come again?"

"I was in his house—"

Nate cuts me off, "It's 5:37 Cole, can we talk about this at school?"

"Yeah." I say, feeling immediate regret.

He hangs up.

I shouldn't be going to school. Blake's going to be there.

Sweetie, you can't not go to school.

I don't have a choice.

What are you going to do, avoid school forever?

No, even *I* know how unrealistic that is. I need to get to Blake before he can get to me. I have the key to his house. I could go back and acquire those pictures.

Outside school, I watch students bolt through the pale, frosty grass toward the building. The heating was fixed indoors, so you'd be a fool to spend more than a few minutes outside, which is what I'm doing. I'm not walking into this building alone. I may not have a weapon to protect me, but I will have the protection of bystanders. And Blake knows better than to abduct me when I'm with other people.

Who says he's going to abduct you?

You, driving me crazy with all your insinuations, implanting the idea in my head.

I notice Olivia descending a discolored bus, wearing low tan boots, hastily zipping up her grape-colored parka.

I call out for her.

Her legs are already speed-walking toward the building, but once she spots me, she changes course and sails in my direction.

She starts, "About the other night…"

"Olivia, I think Blake is going to kill me."

Her facial expression drops, accurately portraying the temperature. "Cole, he's our geography teacher. He's a scrawny, meek-mannered, awkward man. Even with his height, between the two of you, I think you'd overpower him."

She's not wrong.

"So now you're the voice of reason?"

"What?" Olivia asks.

"Nothing," I blurt.

God, these delusions are getting out of hand. Will you please just stay away from me for a while?

Olivia glances at the building. "I found a clue involving my sister. I want your help, but not if your attention is skewed." She wraps her arms around me and we're engulfed in each other's body warmth. "I'm heading to class," she says. "You should, too."

The empty halls indicate class has started. I'm not heading to class, not until I talk to Nate. I pull out my phone and dial his number.

"*Mister* Torsney." Principal Parsons blurts, almost causing me to have a heart attack.

Where the hell did he come from?

"You know the rule. No phone usage in the halls."

"But—"

"No buts." He swings his hand at my phone, grabbing it. "You can collect your phone from the office after school."

192

Before I get a chance to respond, he's already sauntering down the hallway. Nate, walking in the opposite direction of him, glances at my phone in Principal Parsons's hand.

"Where were you?" I ask.

"You know my bus is always running late. I vent to you about it all the time."

"Right," I say. "I forgot."

Nates eyes narrow with skepticism. "Cole, what's going on?"

"It's Bla—Mr. Haynes. He's evil."

"Evil?"

"He beats his son. Not only that, but I think he's connected to a killer somehow. He had my mug—"

"Your mug?"

"Yeah, and these pictures of kids, a baby with blood on her neck."

"Cole, slow down."

"I thought I could help Finn. But I can't, and I think I just ended up making things worse. He called me, threatening to kill me."

"Cole!" Nate interjects. "This isn't real."

"What?"

"None of this is real. You're going into psychosis."

Oh, how I wish that were true. "Not this time. I'm not hallucinating. There are pictures, and Finn told me. Oh, and the phone call. I can prove everything."

"Who's Finn? And what did he tell you?"

"Finn is Blake's eight-year-old son. He said that Blake beats him."

"That's pretty frank for an eight-year-old."

I tug at my shirt collar. "Well, he didn't exactly say those words. He said Blake 'loves' him."

Nate's eyebrows rise. "He said Mr. Haynes loves him?"

"I know how that sounds. You don't understand."

He rubs his eyes, then makes a steeple of his finger. "Did you actually *see* Mr. Haynes beating him?"

"No but I can show you the pictures, they're at his house, and the call log'll show he called me at 5:30."

"We aren't breaking into his house!"

A baby-faced student passes by holding a hall pass. I nod at him and he nods back.

"We aren't breaking into his house," Nate repeats in a softer tone. "And even if he did call you at 5:30, while that is suspicious, it doesn't incriminate him."

"We don't need to break in. He gave me a key; he wants me to watch Finn for an hour on Saturday."

If there was any shred of a chance Nate believed me before, that's disappeared now.

"The guy that wants to 'kill' you asked you to babysit?"

I lied. It doesn't matter. The ends justify the means. Once Nate sees the pictures, he'll know how grave this is.

Nate and I, sitting on the black reception chairs in the school office, wait for my phone. I will prove Blake called me. My foot is tip-tapping against the tiled floor. The tick-tock stemming from the black clock plastered on the wall makes time seem all the slower. Yet, it's just an illusion. One I'm aware of.

Unable to wait any longer, I spring out of the chair and walk toward the oak finish reception desk. There's a mini Christmas tree beside the receptionist's laptop, and I resist the urge to notify her Christmas passed weeks ago.

Principal Parsons exits his office. "Here you go Cole, don't let this happen again."

I want to say: I won't. I'll be more covert next time. Instead, I settle on, "You got it."

I start up my phone. Nate hovers over me, curiously.

"That's odd."

"What?"

194

"My phone is on thirteen percent, I brought it to school fully charged."

"Weird. That happens to me sometimes though."

That's not the only weird thing. His call is missing.

"Cole, where's Mr. Haynes' call?"

Staring at the screen, expressionless, I start thinking aloud. "Blake must have deleted his call from the call log while it was here in the office."

"Isn't your phone password protected?"

"It is, but it was taken away before I got a chance to shut it."

"Don't phones shut off by themselves?"

Told you to fix that.

Nate swings around and sighs. I know his patience is running thin. To be honest, I'm surprised he's put up with me on this *Blake is evil* bandwagon thus far. I just need him to hold out a little longer. Until Saturday. Then he'll see.

I convinced Nate to park down the block. Though it was just a few minutes ago, I don't remember the lie I fed him but I do remember the look on his face— disappointment. I feel horrible lying to him, but there's not a chance he'd follow me otherwise.

A pair of middle-aged women, jogging, eyeball us as I unlock the door to Mr. Haynes' house. Their identical appearances cause me to wonder if just like their pink sprinter jackets, they were bought in the same store.

Sweetie, that makes no sense.

The door clicks, unlocking.

"See? I told you he gave me the key."

"Just show me the pictures," he says.

When I set foot into the house I'm bewildered. This isn't Blake's house. Once again, I enter a land foreign to me. The land of confusion. I visit here so often I'm thinking about applying for citizenship.

"What's wrong?" Nate asks.

I look at the picture frames on the entryway table, the frames hung on the walls, and the flowers sitting on the dining room table. There's a rug now in front of the couch.

I grab one of the smaller frames from the entryway table. Blake and Finn are in the picture. It appears to be recent.

"Cole?"

"These pictures," I say. "They weren't here before."

"Maybe he just put them up."

"No, Nate," I snap. "There were literally no pictures anywhere. The house had no sign of character."

I notice the subtle fragrance of vanilla, which is odd; however, it sends a subliminal message: *no maltreatment occurs here*.

I run my hand through my hair. Maybe I am going crazy. No. The pictures. Downstairs.

I speed to the basement. Once down there I pull the ball chain. I'm in more shock than last time I was down here. There are no boxes. I drop to my knees. The jagged ground lacerates my shinbones, though I don't process the pain. My eyes dart around the room looking for any box, as if they'll magically materialize in this empty, four-wall room.

"Nate, you don't understand. I saw it."

"I believe you saw it. But it wasn't real."

"No. This time it was. This time, it felt real."

I gaze upward at Nate, who is looking down at me. A moment passes before he says, "I can't imagine how hard this is for you Cole."

My eyes fall to the ground. "It's hell on earth."

With heavy steps we plod up the stairs. I haven't flicked on any of the lights, seeing that the house is filled with natural light.

Walking to the front door, I hear a car hum into the driveway. I stop, Nate continues walking until reaching the door. Grasping the handle, he looks backward at me. "What are you doing?"

I can't speak. I didn't think Blake would be back right now.

Do you know his schedule on Saturdays?
No.
"Where's Finn?" Nate asks.
I don't answer. I don't need to, I'm sure he's seconds away from figuring it out.
He rubs his forehead. "Jesus, Cole."
I hear the soft thud of a car door closing.
"Is there a back door?" Nate asks.
"In the kitchen."
We scurry to the back, ripping the white, windowed door open. There's a small charcoal grill, to my right, in the large unfenced backyard. Beside it I notice a scrap of paper with burnt edges. I inch closer, interested. Squinting, I manage to make out a child. It's one of *the* pictures.
Not just any.
It's a picture of...me.
A gust of wind sweeps it away, then Nate yanks my arm. "We need to go, now!"
Nate and I surreptitiously dash from bush to bush, until reaching his jeep. Once in there, I release the deep breath I've been holding in since we arrived. Nate doesn't, he starts the car and it creates a rumbling noise.
While speeding away, he glares at the road. His tense hands, firmly clasping the wheel.
Fidgeting with my seatbelt buckle, I say, "Nate, I—"
"You lied to me," he blurts.
"I thought—"
"I don't care. I went along with you because you're my friend. Friends don't lie to each other. Not with things this serious."
"It all seemed so real. I thought this time it would be different."
"It's never different. This stuff, it just isn't plausible."
He's angry and with reason. It's just all confusing. My life is like the movie *Inception*, only more complex. At times I wonder

if it'll ever get easier, then I look back and know...it's only gotten harder.

I think back to what Mrs. Freed said, *if it sounds crazy, bizarre or far-fetched, then it is.* I need to stick to that. That's how I made it this far. That's how I can dictate between reality and fantasy. It's not a foolproof system, but it's the best one I have.

The day's still young, I should be outside doing something, yet, I'm not. I'm lying in bed, ruminating. I don't know what hope looks like, but I do know the face of desperation. I had become quite acquainted with it by the time I was eight.

It's the face of a housewife, scared of her husband.

The face of a girl, not knowing if she'll ever see her sister again.

The face of a young boy, thinking he's all alone, in a spine-chilling room, with a serial killer.

Sometimes I think I'm still that young boy, all alone. That's why I have the voice of my mom in my head. So, I never have to be alone. I tell people I enjoy my solitude. But the truth is, I've never experienced any real solitude. With my mom in here, I'm never alone. Even when I can't see her or she isn't talking, I never know when she'll pop up.

Knowing that no matter where I am, she'll follow, brings me solace. It's crazy, I know.

No, it isn't.

Ok, no it isn't.

I think that's why I cared for Finn so much. I didn't want him to go through this alone. He has no one.

Now I see he's not going through anything. I don't know if Mr. Haynes is a good dad, but I know he's not abusive.

He loves Finn and Finn loves him. That's that.

My phone starts ringing. **Olivia**. I should apologize for all of this. "Hey, Olivia I'm sor—"

"Cole." She says panting.

"What's wrong?"

"I found my sister."

The Defeatist

Society labels the best marriages are the ones that stand the test of time. After eight years being married to Elizabeth, I reached a shocking conclusion: that statement is fallacious.

People like to cling to the idea that the relationship they're in, is better than the relationship of a divorced couple, on the grounds that they aren't divorced.

It's like saying my car's better than yours because it hasn't broken down yet.

It's a false creed.

In fact, some of the worst divorces I've seen are the ones that never happened. The most mature bonds I've seen, were the ones that called it quits because their interests were misaligned. The most immature bonds I've seen were the ones that belittle their spouse's every move, but stayed together 'for their kids.'

The reality is, the worst marriages are the ones that last the longest.

The best marriages are the ones that die young.

I know eight years isn't a lot of time to be married, but honestly, Elizabeth and I should've called it *quits* right after we called it *starts*.

I woke up and Elizabeth wasn't next to me, which was always a bad sign. It sounds counter-intuitive, but whenever she was out of bed before me, she was going through an episode.

Or on her period.

Or hungover.

And I was never able to tell which was which. Obviously, that put me in the doghouse…a lot. I spent many nights on the couch, not just because of confusion. But, because quite often, I was an asshole.

I didn't mind sleeping on the couch, though. It was more comfortable than our bed. And, honestly, I hated sleeping next to Elizabeth. It was also closer to the fridge, so grabbing a beer before bed was easier.

You'd think now that I had an eight-year-old son, I'd be drinking less. Nope. I was an alcoholic. Having an eight-year-old son only made it worse. That's on top of the fact that he was a schizophrenic.

I'd hear him talking to himself a lot and it would creep me the fuck out. I'd think he was possessed or something. Before he was born, I was excited to be a dad. But by the time he was eight years old, I'd leave the room whenever he entered it, keeping my distance from him as much as possible.

I never hit him; I wasn't abusive. Then again, abuse is a very vague term. I wasn't there for him when he was six years old going through psychosis. He wouldn't stop screaming about bugs all over him in the middle of the night. I'd lock my door placing a pillow over my head, ignoring him. He screamed all night, pounding on my door, begging me to help him.

I acted like the problem didn't exist, because I didn't want it to. It was bad enough I had to take care of Elizabeth's bipolar disorder, now I had to take care of him, too.

This wasn't how I pictured being a dad.

In the kitchen, Elizabeth was reading a newspaper. It was quite odd because she hated reading…and the news. But I didn't question it. I learned not to question anything my wife did—one of my many mistakes.

I opened the fridge door and noticed we were out of milk. We have designated responsibilities in our marriage. I take out the trash, she does groceries. I took out the trash the night prior. She didn't get milk.

"Liz."

She didn't answer.

"Liz?"

Again, no answer.

The hell did I do this time? She's given me the silent treatment before, but never this early in the morning. Not being in the mood for this, I marched over to her and slapped the newspaper out of her hand.

"Pick up some goddamn milk on your way back from work!"

It's not easy being a parent, but if I had to be one, so did she.

When I came home, there was no milk in the fridge. Now, if she was too distracted and couldn't pick up the milk, she could've called me. I would've. I had the time.

She didn't want me to have milk. She wanted to invoke a reaction out of me. It was immature, and like this morning, I wasn't in the mood for it. I don't think I ever *was* in the mood for it.

After calling her to the kitchen, I asked, "Where's the milk?"

"What?"

"Where's the milk?"

"I'm not in the mood for your stupid games."

She turned around, wanting to leave the conversation.

"Don't you walk away."

When I grabbed her by the wrist, I noticed there were red circles on them. I should've asked about it but I didn't. Another one of my mountains of mistakes.

"Where's the milk?"

"Are you drunk again?"

The exasperation in her tone made *me* exasperated.

"I told you to get some this morning," I said.

"You never told me to get any milk."

I didn't know what game she was playing at, why she lied. And I didn't care. We needed to argue as much as we needed to breathe. Both of us always trying to get the last word. Our arguments were more passionate than our sex.

"I told you twice."

"Wow, you really are drunk huh?"

"And you're fuckin' bipolar."

My son was upstairs, crying, yelling about the bugs on his body. It only made my arguing more intense.

It wasn't the last time I'd hear him cry like that. Months later he was going to find his mother dead.

I remembered thinking he was hallucinating.

It didn't make sense.

She wasn't supposed to be there.

I tried killing her in Franklin.

So how the hell did she get back here.

The Stoic

Pacing back and forth, I dial Cole's number. He needs to know.

He picks up, "hey, Olivia I'm sor—"

"Cole," I say, panting

"What's wrong?"

"I found my sister."

24 hours earlier.

Using grandma's car, I drive to the high-rise building Mom told me about. The gray skies, along with the blustery wind, lead me to believe it's going to rain any minute now; however, I thought that an hour ago, too. Regardless, I'm wearing a black rain jacket.

In the car, sitting to the right of me is Mocha. She's scratching the window, wanting to stick her head out. I shut the window because of the aggressive winds. It's staying shut.

Everyone presumes Grace is dead. And I did too, for a while. But what if she's not? What if she's been alive this entire time, while we've been going to school, watching TV, enjoying life? All the while she's been locked away somewhere.

Maybe I'm searching for her in the hope that she's alive. Is that such a bad thing? It's better than sitting on the couch doing nothing. And if she does turn out to be dead, at least then I'll have closure.

However, the curiosity, the lack of knowledge is agonizing. She's my big sister. After all this time...I still need her. I wonder what she'd think of Fairview, of Cole, and Mom finally divorcing Dad. We have a guest room; if she's alive, we could turn that into her room. We'd watch reruns of *Seinfeld* together. Like normal sisters do.

I'm being optimistic; I know it's deluding. I need to expect the worst, that way I won't be disappointed when I find nothing of importance.

Reaching the high-rise, I pull over beside the curb. Upon opening the car door, Mocha leaps out. I quickly grasp the leash. She ferociously tugs at it, trying to run leftward, down the block. I glance right, at the high-rise. Ugh. Mocha has never been this resolute.

She leads me down the litter-filled sidewalk, stopping at a shabby two-story building which has no address. The windows are boarded up and the deteriorated wooden door appears to be infirm. The entire building amidst the downcast weather screams serial killer. There's no way I'm walking in there.

Before I get a chance to turn back, Mocha charges at the building, ripping the leash out of my hand. My palms ache from the rope burn.

"Mocha, no!"

She plows into the door, bursting it open. Sawdust flours the air. My heart is racing faster than Mocha. I look around to see if anyone can help me catch her. The streets are empty, making this all the more eerie.

I don't know what to do. My knees are weak. I should let Johnny know where I am. I take out my phone, sending him a text to meet me here.

I shouldn't go in there. It's rash, I know, but Mocha is the only part of Grace I have left. She was *her* birthday present. Now she's in an ominous house, alone. Except, she may not be alone.

I can't lose anymore of Grace than I already have. I'm going in there, and if in doing so gets me hurt, then so be it. Some things in life are worth the risk.

After I walk in, I survey the building. It seems desolate. The only noise I hear is the wind whooshing against the exterior. There's a glimpse of light emanating from the only window that isn't boarded. The grungy walls are tattered and there isn't a single piece of furniture on the timeworn floors.

"Mocha?" I whisper.

I tiptoe through the building until stumbling upon a doorless frame revealing a little, paved backyard that's incongruously well kept. Mocha lays, whimpering, in front of a rectangular red patch of bricks in the pavement. One brown brick dwelling above the others catches my eye. I glance over my shoulder, inside the building, thinking I heard something. I'm sure it was nothing. Mocha would probably bark if she heard someone.

I creep forward to the patch of bricks. Standing atop it, I grasp the brown one. There's a faded engraving in it. Five letters. What does it say?

I hear another noise in the building but ignore it, focusing on what's written on the brick. My eyes widen when I realize what it says. I drop the brick and jump off the grave I'm standing on.

Grace's grave.

Mocha stops whimpering and starts barking. I hear footsteps prowling closer. My body is too tense to move. I feel as stiff as a corpse.

Facing the building, I manage to pull my phone out of my pocket, wanting to dial *9-1-1*. I look down typing the numbers in and when I look up, there's a gun pointed at my face.

I shriek.

Johnny almost pulls the trigger before realizing it's me.

"Are you insane?" he asks. "Why didn't you wait outside?"

My eyes are burning. I can't speak. Johnny glances at the grave and instantly understands. He wraps his arms around me and with one hand strokes my hair.

I start bawling.

"It's okay, it's okay," he says with a warmhearted voice.

"She's dead," I snivel.

"It's not your fault."

Grace's last words to me were 'I hate you' and because of that, I grew up hating myself. I was too young to save her back then. Too weak. And I thought now, I'd be strong enough. That her last thought wouldn't be of how much she hated me, it would be about how grateful she was to see me. Now I know it was all just a pipe dream. She's been dead for almost a decade and somehow Mr. Torsney knew.

There's about a dozen police officers here now. Some inside the building, some out. Two of them, in white overalls, are currently digging up the grave. Over the phone, I inform Cole on everything that's occurred thus far.

"Olivia. I'm sorry I wasn't there for you."

I draw a deep breath. "It's okay," I say, though it wasn't. I don't have it in me to fight right now.

"There's something else," I say.

"What?" Cole asks.

"They want to know how I found this place."

"Olivia..."

"Cole, your dad knew," I say, "I'm not suggesting he killed her, but he knew."

"I know. There's no denying that now, but he's my dad. I don't want him to get in trouble."

"This is beyond that now."

"Just give it a week," he pleads, "we'll dig deeper and if we don't find anything after a week, you can go to the police."

"Cole..."

"One week." He pauses. "He's my dad, Olivia. He's all I have left."

"Okay," I say. "One. Week."

Johnny saunters toward me with the same sympathetic look on his face he had ten years ago. This is the last thing I wanted: people feeling sorry for me.

"How are you doing?" he asks.

I brush aside his daft question and ask, "Could you wait to tell my mom about this?"

He looks at me like *I'm* the one that said something daft. "Olivia, even if I wasn't obliged to notify her, it's only a matter of time before the press finds out about this."

I chew on a cuticle. This is going to devastate her. She just escaped the prison of grief and started growing; now she's going to be locked up again. My ears haven't bled from the heart-rending sound of her sobs in months. Change is imminent. I remember a time: I was thirteen years old, Mom passed out on the couch, holding a picture of Grace. There was a glass of cabernet on the coffee table beside her. I tossed a blanket over her and poured the wine out in the sink.

Dad should've been the one tossing the blanket over her, spilling out the wine. He was the man of the house. Where was he when his wife needed him? Where was he when his wife passed out on the couch?

Oh right, getting drunk with his bar friends.

Sometimes I wondered if he was happy that Grace disappeared. I mean, he always belittled us, telling us we were worthless. That we "loved spending his money." He would say, "If I didn't have you girls, I could be driving a Ferrari." Ten years without one of his girls and he's no closer to that Ferrari.

After Grace was taken—I mean died—he had less responsibilities. Not because there was one less child, but because my mom—too weak to badger my father—took on more responsibility. I wonder how he'll react to Grace being found dead.

The Stoic

Moms are a different breed of human that science has yet to explain. Their physical and mental strength is unrivaled. While I may often argue with my mom, there isn't a soul I respect more than hers. After everything she's been through, I'm surprised she isn't getting wasted, drinking her sorrows away at a bar. Instead, she's here, at home, on the couch. She's covered by a fleece blanket and clutching a box of tissues. No matter how persistently she wipes her bloodshot eyes, the tears don't fade.

It hurts seeing her like this. What hurts more is seeing Mr. Torsney here, comforting her. He brought her a single stem scarlet orchid. I hate that he knows her favorite type of flower.

It's inconceivable how he has the audacity to set foot in this house. He knew she was dead all along. Not only that, but he knew where she was buried. It would be naïve of me not to assume he killed her himself. But I don't want to go that far, not yet.

Sitting at the dining room table, rage-filled, I watch him, feeling like a ticking time bomb about to explode.

I glance at the carpeted stairs which lead to the basement. Mocha is snarling in her cage down there. She tried to bite Mr. Torsney, which I can't blame her for. However, Mom demanded I lock her up until he leaves.

My phone chimes. Another text from someone wishing their condolences. I received plenty today. These same people wishing me their condolences were spreading rumors about me months ago. High school. People are so authentic here.

I rise from the chair and head out. This house feels suffocating. Mom wanted me to visit Dad, which is why Cole isn't here. She wants me to confirm he's okay and if he sees Cole he probably won't be.

There's a thick morning mist today. I hold my palm out flat and feel a few tentative raindrops. The weather isn't so bad; I'm not going back inside to grab a rain jacket. Using Mom's compact SUV, I drive to Dad.

The horror movie-like fog along with the tree silhouettes on the side of the road are slightly disturbing. I proceed with caution.

Once I reach Dad's house, I park outside and lock the car.

I knock three times. Nobody answers. I'm not sure if I find that odd. I slowly twist the knob, it's unlocked. Gradually opening the door, I breathe, "Dad?"

I hear what sounds like a football game playing on the TV. Entering the apartment I spot Dad on the couch, eyes glued to the game.

"Seriously?" I'm not surprised, His daughter was taken in a home invasion; still, he doesn't lock his doors.

His eyes don't move from the TV. "Hey Gra—I mean Olivia."

"I told you I was coming."

"You did? Right, you did, that's why the door was open."

"Right." I scoff.

He doesn't look the least bit mournful. I have to wonder if he even knows Grace's body was found. "They found Grace."

His eyes finally budge from the tube-shaped TV, acknowledging my presence.

"I told you."

"What?"

"I told you she was dead, years ago. You thought she was out there somewhere." A smirk rises on his face. "I guess she was, just dead."

My back tenses.

This was a mistake. I don't know why, every time I come here, I think he's someone he's not. I think he's my father. Then I leave and I remember, he's *my father*.

My eyes dart to his scarred, wooden table. There's the paper I've seen since I was eight years old. The same paper Mr. Ackerman received from The Cauterizing Killer. Dad isn't sentimental. Besides for him, that paper is the oldest thing in this apartment. I glance at my dad whose focus is still centered on the football game. I creep forward and examine the antiquated paper. It reads:

I hope we can do it again.
-O.M.

Before I can process what I just read, my hair is yanked and my head jerks back slamming me hard onto the floor. Ringing reverberates in my ears. Trying to placate the throbbing, I squeeze my eyes shut and pinch my temples.

"You fuckin' bitch."

My vision blurs. I can't push myself up from the floor, yet my whole body feels as light as a feather. Someone clenches a fistful of my hair, lifting my head up.

When I catch a whiff of vinegary breath, I know it's Dad.

"Get out of my apartment," he says, with disgust.

Then he releases my hair from his grubby hands and I plop onto the chilly floor.

Clarity returns to my eyesight. I glance at Dad, who's returning to the couch, back against me.

I touch the back of my head. I think I'm bleeding. My heart's racing but my body remains still. Panting, I look at the door which seems to be rotating. I stand up with unsteadiness and wobble to the exit.

Somehow, I make it outside and dash to the car. Gripping onto the door handle, my stomach turns and I barf.

I'm never coming here again.

Driving isn't safe, but I can't stay here. I feel more vulnerable here than I did in the abandoned building yesterday.

I get in my car and drive off. The fogginess seems to have increased, intensifying my dizziness. I roll down the windows, the strong breeze is refreshing against my sweaty face.

Noticing that I'm drifting left over the yellow line, I swerve right, which brings back any dizziness the breeze diminished. My phone residing in the cup holder, rings. Why is it not connected to the car's Bluetooth? With clammy hands I grip it and press answer.

"They've positively identified the bones belonging to your sister."

The phone slides onto the floorboard. Crap. I wiggle my left leg trying to feel it. Then with one hand on the wheel I peer down and reach. When I glance back at the road, there's an abrasive honk.

I curve right until I'm off-road, then slam the breaks. I stare vacantly into the distance, breathing deep and exhaling hard. I feel like a balloon someone keeps squeezing, trying to pop. There waiting for air to burst out of me. It's not going to happen. I won't pop. I won't break.

When I return home, Mom's sitting on the couch, looking at her phone. Mocha's half on her lap, half on the cushions. When I was seven and I'd enter the house, she'd storm at me with excitement in her eyes. Now, she barely raises an ear.

"Mr. Torsney gone?"

She looks over her shoulder, then rises. "Yes," she says. "Next time he's here I want you to treat him with more respect.

He's really been helping me get through this, and he's Cole's dad for crying out loud!"

Clenching my jaws, I start tearing up.

Mom's facial expression switches from angry mom to consoling mom. I like consoling mom. "Oh Olivia, I didn't mean to raise my voice." She hugs me. "We're all going through tough times."

Sniffling I say, "It's not that."

Mom bobs her head back and gazes at me.

"Dad, he…he…"

She places her finger against my lips before squeezing me. It's euphoric. All the stress, pain, exhaustion I feel dissolves.

"I'm sorry, honey."

Reaching serenity, I remember the note. "There's something else I wanted to ask you."

"Anything."

"Dad has a note, from when Grace was taken. Why did you keep it hidden?"

A look of puzzlement crosses her face. "I don't understand."

"Mom, I saw the note. You don't have to deny it."

She shakes her head. "I was there Olivia, there was no note that night."

I study her body language before concluding she isn't lying. I'm just surprised she never noticed all the times Dad solemnly stared at it. Then again, she was always preoccupied, slaving away, doing housework on top of her full-time job.

"Maybe Dad found it before you and hid it."

"That can't be."

"Mom, I saw the note."

"I believe you. It can't be that he found it. The police swept the whole house long before he came home."

"It could be that The Cauterizing Killer broke in again and left it."

"I doubt it. We added new locks on the door, and there was also a police cruiser surveying the house the rest of the month."

He has a note from whoever killed Grace. That's irrefutable. How he received it is a different question.

"I could see your thinking," Mom says.

"It just doesn't make sense."

She presses her lips together. "Olivia, I think it's time you drop this."

"Mom, this note—"

"Not the note," she interjects, "everything. This 'investigation' you've conducted. I didn't mind when it started, but it's gotten too far. Your grades are dropping. You're about to graduate, you've worked so hard, you can't just throw all that away right before the finish line."

"But The Cauterizing—"

"Enough about that psycho!" Her eyes widen. "He's taken enough from us."

Mom doesn't seem sad anymore. I think she's really moved on.

"The future is always brighter than the past, especially *our* past. You can't keep obsessing over this. It's not healthy, and it's not what Grace would want." She cups my arm. "He can't hurt us anymore. What will hurt you is chasing this killer. I mean you were in an abandoned building for crying out loud. What were you thinking? There could've been junkies there. And I don't want to know how you found Grace's bones. Johnny told me you wouldn't tell him."

"We need justice for her," I whimper.

"Justice? Olivia, you are talking like a madman. You are seventeen. Let the police handle this."

"I can't do that. Not now. Not after all I've learned."

Mom nods with contemplation. "I don't want you seeing Cole anymore."

"You can't—"

"Yes, I can."

I storm upstairs, to my room, slamming the door behind me. Then I erupt into laughter. Mom banning me from seeing Cole is the most normal thing that's happened in a while. It's relieving. I *must* be a madman because who else would smile at a time like this.

I sit on my floral-sheeted bed, mulling over all the information I've obtained.

Cole's dad lied about his nightmares.

He knew the location of Grace's body.

He presumably knew the date she died.

Whatever is going on, Mr. Torsney is in the center of it. He knows more than he's letting on.

I take out my phone and call Johnny, who answers on the first ring.

"I need you to look up a file for me."

"Hello to you, too," he says.

"I apologize but it's urgent."

It wasn't urgent but it sure felt urgent. And I've learned that if you tell people it's urgent, they'll treat it as such.

"I need you to see if there are any police reports on Robert Torsney."

Without asking any questions, he says, "Okay, I'll get back to you ASAP."

Mom knocks on my door and without waiting for an answer, opens it. "Hey, buttercup."

I roll my eyes. Her nicknames have been worsening with time.

"How are you doing?"

"Hmm, let's see, my sister's bones were just found. By me. My dad threw me on the floor, calling me a bitch. And the one thing my mom is worried about is my friggin' grades. How do you think I'm doing?"

I anticipate a penalizing response for my attitude.

"You are much more mature than I was at your age."

I'm taken aback. Mom sits beside me on the bed. She proceeds, "When I was married to your father, he was physical with me. When Grace aged, he was physical with her, too."

215

"Mom, I was there. He never touched us. If he did, I would see."

"People see what they want to see. What they are led to believe," she says. "I was frail when I married your father. I always resented myself for letting him hit Grace. So, when you were born, I made sure he wouldn't touch you, or at least any of us in front of you."

"But he did worse. The things he'd say, they pained more than fists."

"I know that now. It was just all so much. It didn't happen overnight. It was incremental. Small things I let slide. Once I realized how bad the situation was, it was too big. I felt like I was fighting a forest fire with a water gun. I didn't know what to do."

"You could have left him."

"That was my weakness. You know this. I care too much about the Joneses. I didn't want people in the neighborhood to talk. It was stupid. I'm still like that but I'm working on it. And I hate myself for taking so long to leave him."

"Mom, I respect you so much for leaving him. I can't imagine how hard that must've been for you. What bothers me is why you still care for him now. After everything he's done."

"I can't explain it. Maybe you'll understand when you're older, but when you are married to someone for that long, they are just a part of you. You can't help but think about them. Long after you've separated."

She pauses for a moment.

"Cole's a nice man."

"That's the first time you called him a man," I say.

"That's what he is, that's how he treats you. He is a man. I shouldn't have been calling him a boy. I know that if I restrict you from seeing Cole, you'll just do it behind my back."

True.

"And the truth is, I want you to see him. He's good for you. He's not only better than most teenagers, he's better than most men."

"Thank you, Mom."

She gives me a look indicating there's more she wants to say. "I think it's time I talk to you about what happened that night. When Grace was taken."

"It's okay Mom, you don't have to."

"I want to, I think you're ready."

I slowly nod.

"After you and Grace were in bed, your dad went out drinking. At least that's where I thought he went. It's what he initially claimed. But none of his drinking friends could vouch for him. Eventually the police found his car by some shady motel."

"Why was his car there?"

"I don't know, and I'm not sure I want to. He's been..." she tilts her head, "less then loyal to me before but, if I found out he cheated on me while Grace was taken, it would kill me."

My phone chimes. I ignore it.

"I was sitting on the couch, glass of red wine in hand. Mocha was insistently barking. You don't remember, but before Grace disappeared, Mocha had the tenacity of a lion. Fearing she'd wake you girls up, I put her in the basement, locking the pet gate." Mom inspects her fingernails. "In my slippers, I shuffled back to the couch. The pajamas I was wearing always tired me, but when I saw him, The Cauterizing Killer, I couldn't be more awake. The glass of wine I was holding crashed onto the floor. He was standing in the kitchen, holding a branding iron and rope. Over his shoulder, the window on the backdoor was shattered. His voice was automated as he said, 'I'm going to tie you up. If you try anything, your daughters will die.' Mocha's barking grew deafening. It only made me more uneasy. He tied me up, sitting on the couch, opposite facing the stairs. The rope felt like it was cutting my skin. At this point, silent tears were

217

streaming down my face and I shrugged them against my shoulder.

"I noticed as he walked upstairs, his footsteps were naturally light. I stared at the wall, praying for someone, anyone to save us. My heart was barking as much as Mocha. Then she stopped barking. I looked over my shoulder to see the pet fence busted in. She practically flew upstairs, like Superman. It was then that I truly realized how loving a dog could be.

"She was my only hope. The only glimpse of preservation we had. I heard a loud thud, then The Cauterizing Killer was limping downstairs, clinching Grace. Mocha bit him. He fled with her, among other things like my marriage, my family, and our only sense of security. However, I've recently discovered that that was all my doing. The only thing he took, was Grace and a bit of time. Luckily, we still have that, time."

"Why did he run?" I ask.

Mocha enters the room with her head hung low, as if she knows what we are talking about.

"The police think he was allergic to dogs. He could've gone into anaphylactic shock and died," Mom says.

Mocha scratches my leg. I pick her up and put her on the bed. She's getting heavier.

Mom frowns at Mocha. "I know this sounds stupid, because she's a dog. But I think when Grace was taken, she lost a part of her spirit." Mom wipes her eyes. I hadn't realized they were wet. She continues, "They say it's a dog's job to protect their owners. It's as if she's remorseful for failing." Mom scratches behind Mocha's ears. "She's an old dog now, her disposition matches her age. It's just sad that this has been her disposition since she was two years old.

"Grace being taken hurt us all. But dogs are supposed to be rays of sunshine. I mean, when people are depressed or mourning, they recommend getting a dog, but we have a dog, and she's mourning. What do we do then? She was our only consistent light, and she turned dark."

My phone rings.

"Answer it. I'm going to cook meatloaf for dinner."

A soul-stirring smile rises on my face.

Looking down at my phone as Mom exits the room, I accept the call. It's Johnny.

"I didn't expect you to find the file so soon."

"I didn't."

"So why are you calling?"

"Robert Torsney doesn't exist."

The Defeatist

A week after the milk incident, I woke up from the sun sparkling through the window. I hugged the blanket tight, too tired to get up, but she wasn't in bed. Again. Which meant she was dealing with one of her many 'issues' and I'd have to make Cole breakfast.

Downstairs, Elizabeth was ransacking the pantry, throwing things into a picnic bag. She looked like she was robbing the place.

"What are you doing?" I asked.

"Nothing."

She dashed to the door.

"Where are you going?" I asked.

She opened the door. "To work, honey." Then breezed out.

It was a Sunday.

She never worked on a Sunday.

Nor did she ever call me honey.

Our relationship wasn't sunshine and roses.

We lived together. We had a son together. And, yes, I loved her. But we never really showed affection. We weren't touchy-feely. We were more vulgar than softhearted. I was aloof and inattentive. She was reserved and unresponsive to sentiment.

But she was always frank. If I ever cared enough to ask her how she felt, she would tell me the absolute truth.

Unlike her, I actually worked on Sundays. Late. When I came home, I found her sleeping in bed. Still angry and confused, I shook her.

"I thought you were working?"

It was 11 p.m. Even if she did work, she'd be home by now. She groaned. "Please just let me sleep."

"Where the hell did you go?"

"I was by Ruth's house."

Ruth is our annoying neighbor. We both openly bash her. There's no way she'd have gone on a picnic with her. And besides, she said she was going to work. "You told me you were going to work."

"I did. I was working with Ruth."

I knew she was lying. "You were on a picnic with Jerry, weren't you?"

"Please, just let me sleep."

"I bet Jerry treats you nice, but guess what? He doesn't have to deal with your excessive alcohol consumption, or your bipolar disorder." A moment passed before I asked, "Does he even know you're bipolar?"

Yup, I was a certified asshole.

I think that was the first time I really hurt her. Now I know what you're thinking, we argued all the time. But all those arguments were just that, arguments. Always about stupid things. She was numb to *those* arguments.

She never let out a tear.

Until now.

That was the first time a part of her soul was ripped away.

By me.

And the worst part was...

At the time...I liked it.

She rose from the bed and said, "Fuck you." Then stormed out.

I fell asleep that night unaware of where she went. And I was okay with that.

I didn't know where she was the following day until the night. I woke up at 12 a.m. and there she was, standing in front of me, naked.

I stood up and she pushed me back down, then climbed on top of me.

We didn't say anything.

That was the greatest sex I ever had with Elizabeth.

The Stoic

"What do you mean he doesn't exist?"

"Kidding." Johnny giggles at his own joke.

I'm glad he's enjoying himself at a time like this.

"I thought that would sound cooler."

"Johnny, don't do that to me." I huff out a sense of relief.

"I wasn't entirely kidding. His name isn't actually Robert Torsney, its Robert Dalton. He changed it almost eight years ago."

Why would Mr. Torsney change his name?

"There's more."

"Yeah?"

"Ten years ago, he was arrested but not convicted. They found his DNA at a crime scene. They thought he was The Cauterizing Killer."

"Why wasn't he convicted?"

"He had an alibi."

"Johnny, please stop beating around the bush and just rip off the bandage."

"Okay, okay," he says. "His schizophrenic son covered for him."

Johnny doesn't speak; he lets his words sink in.

The same person that sees his dead mother on a daily basis said he saw his father at home.

"Olivia, I've seen this happen a lot, kids covering for their parents. It's a weak alibi, but it's effective."

"How'd his DNA end up on the crime scene?"

"Afraid I don't know, and neither does he, or the Greenville Police Department."

Why wouldn't Cole tell me this?

"You know, Olivia, I'm a detective. I know this has to do with Grace as much as I know you're hiding things from me."

"Johnny—"

"Stop, this isn't safe," he says. "I'm going to ask this last time; how did you end up in that building?"

It seems like everyone's concerned for my safety. The rational thing to do would be to reveal all my knowledge to Johnny, and that's what I do. I'm a teenager; he's a cop. He's more capable of solving this than I am.

I disclose all my discoveries: Cole's branding, the frame, the dreams, everything. After absorbing the overwhelming amount of information that I relayed, he says, "You know, I've heard a lot of people wholeheartedly believing victims becoming abusers, but I gotta tell you. It's a load of bullcrap. Let's just say, my dad wasn't so loving to me and I'd like to believe I turned out fine."

"Eh, you're kind of an asshole but…"

"Ha-ha."

"Kidding," I say. "You know, you are more of a dad to me than my actual dad."

"That's really sweet Olivia, but you only get one father and he isn't me."

I look down at my bedroom floor. He's wrong but I don't say it.

"We're getting sidetracked," he says. "Cole and his dad must've been in Franklin that night. Will Cole come in for questioning?"

"Doubt it, and the dreams or distorted memory, whatever they are, is all a haze to him."

"Ok, I think this is our guy."

"When are you going to arrest him?"

He doesn't speak.

"Johnny?"

"It's complicated. There's a process to this, and to be frank, a legal name change and a few coincidental numbers isn't grounds for arrest."

I let out a sigh.

"I have some vacation days saved up. I'm going to come down to Fairview and do some freelance work."

"Freelance work?"

"I'm going to gather enough evidence to make an arrest stick."

Before he hangs up, he says, "Good job. Grace would be proud."

After a shitstorm like today, that's all I needed to hear. Actually, that's all I ever wanted to hear.

I glance at the bottom shelf on my nightstand, where a photo album of Grace and I stands. Wanting to reminisce, I reach for it, then flip through the pages. I land on a picture of us on my sixth birthday. There's a round cake iced pink. I remember this day. Grace and I were bickering like the children we were.

I teased her. "I get to make a wish and you don't."

When it came time to blow out the candles, she did it for me. I was infuriated.

She matched my teasing with some of her own. "Now my wish will come true and yours won't, ha!"

Mom didn't punish either of us. She sat on the couch, with sheets spread out on the coffee table in front of her. I assume doing taxes.

I wonder what it is Grace wished for. What problems was she facing? Mom and Dad fighting? A Boy? Grades? Or maybe her wish involved me. I'll never know now.

My phone chimes for what feels like the 100th time today. It's a text from Cole. .

Wanna come over later?
It's already pretty late. I check the time: 2:37. On second thought, I wouldn't mind going to Cole's.

Cole and I are relaxing on his contemporary couch, facing each other. I've gotten used to how uncomfortable it is.
I vent to Cole about how awful today was.
He empathizes, "Bad days come and go. I know you've had more bad days than good recently, and that sucks. Life can suck sometimes."
He rests his hand on mine.
"That it can," I say.
Our steady eye contact is soothing.
One of the many things I adore about Cole is his cognizance of knowing when to offer advice and when to make me feel heard. Today he's making me feel heard.
I shouldn't bring up the name change or his dad's criminal history. It's not the right time. Then again when is the right time for this stuff?
"Cole, um." I look down, breaking eye contact. "I have a police friend, Johnny. He told me your father changed your last names."
Cole straightens.
"He also told me he was arrested on suspicion of being The Cauterizing Killer, yet you covered for him."
I touch my throat, massaging it. I feel awful talking about this. I'm not trying to insinuate that he's lying or keeping things from me, I just want to clear things up.
My eyes are still facing downward. I can't bear looking him in the eye right now.
He puts his index finger below my chin, lifting my head. "Olivia, my dad...he's a paranoid man." He turns away,

exhaling a harsh breath. "I'm sure you've picked up on that already."

I don't respond, out of fear of sounding presumptuous.

"After we moved here, he changed our last names and made me promise not to tell anyone. Out of trust and respect, I kept that promise." He gulps. "And as for the police incident, well, I didn't cover for him. I told the truth. And I didn't know why he was arrested up until this very moment."

I place my hand on his tense lap, trying to comfort him.

"You know, Olivia, I may hallucinate my mom, but I...I don't my dad."

I rake my hand through Cole's brown hair. "Okay, I wasn't implying anything, really. I just wanted to understand." And sadly, I still don't. All I know is Mr. Torsney is exploiting Cole's confidence in him. He's The Cauterizing Killer, I'm certain. I don't know why he branded Cole, yet didn't kill him. Why he had the location and address framed on his door. Or why Grace was the only victim that was buried.

"I know you're trying to figure this out, but I'm on your side." Cole stands up. "If you're done interrogating me, I'd like to go the bathroom."

I trust Cole, he's a trusting person. I just fear he's too trusting.

I hear a forceful clink stemming from the basement. Someone unlocked the basement door.

"Cole?"

No response.

I don't need to go down there. Johnny has this entire situation under control. It's unnecessary. Yet, my body doesn't correspond with my mind. Before I know it, I'm off the couch, cautiously walking toward the basement stairs.

While descending, I lower my head and whisper, "Cole?"

No response.

When I reach the bottom, the vault-like door is slightly ajar and the numbered frame is gone. Mr. Torsney knows I saw it. I expect to hear sounds of agony on the other side of this door.

Instead, I hear a light snivel. My sense of alarm dissipates and bewilderment strikes me.

With two hands and a good deal of force I push the heavy door open.

Every bone in my body jolts back. Mr. Torsney's here, standing on the glossy concrete ground. He notices me and wipes his eyes. Was he crying?

"What are you doing down here?" he hisses.

I don't answer. Instead, I focus on every detail in this dank room. It's bare besides for a picture-littered desk and a tall closet which is open. He's actually clasping the doors, obscuring whatever is in there.

I take a step forward and that's when I realize I should've taken one back. There's a blood-stained kitchen knife in his hand, and judging from the way he's staring at me, he's aware I spotted it.

"You shouldn't be down here." He violently slams the closet doors, causing me to shudder.

Cole's upstairs and Mom knows I'm here. He's not going to lay a finger on me with all these discoveries transpiring.

"I was looking for Cole, thought he went downstairs."

"Nope," he says. "But while you're down here, I wanted to ask you something."

I throw him a tight-lipped smile. "Anything."

"I'm sure it's been hard with Grace's body being found. How are you doing?"

He smirks. How dare he bring up her name.

He takes a step forward holding the knife. My breath quickens and my eyes focus on the blade. Focus, focus. He's trying to intimidate me.

"I am okay," I say, sounding like a robot. I draw a deep breath. "The police are closer than ever. Someone is going to be locked up real soon."

He shrugs. "Perhaps, but I'd be careful." He gazes at me, dead center in the eye; those same eyes that witnessed Grace's death. "The killer may decide to go after you."

My eyes widen and my legs start convulsing. Those threatening words make it difficult to stand.

I swallow hard and say something so audacious I may as well plan my funeral now. "I saw Cole's branding, there's no police report of it."

His eyes pop out and he drops the knife. It clashes on the ground. If I didn't know any better, I'd think he was about to charge at me.

"Olivia?" Cole calls out.

I turn around and plod up the stairs. Mr. Torsney doesn't do anything. He can't do anything. He's on borrowed time.

I don't share with Cole what just happened. His loyalty is fogged. He wants his dad to be the hero he treats him as. But he's not, he's the villain. He's the killer in this story.

He's...*The Cauterizing Killer.*

The Stoic

The following night, after my encounter with Mr. Torsney, Cole spends the night at my place. I thought convincing Mom to agree to this would be like convincing an astronaut the earth is flat. It just wouldn't happen. Yet here he is, one arm around me, on the couch. However, he will be sleeping in the guest room. His father's killed countless children. I care about Cole. I don't want anything bad to happen to him, and living with an avid serial killer, something's bound to happen. Given, me provoking Mr. Torsney definitely didn't help the situation.

I also feel safer with him around. Now I know what you're thinking: *feminist of the year*. But Mr. Torsney let him go all those years ago. He doesn't want to hurt him, at least I think he doesn't, and Cole will do anything to protect me. Mr. Torsney can't fight his son. On top of all that, it's comforting having someone you love sleep under the same roof as you. And right now, I need as much comfort as I can get.

We're watching a movie: *Seven*. Cole's droopy eyes keep shutting.

"Cole, you keep dozing off."

"No, no, I'm not," his voice is muffled by the throw pillow he's rubbing his head against.

A car whirs into the driveway. I infer it's Mom, from the swift double honk. "I'll be right back. I'm going to help her with the groceries."

Cole's warm hand grasps mine. "Don't be silly, I'll take care of it." He rises then heads outside.

Cole's sweet, he's been here often enough. Still, he won't know where to place everything. Mom generally goes to the supermarket with a list of five things, then returns with twenty, all random, all never on the list. In my fuzzy slippers, I shuffle to the kitchen. Mocha is guzzling water out of her stainless-steel bowl. Mom enters the kitchen with no bags in hand. I tilt my head at her.

"In all our years of bringing groceries in, no man has ever offered to help," she says, "so you can bet when one does, I'm going to let him."

I shake my head, eyebrows raised. She turns around and leaves the kitchen. I hear her flat footsteps ascending the stairs.

Cole returns with three brimming bags dangling on each forearm. I cover my mouth, suppressing my laughter. "Oh my god."

He sets them down on the marble counter, then exhales, exhausted. Mocha takes that as an invitation to be pet and mounts up his leg. While stooping, caressing Mocha, Cole looks at me. "I'm always willing to help out, but I'm also very lazy. If there's a chance I could bring everything in, in one trip, I'm taking that chance."

I giggle. "I'm just amazed you could carry all that and manage to close the trunk."

Cole's smile drops. "The trunk?"

"You did close the trunk, didn't you?"

"Um, yeah." His eyes dart left. "Of course."

"Cole…"

"You know, honestly, this neighborhood is really safe. I think it's okay to leave the trunk open."

We chortle.

"I'll go back and close it now."
I nod.

Before bed, Cole taps on my bedroom door.

"It's open," I say.

He nudges it a drop, standing half behind the door, peaking at me. "I'm going to bed now. I just wanted to wish you a good night."

"Ok, good night, Cole."

He gnaws on his bottom lip. His sensuous eyes focus on me. My heart's pounding and I bet his is too. I warned him before he came over: touching must be kept to a minimum. Yet right now, all I want him to do is burst through the door and grab me.

"You need to stop gnawing on your luring lips because I'm a second away from making love to you," I say.

Cole chuckles. "Fine, but you need to stop dressing so seductively."

"I'm wearing flannel pajamas," I say, smirking.

"And you look damn *good* in them."

I chuckle. "Ok, Cole, you really should head to bed before Mom sees you this close to my bedroom."

He nods, then closes the door, going to bed.

Recognition flows over me like a tidal wave. I've blindly focused on exposing this killer, Cole's dad, for so long, I never thought about what it would do to Cole.

You can't ignore what Mr. Torsney has done, but if you could, you'd see what a great father he's been to Cole. Better than my dad. And that sickens me to say. *A serial killer is a better dad than my dad.* A better father than Otis Moore.

It baffles me how someone so paternal, so protecting, so loving is capable of something so diabolical. The worst part is, after everything goes down, Cole will probably be harassed everywhere he goes. He's the son of a serial killer. He's strong yet fragile. And even if he could handle his father lying to him, I doubt he'd be able to handle the harassment.

Maybe this is a mistake. Maybe I should tell Johnny I was wrong. I reach for my phone on the nightstand. Standing next to it is a picture of Grace and me.

Grace.

This is graver than me. Graver than Cole. Than any one of us. He's killed dozens of children. And he's still doing it. I love Cole, but some things are more critical than one person. As I drift off, I think to myself, I'm sorry Cole.

I awaken from Mocha's barking, something she's only started doing recently. She used to snarl from the couch. And if she had the energy, she'd let out a small bark that sounded more like a light cough. Now I wonder if this is a light cough.

I hear her again, but this time it's not a bark, it's a yelp.

What time is it?

I rub my eyes, then reach for my phone: 2 a.m.

God.

What have I done to deserve waking up at this hour?

I rise from my bed, and shuffle out of my room. The barking that's been pestering me has stopped. Someone must have brought her to their room. I should check to be sure.

I make my way to the guest room. Cole's asleep; no Mocha.

Then Mom's room. She's sleeping too; no Mocha.

My heartbeat quickens.

I need to relax. I'm sure she's just downstairs, resting on the couch.

Trudging downstairs, the ice-cold oak stairs send a shiver throughout my body, waking me up. I should've worn slippers.

An invasive gust of wind whooshes at me.

The door is open.

Who left it open?

Mocha must have run out. I head outside, too tired to put my jacket on.

It's foggy and somber outside. Standing on the porch, arms wrapped around myself, I call out, "Mocha, Mocha?"

My body is shaking uncontrollably, it must be subzero out here. I glance at both ends of the moonlit road, not seeing her anywhere. Having watched enough horror movies, I know not to go wandering the streets at 2 a.m., looking for your dog.

I'm not dealing with this right now. I'll search for her in the morning.

Inside, I lock the door behind me. The house is dark and hush. Trying to keep it that way, I tip-toe to the stairs.

"Shit!" I exclaim while jerking my leg back.

What the hell is that?

I stepped on something sharp. I need to stop walking around the house barefoot. After flicking the light switch on, the room doesn't brighten. Fidgeting with the switch, nothing changes. The power is out.

My shoulders tighten.

Whatever I stepped on is going deeper into my foot with each stride. Needing to yank it out, I drop on the stairs and place my hand on my foot.

My foot is dripping. Oh god, that's blood.

Reacting on instinct, I cover my mouth with my blood-soaked hands.

I cringe. As if this situation couldn't get worse.

I put my hand back on my foot.

What the hell is this?

Holding the pointy object, I waddle up the stairs, leaning against the railing for support. My phone has a flashlight. I could use that to see what I stepped on.

When I reach the top, I hop toward my room, where my phone resides on the nightstand. Holding the flashlight to the item I'm holding, I'm taken aback.

It's Mocha's tooth.

I turn around and—

"Jesus!"

My phone falls onto the floor.

There's a…there's a masked figure standing by the entryway of my bedroom, not moving.

My heart rate accelerates.

He's just… staring at me.

I want to scream, yet I can't.

I want to bend down and pick up my phone, yet I can't. Why am I just standing here? Do something!

There's a gleaming red branding iron in his gloved hands. This is it. It was stupid of me to think I'd be safe with Cole here. Mr. Torsney killed Grace when Cole was with her, why wouldn't he do the same to me? I've worked so hard to try to put this killer away. To find out who he is. I was so close.

He takes a step forward, resulting in me shrieking.

He locks the door and charges at me. Then swings the branding iron at my knee, making my leg spasm, and I nosedive onto the carpeted floor. With the branding iron, he thrashes my leg. The metal against my bones feels sharp. I clench my jaw, trying to bite down the pain. He stops as I hear a cracking noise. Eyes fixed on mine, he slowly twirls a strand of my hair.

"You poor thing," he says with an automated voice.

Tears are streaming down my face as he holds the searing branding iron close enough to my cheek for it to tingle.

Shutting my eyes, I think about Grace. Is this what she had to experience? Did she put up a fight or was she paralyzed with fear like me?

I guess I'll be seeing her soon.

The door bursts open, though I keep my eyes shut, petrified to open them.

Mr. Torsney is yanked off me and flung against the wall, causing it to reverberate. I hear the coughs of someone struggling to breathe. As if they're being choked. I should open my eyes, but I can't.

Seconds later, I hear gasps for air followed by an intense groan. It sounded like Cole. I open my eyes. Mr. Torsney's fleeing and Cole's on his knees with a syringe in his stomach. He pulls it out. Gazing at me with wide eyes, he murmurs, "Protect…Olivia."

Then he thuds onto the floor.

Part 3

Love is a serious mental illness.

-Plato

The Defeatist

There's nothing more disappointing than sharing a memory with someone, and cherishing it more than they did. Scratch that, there are a lot of things more disappointing than that, but it still feels like shit.

You'd like to believe just because a person means a lot to you, that you mean a lot to them, too.

You'd like to believe when something important happens to the both of you, it's important to the both of you.

But human beings are forgetful, and ignorant, and just don't care. I thought Elizabeth didn't care. Or at least acted like she didn't care to get at me.

The following morning she wasn't in bed. Unlike usual, I wasn't scared for what was in store. After last night, and the amazing sex we had, I felt like proposing to her all over again. It felt like she was a whole different person.

This time, if depression crept in, I'd hug her all day.

If she was on her period, I'd get her Chinese and coddle her.

If she was hung over, I'd bring her Tylenol and make her a coffee.

I wanted to *love* her in any way I could...or so I thought. In the kitchen, she had a solemn look plastered on her face. Ok, this is what I prepared myself for.

I loomed in from behind and start passionately kissing her neck.

Her body stiffened. "What the fuck are you doing?" she asked. "Get off of me."

This, I wasn't prepared for. "Oh, come on, last night was amazing."

"What the hell are you talking about? Are you drunk?"

That was something she did, often. Whenever she was mad at me, she'd label me drunk. But I wasn't…not this time.

"You came back in middle of the night. We made love."

"Made love," she repeated with air quotes. "What are you, a sixteen-year-old girl? Why would I ever fuck you after you antagonized me for being bipolar?"

Just like that, all my hopes faded. All my promises to be better, gone. Sex—it makes you believe crazy things. Makes you want to do crazy things.

It's stupid I know, but I thought the sex we had that night was an apology for the last eight years and a promise for a better tomorrow. It wasn't. She just wanted to mess with my head. She wanted to play mind games with me.

You know, we fought a lot, but she was never this devious. Never this *deceptive*.

The Stoic

I've been in this cramped hospital bed since last night, 2 a.m. to be more accurate. Mom brought me my henley sweater and ripped jeans to change into so at least I don't have to wear that airy gown any longer. Looking around the sterile room I'm in, I see: water leaking from the faucet, tip-tapping in the sink; a mute TV playing a show I've never heard of or seen before; and half white, half teal walls. I need to break out of here. I need to find Cole. Wherever he is. He could be beside his father, not even realizing that's the same man that stabbed him. Mr. Torsney was wearing a thick black puffy coat, boots and mask. His entire figure was concealed, like most burglars.

When Cole's body went limp, I thought it was too late. I thought he died. And if the police didn't come when they did, maybe he could've. Mom woke up when I hissed a curse, and seeing someone in the hallway, she hid in her room and called the police. They arrived minutes after Cole fell and carried him to their car, escorting him and I to the hospital. The doctors said Cole is fine, it wasn't anything serious, though it seemed like it was. It wasn't injected in any vein and if it was, it wouldn't have caused serious damage; it was a very small dosage. The reason he fainted was more psychological than physical. Still, trying to assure me of his safety, the doctor said he was the most unlucky

lucky man he'd ever seen. Which made me more uneasy, having the opposite effect of what intended.

Meanwhile, a wheelchair brought me to a different room, where, after a glance, a doctor said my leg was broken. He's stressed me to relax and stay home when I'm relinquished from this hellhole. What he fails to grasp is that my home is a crime scene now. Johnny notified us that we can't return home, not yet. They are searching for fingerprints or anything the killer may have dropped. They also sent the syringe Cole was impaled with to forensics.

I've been brooding over what happened since I got here. The glowing branding iron. Mocha's tooth. Those blood-curdling words.

You poor thing.

They dreadfully echo in my head. Powerless, I thought I was going to die.

I was going to die. Just like my sister. If it weren't for Cole... No, I can't think like that. I just hope he is okay.

Earlier, two officers interviewed me, while the events of what happened were still 'fresh in my mind.' As if tomorrow I'd wake up blessed enough to forget all this. I told them everything that happened: waking up that night, door open, Mocha's tooth, light switch. I even went as far as telling them about Cole's dad threatening me. They brought along a sketch artist, thinking he'd be of use. He wasn't. There wasn't a single distinctive feature about Mr. Torsney when he attacked me.

Johnny opens the teal-colored door, looking at me with a half-smile on his face. "How are you feeling?"

"I'm okay."

He nods with a full smile. "Of course, you are, a serial killer breaks into your house, breaks your leg, almost kills you, and attacks your boyfriend. I wouldn't expect you to be anything less than ok."

"How is Cole?"

241

"They just finished talking to him. He's in room 405. He's ok, just really shaken up."

That makes sense. I think anybody would be. "Did he tell them anything useful?"

"Nothing really, more of the same things as you already told them." Johnny sits on the armchair beside my bed. "They saw the branding on his skin, the one you told me about. Unhappy his dad never reported it, they are actually looking deeper into his dad because of it."

"It's him Johnny, he's the one who killed Grace, I know it."

"I think you may be right." His focus drifts to the window.

"There's something else, isn't there?" I ask.

"I shouldn't be telling you this, but...the killer didn't break in."

Johnny, the king of allusiveness. "What do you mean 'didn't break in'? We sure as hell didn't invite him in."

"That's not what I mean," he says. "It's the door...it wasn't busted in."

"My mom must've forgot to lock it."

"We talked to her already, and she told me she's locked the door every night since Grace was taken. She remembers locking it last night."

"So, what are you saying? You think someone unlocked the door?"

Johnny doesn't respond.

I know what he's thinking. "Johnny, Cole didn't unlock the door."

"Listen, Olivia, if his dad is the killer, it wouldn't be a stretch to assume he unlocked the door to let his father in."

"Cole would never. He's a good person. He knows what's right. He wouldn't let a killer in my house."

"He may not know his father is a serial killer. And even if he did, to be 'good' is objective. What really defines it? I know Cole seems normal, but he's schizophrenic. His mind is a lot

242

different from ours. It's distorted. His morals, his ideas of right and wrong, they're different than ours."

"Johnny, that has to be one of the most offensive things I ever heard."

"I know it sounds crazy, but someone had to unlock the door. It wasn't you. It wasn't your mom…"

"I can't listen to this anymore. If you really think he unlocked the door, I'll go ask him. He wouldn't lie to me." I rise from the hospital bed, leaning forward reaching for my crutches. I almost fall before Johnny grabs my arms.

"Careful." He hands me the crutches.

I hobble towards the door. Struggling to open it, Johnny dashes there and opens it for me. "You know, it's okay to ask for help."

Not knowing if that's a question or a statement, I don't respond.

I limp down the corridor in search of room 405. Johnny doesn't follow and I can't say that I want him to. Not right now at least. The crutches dig into my arms, infuriating me more than the turtle-like pace I'm moving at. There's no way this is normal. Before receiving these god-awful crutches, one of the nurses walked me though using them. But in spite of that, I still struggle.

I shift my body weight against the crutches and swing. Then repeat. I start to gain momentum. I'm going faster.

I pass room 403, push against crutches and swing.

I pass room 404, push against crutches and swing.

As I reach room 405, trying to stop the momentum, I put my foot down.

Fuck!

I lose my balance and flop onto the tiled floor. My hair shutters my eyes, obscuring my vision. I push against the bleach-reeking floor, trying to stand up. A calloused hand grabs my arm, trying to help. "I don't need help."

"You sure about that?"

It can't be. I whip my hair behind my shoulders. It is. It's Cole, standing tall, with an affectionate smile on his face. I almost rub my eyes, thinking I'm seeing things. Cole looks more than healthy.

"You really should be careful."

So everyone keeps telling me.

"I was looking for you," he says. "You wanna go grab a bite?'

My stomach growls, answering for me. Its 11:45, I haven't eaten anything since last night. I'll ask him about last night after we eat.

As we walk to the hospital cafe, I notice Cole's charcoal joggers and white hoodie look cozy. I wonder if he'd lend me them. After finding an elevator and descending to the first floor, we make our way to the café. Cole's beside me limping with his arm compressed on his stomach, the same spot the syringe was in. I'm beginning to think maybe he isn't so healthy and that maybe, he should've stayed in his room.

"Where's your dad?" I ask.

"The police are talking to him now." Cole's body language is constricted. He manages to ask, "What about your mom?"

"Pretty sure they're talking to her now, too."

Cole's arm convulses as he points to a corner with six tables. Oh god. Don't tell me this is the cafe. The hospital is large yet the cafeteria remains empty, making me concerned, though, the carpeted floor feels nice against my crutches. At least there's that.

After ordering, we sit by a table beside a wall. I rest my crutches on the side of the table. A chipper cashier serves us our food. This isn't a kitchen-to-table type of cafeteria, it's barely a cafeteria, but after taking one look at us, the cashier insisted. Cole sits back hunched with a hand pressed against his wound.

A pallid, thin-lipped woman sits on the table furthest from us, staring at Cole, head tilted. I'm not sure if her stare is on account of our mangled appearances, or if there's something more deep-seated at play. All the same, the way her unblinking eyes fixate on Cole sends spiders crawling up my spine.

"I wanted to order French toast," Cole says, "but I was worried they'd mess it up."

Smart, though, I'm not doing this. I'm not dwelling over small talk. Not right now. Any energy I have left will be exerted towards twigging at whatever Cole's hiding. "What happened last night?"

"What do you mean? You were there."

"Johnny thinks you unlocked the door to let your father in."

"Olivia—" Cole chokes up. "I didn't know The Cauterizing Killer was outside."

"So, you did unlock the door?"

"Yes."

My eyes dart to the distant thin-lipped woman. With her eyes set on Cole, she tentatively stands up, then sits back down. I wonder if she can hear what we are discussing.

Bringing my absentminded attention back to Cole, I ask, "Why?"

Cole struggles to grasp his milkshake. His hand is wobbling as he brings it to his mouth and it spills on his lap. "I'm not feeling well."

"I know Cole, we'll go back soon. Just please explain this to me."

"Okay," he wheezes. "I remember what happened, at least I think I do. The person standing outside wasn't The Cauterizing Killer."

"But why'd you let him in?"

"I was told to."

"By who?"

"You're Cole Dalton, right?" The thin-lipped woman asks, now standing by our table.

245

The Stoic

Too immersed in the conversation, I didn't see her walk over here. The thin-lipped woman is waiting for Cole to respond to her question: *Are you Cole Dalton?*

Cole shifts his eyes from her to me. I think he wants affirmation of her existence. I nod.

Cole proceeds, "Yes."

"Oh my god," the woman says, "what a small world. I was your mother's psychiatrist in Greenville." She extends a hand to Cole. "My name is Moira Miller."

Cole's frail arm reaches for her hand. I can see the exhaustion on his face.

"She used to show me pictures of you as a kid."

"That's great," he says, in the same tone you tell a kid his drawing is great.

"I always wondered where you guys ran off to. So, you guys are living here now, huh?"

"Yes," Cole says. I can pick up on his hesitance and I think for a psychiatrist she's horrible at reading people.

"How is he, your dad?"

"He's good."

She glances at me, then back at Cole. "Well, I can see you're busy. I'm in town for a bit, covering for a friend who got hurt.

She's actually the reason I'm here." She hands him a card. "You and your dad should stop by sometime; I'd love to catch up."

Cole takes the card and as she walks away flings it on the table. I grab it, investigating it.

Mrs. Miller –Psychiatrist–

Seems like a very…*informative* business card.

"What's wrong?" I ask Cole.

"It's nothing, it's just, I'd like to believe Mom cared about me enough to show pictures to people, but the reality, as horrible as it is, is that she wasn't tender-hearted enough to do that."

"You think she was lying?"

Cole rubs his dry eyes. "It's not just that. My mom, she never had a psychiatrist."

I scratch the side of my head. God, that feels satisfying. I could use a massage, too, right about now. "Listen Cole, that's all very peculiar, but you were about to tell me something before she interrupted."

Cole starts coughing. "Olivia, I don't know what I'm witnessing. It kills me not being able to help you. These hallucinations are parasites, slowly deteriorating everything. Why would I spread them onto you?"

"Because I love you. We can get through this together," I say. "Just tell me what you saw."

"And I love you, which is why I want you to," he grunts in pain, "find this killer." His face scrunches up.

"Cole?"

He falls unconscious, out of his chair, onto the floor.

The Defeatist

After what she did to me, I needed to get away for a little bit. I couldn't be in the same house as her. My boss wanted me to meet a client in New York. I was supposed to be away for a week. That's what I told Elizabeth. But being away, it made me realize how much I wanted to be back home. I actually missed Cole. I was going to surprise him. Try being a real father. That didn't last too long.

There's a famous proverb. You've probably heard of it; it goes: *Fool me once shame on you, fool me twice shame on me.* At this point, I was only setting myself up for failure. Like I stated earlier, we weren't a lovey-dovey couple. And you can't be what you aren't. You can try to act, but never fall fool to believing it's anything more than that: an act.

A taxi dropped me off by the curb. The pavement glimmered amber from the kitchen lights shining through the window. The black sky made the light seem brighter outside than it was inside.

I stood confused, gazing at the driveway. Elizabeth's car was gone. Where was she?

With slow steady steps, I walked toward the entrance. When I touched the knob, I saw the door was slightly ajar. Why was the door open? Her car's gone, maybe something happened and she had to leave in a haste.

Inside I flicked the lights on. "Cole? Liz?"

Cole stood by the railing with fearful tears. "Dad?"

He sprinted to me, then hugged me. I stood frozen for a minute before I wrapped my arms around him.

"W-where's your mother?"

He shrugged.

After lying with Cole until he fell asleep, I waited downstairs, on the U-shaped sofa. Hours later, her car lights flared through the windows. Then I heard her car engine shut down.

Elizabeth scurried in, without noticing me. She slammed the door shut, making sure to lock it.

"Where were you?" I asked.

She flinched, startled by my presence.

She was holding a laundry bag, but it didn't look like laundry was in there.

"Honey, I didn't see you there."

I rose from the sofa, drawing closer to her. "Why was Cole left alone?"

Her eyes darted to the side. "I had to run a few errands." She clasped the bag tighter.

"What's in the bag?"

"What? This? Nothing." She chuckled.

I tried to snatch the bag but she recoiled.

What the hell is going on? I thought.

The Cynic

People fear death. I welcome it. Not to me of course, but to others. Initially, I was against the idea of killing children. I still am, however I have to admit, for kids like Tyler, well, it's not so bad.

Some people are born to create order; others, chaos. And me? Well, I'm just a beneficial spectator.

Tyler was an open wound, left untreated for years. He was infected and the only solution was ridding that infection. Cutting off the limbs.

The corners of my windshield are frozen. I'm driving to the hospital to pick up Finn. One of his teachers called earlier telling me he fainted. No matter how many aspects of my life improve, certain things will always remain the same; Finn will always be a nuisance.

After circling for twenty minutes, I park in the far end of the teeming parking lot. The pavement is recently wet, so I take large steps trying to avoid puddles.

Entering the hospital, the doors automatically slide open. A rush of cozy warm wind blows from above. The noisy lobby is large with ceilings that must be two stories high. A steady stream of people flows in and out of different doors. Robert Langdon had a better chance at finding the Holy Grail than I do Finn.

A square-built, unshaven man bumps into me. His eyes focus on the ground.

"My bad," he says.

"Robert."

His eyes ascend from the floor. Tilting his head he says, "Yeah...who are you?"

You're Cole's father. I've been keeping tabs on you. For someone as paranoid as yourself, I'm surprised you haven't noticed. Yet, I'm sure after this conversation you will. "I'm Cole's teacher. My job requires me to know all parents' names."

His eyes are weary, forcing me to ponder if it's a side effect of his lengthy lies or if the cause is something more recent.

"Well, it's great to meet you, Blake."

I jolt. I never mentioned my name. Whether he slipped up or disclosed it deliberately, I take it all the same; it's a threat.

"You know, Cole asked me about this interesting birthmark he has."

His face pales. Though we are in a hospital, I don't need a stethoscope to hear his anxious heartbeat.

His mouth hangs ajar before speaking, "I lied earlier, when I asked who you were. I already knew." He throws an arm over my shoulder and guides my focus to the corner. There's a woman sitting on one of the lobby chairs, wearing a cheap suit, writing something in her notepad. She fingers her glasses up her nose as she looks down. "That woman over there was asking about you. I informed her on what a *loving* teacher you are." Robert vehemently pats my back, then whispers in my ear, "I don't know much about you, or how you know what you know, but Finn's going to be taken away long before he ever gets the chance to be branded." The aggression in his voice makes my knees lock up. He continues, before dashing out, "Stay away from my kid or so help me god, *I'll kill you myself.*"

My eyes remain unmoved from the social worker. She glances at me, then down at her notepad before proceeding my way.

"Excuse me, you're Mr. Haynes." She tells me as if I didn't already know. I don't respond.

"Your son's upstairs."

Again, I already know.

She begins writing in her notepad. "Not.very.talkative."

"This isn't my fault."

"Oh, really?" She smiles a sarcastic smile.

"The school should be making sure he drinks enough, not me."

"I entirely agree."

"Good."

"Which is why they've been informing parents for the last week of a broken water fountain, telling them to send kids with a drink."

Crap. "So, I forgot once, is that a crime?"

"Mr. Haynes, look outside, it's frigid. For a kid to pass out as bad as Finn did, in this climate, he'd have to have been deprived fluids for more than just one day."

"What do you want me to say? You've clearly already painted me as the bad guy."

She scoffs, eyes drifting to the side then back to me. "Are you aware that Finn's forty-two pounds?"

"So? I'm skinny, he takes after me."

"He's twenty pounds underweight."

Again, I don't respond. I feel like I'm being tested and colossally failing.

"Enjoy the rest of your day. Something tells me I'll be seeing you again soon." She disappears into one of the many doors.

Christ. Fucking Finn.

After finding Finn, I drag him outside, against doctor's orders. He can barely walk, and I'm practically carrying him. In the parking lot, I conceal him between two cars. He collapses onto the ground before I lay hold of him, lifting him against a Camry. He's not escaping that easy. The car alarm starts beeping.

"How dare you, Finn," I burst. "Do you want me to get arrested?"

He slowly blinks, drifting off. "I...I couldn't help it."

The car alarm is still blaring.

"Don't feed me that weak excuse. How hard is it to take a water bottle to school?"

His eyes shut; he isn't speaking.

I rock him. "Wake the hell up, Finn."

Looking around, behind me I spot a familiar onlooker watching: Katherine.

"I can explain." No, I can't. At least not in a way the average person will understand.

Katherine stands there with a hand covering her mouth.

After dropping Finn, she runs.

I'm not going to kill her but I can't let her get away; I chase after her.

She sprints between cars and in my efforts to catch her, a side mirror bashes into my stomach. I ignore the pain.

I've calculated every move thus far. My freedom lies with her. She's no longer a person to me. She's another threat. A means to an end.

She stops by a white Honda and starts frantically searching though her purse. She finds a key and inserts it in the car door. Then enters, thinking she's going to escape. She won't. Before she can close the car, I lay hold of the door, tug it open and yank her out. Her head crashes onto the damp ground.

"You aren't getting away," I say.

Her red hair covers her face. She brushes it to the side, but several strands remain plastered to her blood seeping forehead. "You're sick," she stammers.

There's no convincing her of my high-minded thinking, not after what she's witnessed. If she won't see me as good, I'll show her others are worse.

"You think foster care is better? They molest kids there. Is that what you want for Finn?"

"Your shrewd words won't make a difference now."

"What do you mean?"

Still on the ground, she looks to the side.

I grip her arm, firmly, and heave her up. "What do you mean?" I repeat myself, steam storming out of my ears. My face is close enough to feel her rapid breathing, her breath smells like peppermint. I stare in her frightened eyes, waiting for her to continue.

"The social worker. I gave them everything."

"You wouldn't."

"I'm the one that called them."

She's lying. There's no way. She cares too much about me to do that. Testing her, I ask, "How long did you know?"

She doesn't answer, but swallows an audible gulp of air, which in its own regard, is answer enough.

Still, I yell, "Answer me!"

A few suspicious bystanders walking by begin to ogle. Now I know there's no putting the genie back in the bottle.

"Since before I met you," she blurts.

Taken aback, I unclasp her.

"You're a monster," she mutters.

I gaze off into the distance, past the crowd of bystanders, searching for Finn: the cause of all this.

"You think I'm a monster? You should meet Finn's mother."

The Stoic

The walls in this waiting room are a placid yellow, and soft white lighting calms me, making me think the design was deliberate. This is a therapist's office after all.

I massage my armpits. They have been aching for the last five days since I was released from the hospital. Cole's still there, in the hospital. He's passed out a few more times. The physicians don't understand why, considering a majority of the pentobarbital has been ridden from his system. They figure it's psychological, but want to observe him a little longer.

He saw something that night The Cauterizing Killer broke in. And even while he's in the hospital, I know it's messing with his head, making him question reality all the more often. I've tried pressing him to reveal what he saw, but still, he won't budge. And I know why. It's his father. The love he has for him is alarming. I don't understand it. But that's why I am here; to learn more about his parents.

After meeting Mrs. Miller in the hospital, I called her. She was surprisingly keen on meeting me. In fact, I'd say she wanted to meet me more than I her. Cole warned me not to trust her, saying she's not who she says she is, yet neither is his dad.

A white paneled door opens. "Olivia, you can come in now." Mrs. Miller holds the door open for me.

I don't know the color of the wall; however, I do know the color of the bookshelves in front of the walls: cherry oak. I glance at a camel-colored armchair, which I assume she will be sitting on, then a plastic-covered cream couch: patient's seat.

Mrs. Miller glances left then right, outside the room, before locking the door. "Just don't want anyone interrupting."

Walking in here, I didn't see a soul. The last thing you need to fear is someone interrupting.

With my crutches I hobble to the couch, then back up in front of it, like a car backing into a parking spot.

"My friend's a neat freak; you'll have to forgive me for the plastic."

I figure she's referring to the couch, but I notice there's a plastic sheet on the rug below us, too.

"Tell me about Cole," she says.

"Um, well, he's a really nice man," I say.

I glance over my shoulder to the door, starting to feel uneasy. It's a bit odd she locked the door.

"Is he...like his father?"

My eyes widen. "What does that mean?"

"Nothing, just, do they share any mannerisms?"

"Cole's charming, caring, funny. He's a good guy." I don't say: he's nothing like his psychopath of a father. "Could you actually tell me a little about his father?"

"I don't know his father too well. Just what Elizabeth told me."

"And what did she tell you?"

She tightens her lips. "Too much."

The shades are down. Part of me wants to leave, but the other part of me knows this woman holds answers to my questions. And whether I want to receive them or not, I'm going to.

Mrs. Miller continues, "I was shocked when I heard Elizabeth killed herself."

Cole told me about her death. "Wasn't she bipolar?"

"Yeah, someone with her history, it isn't uncommon. Yet something she told me, it…" she looks to the side, "well, it makes me think."

Her reluctance is transparent and I start to doubt her knowledge. "What was she like?"

"I'd like to tell you she was full of life, after all, that's what we're meant to say when someone passes away."

"But?"

"She wasn't a great person. In fact, both she and Robert were horrible people." She squeezes her eyes shut, as if she's remembering something. "Horrible parents," she reiterates.

"Did that ever anger you?"

Her eyes narrow at me. "Does a child being neglected anger me? Yeah, I don't know a person it wouldn't."

I'm not asking the right questions. It's hard for me to focus when the thought of this place being something other than a therapist's office keeps creeping in.

"Listen, I'm familiar with the cycle of abuse. Most of my clients have been maltreated by parents, loved ones, and frankly, people in general." A moment passes before she says, "And that includes Elizabeth."

Is she referring to her being abused or her abusing Cole? "How do you know that?"

"I was her therapist."

God! I could never be a detective; I can't formulate pertinent questions.

She peeps at my crutches. Then stands and my heart flinches. She grabs my crutches and my eyes follow her as she carries them to the other side of the room. "Sorry," she says. "My friend, she would *murder* me if she saw them leaning against there."

I nod but I shouldn't. I should ask for them back. I should leave before it's too late.

"I know why you are really here." Her face turns sour. "You think Robert killed Elizabeth."

257

"That wasn't what I was thinking," I blurt.

"Well, if it was, you should know he didn't kill her."

"Then who did?" I ask.

"She did, of course."

I let out an exhale of relief as she sits back down on the armchair. I look at one of the many books on the bookshelf. *The Ethics of Killing Animals.*

"Physically, at least," she clarifies. "But it's Robert who drove her to suicide."

My focus flashes back to her. She has to be the most ominous person I have ever met. Either she's going to kill me or delude me to death. Either way, I need answers. "Can you just tell me what it is you've been holding back from saying?"

She lets out a faint smile. "Okay. It's hard for me to talk about this. Not just because of confidentiality, but because, I'd sound crazy. I mean, Elizabeth sounded crazy."

"What did she tell you?"

Mrs. Miller undoes her ponytail. "I diagnosed Elizabeth with schizophrenia, but...I don't think she was schizophrenic."

The Stoic

"Elizabeth was one of my tougher patients, and I was assigned to her after the death of her sister. They were both split up into foster care at age seven, after being taken away from their parents."

"How'd she die?" I ask.

"The foster home she was in burnt down when she was thirteen. It was so bad that the firemen couldn't take the fire out. They let the entire home burn down while making sure it didn't spread. Elizabeth's past, along with her bipolar disorder, were a terrible combination. Her drastic mood swings were like none I've seen before. Certain days I could've sworn she was a different person. But that's what being bipolar is like. And her episodes, well...they were extreme to say the least. The number one thing I suggest to someone struggling with bipolar disorder, is to have a supportive partner. Elizabeth didn't. Instead, she had Robert. He'd degrade her, belittle her, and mentally destroy her. The things she told me he'd say, it made me cry."

I'm a bit floored at how much she's willing to reveal. I assume this breaks some type of confidentiality, unless she isn't the type to value those principles.

She continues, "And poor Cole. She told me he wouldn't even acknowledge his existence. He was nothing more than a wall to him. Something in the room that you don't talk to. Though, she wasn't any better. She wasn't a mother. She dressed him, made him breakfast, dinner, and lunch, but she told me she didn't feel comfortable hugging him. Hugging her son."

This is all so heart wrenching, but I'm still focused on what she said earlier. "What made you diagnose Elizabeth with schizophrenia?"

"Right. Towards the end of her life, her mood swings were more predominant and she was acting more...erratic. She'd disappear and..." Mrs. Miller tugs at her pierced earlobe.

"What is it?" I ask.

"She told me she was being held captive. Repeatedly."

"Repeatedly? Like someone was kidnapping her and letting her go?"

"Yes," Mrs. Miller answers. "And doing it again days later, sometimes for a few hours, other times weeks."

"And she didn't go to the police? You didn't go to the police?"

"No, because she wasn't being held captive."

"What do you mean?"

"Cole and his father would see her at home on days she said she was kidnapped. So did her work and me. She was lying."

Each answer this woman gives, while enlightening, sprouts ten more questions in my brain, making me wonder if I'm inept at asking questions or if she's incompetent at answering them. Regardless, I ask, "Why would she lie?"

"Unintentionally. She genuinely believed she was being kidnapped, that someone was out to get her. It went on for a few weeks and I brushed it off as delusions. But the last week or two she was alive, she told me her husband was following her everywhere, that he was ransacking her drawers, and that he would pat her down whenever she'd come home. She told me she thought he would kill her. And then...she died." Mrs. Miller lets her words dry for a moment.

My phone goes off insistently buzzing; someone is calling me. Too focused on the conversation, I ignore it.

She continues, "Then again, the police found Elizabeth and they were 110 percent sure she killed herself. I trust the police, but another concerning thing was how fast they moved away. I know how hard it can be living in the same place as your dead loved ones lived, but the way they just fled," she fiddles with her bracelet, trailing off, "it was just, *questionable.*"

My phone chimes. It's Cole: **Finn is missing.**

The Existentialist

My father, Robert Torsney, Robert Dalton, whatever you want to call him, he killed Grace. I've known for a while now. I saw it with my own eyes. My father there, holding the knife. Grace's muffled screams, the knife slicing her throat. I know now, this isn't something a kid's imagination fabricates. Neither is it something a kid can forget. Yet I did, until the night someone broke into Olivia's house. It's why I woke up a second time, after I unlocked the door.

Why did you unlock the door?

You know why; like always, you were there with me.

Regardless, I've kept this secret hidden from Olivia for long enough. Once I woke up, I was going to tell her, instantly. Then I was stabbed by someone that isn't my father. And I was forced to doubt what I witnessed. Reality is contradicting itself, which is making me unsure of myself. It unveiled my father killed Grace. Directly after that, I see someone else trying to kill Olivia. Not just anyone else. A person that could never hurt Olivia.

All of this uncertainty makes me ponder a tantalizing question: what is worse—to convict an innocent man, or to let a guilty one run free?

If I confess what I witnessed my father do, he'll be arrested. But if he didn't attack us that night, then he may not be The

Cauterizing Killer, and my father—an innocent man—would be convicted.

And what if he's guilty and you don't confess?

Then I'm letting a guilty man run free...

At times I think it's better for me to keep quiet. Kind of like what I did with Finn. But now Finn's missing. Mr. Haynes was arrested for assaulting some teacher from Finn's school, and they also suspect him of negligence. Though, they are restrained by the fact that they don't have a warrant to search his house.

My phone rings: Olivia. I swipe answer.

"You can't just send me a text saying Finn's missing and not follow up."

"Olivia, I remember."

"Remember what?"

"What happened ten years ago. Not everything. But most of it."

"And what do you remember?"

"My mom, on the ground, battered, pleading for her life. My father standing tall, above her, fury-eyed. He turned to Grace, walked up to her and killed her."

"I don't understand. I thought your mom killed herself in Greenville. That the police said she was dead for a couple days."

She was. She did. How she managed to be in two places at once is beyond me. "This is all so confusing. I don't understand how he did it. For all I know, I was hallucinating my mom. But he killed your sister; he killed Grace."

"Then we have to go to the police, tell them what you just told me."

"We can't."

"Why?"

"Because, whoever attacked us last week wasn't my dad."

"How do you know that?"

"I just do."

"Cole, Finn's missing. If you have a lead, you need to tell the police. Before he gets hurt."

263

"You don't need to lecture me on Finn getting hurt. I was there, I saw what his dad did to him. If they arrest my dad, they'll stop looking for whoever attacked us last week, and that same person could be the person who took Finn."

"Cole, you just told me your dad killed my sister, we need to tell the police."

"I'm also telling you he isn't the person who broke into your house last week.'

"How do you know?"

"I just do."

She breathes a sigh of exasperation. "I always get the feeling you're hiding something from me."

"Just because I don't tell you every little thing doesn't mean I'm hiding things from you. "

"No, but you evading questions does."

"I see things. Things that aren't real. If I told you every little thing I've seen, you'd think I was crazy."

"No, I wouldn't."

"Yes, you would."

"I wouldn't—"

"Olivia. You're doing it now!" A moment passes. "I've lived a life where everything I see, I second guess. People who know of what I have, take my words with a grain of salt. So, if I have trouble opening up to you, it's because of that. But right now, I'm telling you what I believe. I'm opening up to you like you wanted and you refuse to listen, to believe me. My dad…he killed Grace. I remember it now. But he is not the one who attacked you."

"Okay Cole, I believe you," she says, sounding anything but in belief of me.

After Olivia hangs up, I toss a coat on, heading outside for fresh winter air. Dad watches me from the kitchen window as I sit on the curb. The moistness slowly wets my pants.

I wonder what he's thinking.

Shallow puddles along the road reflect gloomy skies. Above me a thump-thump sound catches my attention. Looking up in the distance, a helicopter fades in, zooming nearer. A low rumble makes me glance down the block. A continuous stream of cop cruisers rolls in, bouncing on the bumpy road.

This isn't real. This isn't real. This isn't real.

I jump to my feet, huffing uncontrollably. They stop by the curb, inches in front of me, causing me to spring backward, toppling over onto the ground. Officers in tactical gear burst out of their cruisers, grasping guns, pointed at my house. Everything is happening so fast. Too fast. I thought I had time. Time to find the truth. Time to find Finn. Time to...to spend with my dad.

A brown-haired officer extends a hand. "Cole, my name's Johnny," he says, as if that's an explanation.

Still on the ground, I don't reach for his hand. Not wanting to face reality, I don't get up.

Johnny retracts his hand. Crouching, he asks, "Is your father inside?"

I open my mouth, as if to speak, but words don't come out. Words can't come out.

A memory pops up in my head. In sixth grade, the latest fad was sleepovers. Everyone was having them, and if you weren't, you bet you'd hear about it at school. Fearing I'd wake up with a nightmare, I never went. Seeing everyone have fun without me stung more than the pentobarbital.

That's not true.

Ok, it's not. Anyways, one day Dad called me to the living room where a pillow fort, sleeping bags, and French toast waited for me. "I know you're scared to sleep away from home. I'm hoping we could have a sleepover, just the two of us." That's the dad I know. Caring, supportive, empathetic. He's not a killer, yet everyone including my own mind is telling me he is.

"Cole?" Johnny says, bringing me back to reality.

Staring at the ground, I gulp. "He's inside."

The Existentialist

There're more officers outside, holding off the press, than inside, surveying a serial killer. My father. My stomach feels like there's a giant hand clenching it tight, suppressing my breathing. I hook my feet around the legs of the black chair I'm sitting on. I've been waiting to speak to my father for three hours now. Each passing minute, my nerves worsen. My hands grip the slanted arms, tightly.

Fixed in the corner, a small antiquated TV is playing Channel 7 News. A clean-shaven man holds the microphone to a teary-eyed woman's face. The man has the appearance of a 30-year-old and 50-year-old at the same time. I take it he's the reporter. The teary-eyed woman's face is puffy with makeup running down it. She begins, "That monster took my Douglas from me. He branded him. He was only four years old. Four years old," she repeats, in a louder tone. She yanks the microphone out of the reporter's hand. "His son should die; they both deserve the death penalty!"

The screen goes dark.

Olivia emerges to my left, holding a remote. She places it on a round table that sits between two chairs. "You shouldn't be watching this."

"What did Johnny tell you?" I ask.

She sits beside me. In a lower tone she says, "They found a knife in the woods, around the same area they found Tyler. It was a combat knife, the type you use for hunting. It had your and your father's fingerprints on it, along with Tyler's blood." She takes out her phone. "The picture was somehow leaked online a couple of minutes ago. Some money-hungry CSI must have taken a picture of it."

She shows me the blood-stained knife. I shake my head. "That doesn't make sense."

"What is it?"

"That knife, I lost it."

"Cole," she says with concern.

"I'm not hallucinating. I had it."

"I believe you," she says. "But don't you think, just maybe, you're finding ways to disprove this reality, because you're having trouble coping?"

I inhale a long breath and peer at her hands which are covering mine, supportively. I thread my hand though my hair.

"Why is it," I ask, "that my mind is always so clouded, even when I'm not hallucinating?"

Her eyelids begin to droop. "I don't know, Cole, I don't know," she says. "But I'll always be here for you, to help you uncloud it."

The world is just such a hard place, but gazing into her trusting eyes, I realize with her by my side, it doesn't have to be. She's my glasses. The one person I can put my faith in, to tell me what's real and what isn't. It's time I tell her what really happened the night I slept over.

"Olivia, my m—"

"Cole!" Johnny calls out, holding an ocean-blue door open. "You can talk to your father."

"I'll be waiting right here," Olivia says.

I use my arms to lift myself up from the chair. My legs are too apprehensive to help out and only begin walking to the interrogation room a minute after rising.

Johnny seizes my arm, making me flinch. "He only agreed to talk to us if he could talk to you alone first. We'll be on the other side. If anything goes wrong, we'll burst through that door."

I give a quavery nod.

The door squeals as Johnny shuts it behind me.

A dim light mounted directly above the table shines down on Dad. He's handcuffed to a table with his head hanging low. I glance behind me at the reflective one-way window, then sit on the metal chair.

Looking at dad now, all my trepidation dissipates. What replaces it is indignation.

He doesn't speak. The lack of eye contact tells me he's sheepish. I'm going to have to initiate the conversation.

"Dad," I say in an undertone.

He doesn't respond. There's no indication he even heard me. But I know he did. For the last three hours I thought when I'd finally see him, I'd be too scared to speak, however, now all I want to do is scream.

"Dad, look at me," I demand.

His face rises and I see it's lost its color.

"What happened to our rule?" I ask.

"I'm sorry," he says. "I didn't mean for any of this to happen." His consoling voice almost makes me forget this is his fault.

"Except you did," I say. "You killed various children on various occasions. That's not something that happens by accident."

"No," he says, sounding depleted. "It's not."

"So why? Why did you lie to me? I was honest with you. I vouched for you. Everyone already thinks I'm crazy, what will they think now?"

"I'm sorry."

I wipe my watery eyes. "I don't care what they think. All I cared was what you thought. I trusted you like you asked. Why couldn't you trust me with the truth?"

I'm panting and I feel like I'm going to start bawling if I continue pressing him.

I loved him. I still do. He's my father.

He nurtured me. Shielded me. Loved me.

And deceived you… about everything.

My throat feels tense. I need to fill my lungs with air because right now, all it's filled with is disparity.

I draw a deep breath. "We had one rule, Dad. One. Rule." I shake my head. "I'm going to ask you this last question, and don't break that rule. Did you kill Grace?"

"Yes," he says. "I slit her throat."

The Existentialist

It's been a day since Dad confessed, and like many things in my life, I don't understand it. I mean, he didn't have that knife, I did. I stole it after it was suggested I use it for protection at Green Point Lake. Which is also where I believe I lost it.

Finn is still missing. Just like I feared, the police resources have been focused more on Dad than Finn. I get the picture; a neglected child has been missing for more than twenty-four hours. He's either ran away, is dead, or both. All the same, I'm going to continue my search for him. That's why I'm on the way to Mr. Haynes' house right now. I hope to find something of use.

I didn't want to go alone, but Olivia isn't answering her phone. She's likely too distraught to deal with anything. Regardless, I left her a message asking her to meet me there.

I park a few houses away from Mr. Haynes'. I still have his key, whether his negligence is to my benefit all depends on what's waiting for me in his house, if anything.

The door clunks when I unlock it. I shut it behind me then lock it. Everything looks more or less the same. Actually, I think there may be more pictures. He's really tried to appear as normal as possible. With the seemingly endless amount of photos, I have to wonder why there are none of Finn's mother.

I head upstairs to Finn's room. The creaky stairs make me think this place is haunted, yet I know, the only ghost I see is the one in the back of my head.

Turning into Finn's room, I freeze. The entire room is flooded with drawings. All of the same place: Green Point Lake. I snap a picture and send it to Olivia. These drawings aren't from one trip. They are all of different climates: sunny, rainy, snowy and cloudy. He's likely been there more than I have. The question harassing me is who took him?

There's a familiar drawing on his thin, stained mattress. I inch closer, too scared to lift it. I don't want to know what's on there for the same reason I never questioned how my mom led me to Green Point Lake if she was dead and I had never been there before.

The drawing on his bed is of me, sitting on a log. It's fall time and there's a tall woman standing beside me.

Before I can gather my thoughts, I hear the clunk of the door unlocking. No one else has the key. At least, I think no one else does.

"Hello?" A familiar honeyed voice calls out.

This voice eases my nerves.

"Cole?"

The footsteps are approaching. I know I should hide. That would be the sane thing to do. But, by now, you know me. I'm not sane.

"Cole, come out." I'm drawn to that voice like a son to his mother, and when I exit the room, I understand why that is.

"Mom?"

The Stoic

I can't stop thinking about what Cole said. About the knife. Is there really a chance Mr. Torsney didn't kill Grace? No, there's no way. I know it was him. I'm just curious why he had her death posted on his door like a reminder. Why, when I walked in, I found him crying. Whose initials are on the branding? And why did he brand Cole yet never kill him?

I feel as if we solved a puzzle only to realize there's a piece missing. After looking everywhere for it, I've come to the conclusion that our answer lies under the puzzle.

The press still remains camped outside the police station like teenagers waiting to enter a concert. I sit in the same place as yesterday waiting to speak to Johnny. An ocean blue door opens and Johnny emerges slouching. He's wearing the same button-down shirt as yesterday except it's untucked and open-collared.

"Olivia, I'm short on time."

"I need to see Cole's dad."

"I'd laugh if I could."

I stare at him.

"It's not happening," he clarifies.

"It's for Cole, not me."

"I'm not sure that's better," he yawns, "and if it is for Cole, why isn't he here?"

"His dad lied to him his whole life. Would you be able to sit across from him?"

"Ok," he nods in concession. "That doesn't change the fact that I'm not letting you speak to him. Listen, Olivia, you act older than you actually are, so I treat you older than you are. But you aren't my partner or a sidekick, you are a kid." He sighs. "I have my limits and you talking to a serial killer, well, it's beyond them."

"Johnny, I've slept under the same roof as him. I've been alone with him in a basement. He's had chance after chance to kill me and hasn't. Something here isn't adding up. He didn't confess to you, he confessed to Cole. Let me talk to him. He's going to reveal something to me, I promise."

"Aren't you supposed to be seventeen?"

"So when can I talk to him?"

"It's complicated."

It always is with him.

"I'm not the leading officer in this investigation; in fact, I shouldn't even be here. While Robert confessed, he hasn't actually given us any information. I'll see what I can do."

An hour and many favors later, I'm sitting across from Mr. Torsney in the investigation room with two officers beside me—per Johnny's request. Mr. Tornsey, like Johnny, is wearing the same clothes as yesterday. His eyes have bags under them and his black hair is ruffled and unkempt.

"I figured you'd want to talk to me," he says.

"I didn't think you'd want to talk to me."

"Olivia," he stares in my eyes. "I am sorry for what I did to Grace." His voice is remorseful, making me all the more confused.

"If you really killed her, don't say her name. You don't deserve to say her name."

He looks down, not speaking. The dim light glistens off the cuffs attached to the table.

"Did you stab Cole that night? The night he slept over."

His bottom lip quivers, just slightly.

"You know, my mom, she really cared for you. I'd never seen anyone treat her the way you have. I didn't understand it at first, but I think I do now. You were trying to make up for what you did."

He doesn't respond.

"You can't make up for anything. Not unless you give us the truth."

"I gave you the truth," he mumbles, face down.

"What?"

He looks up, with glossy eyes. "I killed Grace. I'm the monster in this story."

Hearing him say those words aloud disperse chills throughout my body. I believe he killed her as much as I believe he's sorry for killing her. "But why didn't you kill Cole?"

He doesn't respond.

"You lied to him. You broke him down. You told him the nightmares haunting him were fake. Invalidated his experiences. You mentally destroyed him. If you are The Cauterizing Killer, why don't you kill him, for all the abuse you put him through?"

"I never abused him," he blurts. "Not ever since…"

"Since when?"

A look of defeat overtakes him. He tries adjusting his handcuffs. "Since I killed Elizabeth."

"What really happened to Cole's mom?"

He grits his teeth. "I'll tell you everything. However, I must warn you, this story I'm about to share has an awful message. One I do not agree with. One you might not agree with. It's riddled with twists and turns, and will leave you guessing until the very end. You may get irritated at certain points. But you wouldn't be here if you weren't curious. Curious for this story. Curious for the truth. Curious for what really happened that night. I buried all the answers alongside your sister and my wife, long ago. Hoping they'd never resurface. But they have. Children are dead. Finn is missing. And sadly, Cole's at the center of it all. You're not going to like what I have to say, but remember: no one is forcing this onto you. You asked for this…"

The Defeatist

Our love faded over the years. I'd like to think that was one of the more normal aspects of our relationship. Though, even with the faded love, I was always able to rely on her. Trust her. Yet in these last weeks, that trust fractured. My confidence in her mental stability became minuscule.

I didn't trust her as a wife.

I didn't trust her as a parent.

I didn't trust her as a person.

I didn't want to leave Cole with her. Ever. As challenging as it is for me to be in the same room as Cole, he couldn't be alone with Elizabeth.

Neither Elizabeth nor I usually walk Cole to the bus stop, but that day I decided I'd give it a try. It was pouring, and I noticed he wasn't wearing a raincoat.

I dashed upstairs, searching for a raincoat. The bed in his grim room was broken-down. His drapes were threadbare and hanging askew above his scratched-up window. I thought, *how did his room become this neglected?*

But I knew the answer. This was the result of my doing. *My* neglect. I foraged through his narrow, built-in closet. There was no raincoat.

Downstairs, I asked Cole, "Where's your raincoat?"

"I don't have one."

"Don't be silly, of course you have one. What else do you do when it rains?"

He shot a blank look my way.

When it rains, he wears the same clothes he wears when it doesn't. When it rains, he gets wet. He gets cold. He gets sick. He gets *neglected.*

"I'm going to get you a raincoat today," I assured him.

When I opened the door, I was taken aback. Two police officers were standing there.

"Can I help—"

"Are you Henry Dalton?" one officer asked.

"Yes..."

"You're under arrest on suspicion of killing Liam Allen."

Liam Allen. That name rang a bell. He was murdered a couple days prior. It was on the news. He was branded O.M. I remember thinking those initials were familiar, but I wasn't sure from where.

They arrested me in front of Cole. I couldn't imagine what that was like for him. I told the officers to bring him to the station with me, but because Elizabeth was home, they said that wasn't necessary.

At the precinct, they asked for my whereabouts the night Liam was murdered. It was the same night I came home early to find Cole alone.

They found my DNA in the Allens' house. I didn't know Liam or where he lived. To this day it shocks me how my DNA ended up there. Though, looking back it, all makes sense.

My only alibi was Cole. A schizophrenic child who would probably lie to save his father. It was a weak alibi. Yet it worked. But I knew, another slip up, another piece of evidence and I'll be put away.

When I returned home, Elizabeth was gone. Again.

When she returned—a week later—furious was an understatement as to what I was feeling. Cole was in the living room, sitting on the couch. Elizabeth and I were in the kitchen.

"Who do you think you are? How could you leave a child alone while his father is 'detained'? How could you leave your son without letting anyone of us know?"

"I didn't."

"Don't you dare lie. Not to me. Not to Cole. We may have our ups and downs, but Cole, he never wronged a soul, how could you just up and leave?"

"I would never."

"Liz, you were gone for a week. I was here. You weren't," I say. "Cole deserves better than you."

She broke down, bawling. "I don't know what's going on." She collapsed onto the kitchen chair.

"Don't you dare act like you're the victim in all of this."

Her chest rose and fell with rapid breaths. "I...I...I would never leave Cole," she wailed.

"Then where were you?"

After regaining her composure, she said, "You wouldn't believe me if I told you. I'm not even sure I believe myself."

"Liz, what are you talking about?"

She shook her head. "I...I...I was held captive. For the last week."

I squinted my eyes. "What?"

"I told you. You wouldn't believe me."

"Can you blame me?" I said. "You sound delusional."

"Well, maybe I am."

"Who was holding you captive?" I asked, humoring myself.

"I-I-I..."

I peered at her, waiting for a response, a name, anything. She couldn't give one. "I don't want you in the house anymore. I don't want you near Cole. I. Don't. Want. You."

Her body tensed. "Please, please don't leave me."

In all my years knowing Elizabeth, I'd never seen her plead the way she did that day.

I called up Mrs. Miller. She told me she was suffering from schizophrenia. The same as Cole, only much worse. The way she's disappearing, believing in delusions and hallucinations. She may need to be put in a hospital. When I brought up the hospital idea, she was extremely against it, claiming she was feeling better. Then days later told me she was being held captive again.

I didn't understand it. Why would anyone kidnap a person just for a day or two, with no ransom note, then let them go, only to kidnap them again days later?

She'd also tell me she was being held captive on days I saw her, in the house.

Though I thought it was schizophrenia, part of me was curious. No, that's not right. Part of me was paranoid. I was never an invasive person, yet weeks before Grace's death, that word suited me best.

At home, I'd examine everything Elizabeth owned. I ransacked her drawers, looked through her phone, I even searched through her wallet. I didn't know what I was looking for, the only thing I knew; I couldn't trust her.

Whenever she'd come home, I'd stop and stare at her, mentally patting her down.

"I fuckin' hate you," she'd say.

"Well, you're the one that married me," I'd reply.

I bought a tracker online. While she was sleeping, I placed it in her car. I took a week off and from afar, I'd tail her wherever she went. Grocery shopping, work, Mrs. Miller. Certain times I even thought she saw me.

A couple days into tracking her, she was fixed at a specific spot in the woods. As soon as she left, I rushed over there.

I discovered a placid tent secluded by thick trees. What I found in that tent bred a plethora of questions.

Questions I didn't want to ask.

Questions I didn't want answered.

I shouldn't have traced her here.

I shouldn't have come here.

I ignored what I saw. Telling myself the police would find The Cauterizing Killer.

They'd deal with this.

My trust in the police's capabilities were naïve. It was weak. Feeble.

Have you ever wished your problems didn't exist, to the point you believe they don't?

That's what I did.

That's what I tried to do.

The thing is, you can't wish your problems away. All that does is exacerbate them.

It's like adding fuel to the fire.

You see, wishes…

Wishes are for the optimists, the hopeful…the *lazy*.

True action, initiative, willpower, those are attributes possessed by pessimists.

Optimists fail to comprehend the way the world works.

They can't.

I couldn't.

When I opened up her tent, why did I find rope, a shotgun, and a branding iron?

The Defeatist

They say ignorance is bliss. I can't say I find that to be true. Then again, the knowledge I've possessed for the last ten years has been slowly draining my soul. I think ignorance is just less sufferable.

But, just because you're not aware of something doesn't mean it's not happening. Just because you think there's peace doesn't mean there is. Just because you believe things are well doesn't mean they are.

Convincing myself I didn't discover what I thought I did that day in the tent helped me sleep better. But how many kids were dying while I was in bed, getting better rest? How many could I have saved? What could I have prevented? I'll never know how different things would be if I just dug a little deeper, a little sooner. Though, I do know two people would be alive right now if I did something, anything, different.

My boss wanted me to go to Franklin for a week to meet with a client. To be frank, there was a higher chance of me winning the lottery than there was of me leaving Cole with Elizabeth.

I brought them both with me to Franklin.

The drive there was the longest time I spent in a car with Cole, ever. The showering sky sourced slippery streets. It was strenuous trying to see what was in front of me, but I was more concerned with what was sitting beside me. Feeling apprehensive about Elizabeth's presence, I sped the entire ride.

The rain drummed against the roof of the car. I glanced back at Cole several times, checking on his well-being. He was sleeping, head drooping onto his shoulder, mouth ajar.

We arrived at our four-star hotel. Cole was wearing the rain-jacket I bought him. We sprinted into the western-style high-rise, trying not to get soaked.

Our fifth floor penthouse had two carpeted bedrooms and an open kitchen. The fridge had a tablet-sized whiteboard.

Cole was mesmerized. "I've never been to a real hotel before." He wrapped his arms around me. "Thank you," he said.

That evening, we were driving to a restaurant named Spicy Dragon. The roads were still drenched. I noticed Elizabeth's eyes focused outside on a specific derelict building.

"What is it?" I asked.

"Nothing," she said. "That building is just…interesting."

The car swooshed through a puddle, spraying our windshield.

Cole eyes widened with amazement the entire ride, in fact, the entire trip. He'd never been this far from home before. Things as simple as trees, which were the same ones you'd find in Greenville, would astonish him, merely because this wasn't Greenville. The endearing look on his face captivated me.

On this trip, for the first time, I didn't see him as my *schizophrenic son*. I saw him as just, *my son*.

He wasn't a burden, or a challenge. He was relief. He was love and joy; what I've been lacking my whole life. Except, I was never lacking it. He was always right there.

I've spent my life thinking I was locked in a room, when the whole time the key was in my pocket. If I was only observant enough to check.

As I gaze at him, sitting in the backseat, ponderous eyes peering out the window, I can't help but smile.

The light flashed green and a car behind me honked.

"Wake up!" Elizabeth exclaimed.

I realized while I was in seventh heaven, she was in marital purgatory. She initially refused to come, but I didn't give her much choice. I practically dragged her here against her will.

While she was with us in the car, I couldn't help but feel she was thousands of miles away.

She couldn't care less for Cole's palpable sense of euphoria.

"You know, Cole's really enjoying himself," I say.

She let out a sigh. "How much longer until we reach the restaurant?"

"We're almost there."

At the restaurant, we sat in the corner. The room was spacious, yet there were only a few tables. All of which were occupied. Our linen covered table was square shaped. It was well made with menus atop the plates.

Cole sat awe-inspired, watching all the waiters dashing from table to table as if they were flying.

I explored my menu which was five, double-sided pages long. "What would you like to eat, Cole?"

His eyes flashed to mine. "Um, water."

"We are at a Chinese restaurant; you can't just get water."

His eyes dropped. "I don't know what there is."

"Look at the menu, I'm sure you can find something you like."

He opened the menu, but the way he stared at the center suggested he wasn't reading anything.

I glanced at Liz, who was staring across the room at a visibly dysfunctional family. Two sisters sat there bickering like cats and dogs while the mom closed her eyes and rubbed her forehead. The saint of a father was mentally undressing a waitress walking away. He was holding a beer, though, there was no beer listed in the lengthy menu.

I heard Elizabeth's stomach growl. "Liz," I said.

Her nose crinkled.

"Liz," I repeated.

I set my hand on her wrist and she flinched. She reacted as if I just appeared from thin air.

"What do you want to order?" I asked.

"Nothing," she let out.

"You told me you were starving in the car."

Her focus floats back to the dysfunctional family. "I lost my appetite."

"I don't know how to read these words," Cole said with a delicate voice.

I looked at him. My son. His ears were Rudolph red and his eyes rounded. He was ashamed. He had nothing to be ashamed of; he was dealing with so much more than any one of us.

"It's okay, show me which words you are struggling with."

He leaned closer and pointed to the word Lo Mein.

"The L and the O together, sound low. And the M E I N together sound main."

He looked up at me twinkling.

"So, it's lo mein?"

I nodded.

Then an ear-piercing slap startled us. I glimpse around the room to see everyone staring at one table. One man. Your father, Olivia. His hand was set against the table.

"Enough with the goddamn yammering," he fumed. "I take you guys out and this is the thanks I get?" He stormed to the bathroom, slamming a beer in the trashcan before entering.

A moment later, Liz, holding her purse, breezed to that same bathroom.

Twenty-five minutes.

That's how long they were in the bathroom for. Together. It was also long enough for Cole to please his childlike uncertainty, settle on something to order, and finish half of his plate.

If this had occurred weeks earlier, I would've left right then and there, but Cole was so goddamn happy. I couldn't leave.

However, I never forgot that father or the look of those two girls. Not because of what happened that day in the restaurant, but because of what was going to happen later. I didn't know it at the time, but the next time I'd see Grace, it wouldn't be in a restaurant. It was going to be in a decrepit building. With Cole and Liz. And with a knife in my hand, I'd kill Grace.

The Defeatist

A week passed and in that week my connection to Cole strengthened, though, Elizabeth's weakened. She fled the hotel room in the middle of the night multiple times. And, when she was with us, she was primarily on her phone, texting someone. It was more than irritating. But I was focusing on Cole. Not his mother. Even so, telling myself I was going to be more attentive, it wasn't enough.

When the trip grew closer to an end, I woke up disoriented. Cole and Elizabeth were missing. I knew Elizabeth left hours at a time each night doing God knows what. I didn't care because honestly, I didn't care for her. However, now Cole was missing.

First thing I did was call the police. Despite the fact that they falsely arrested me, the little trust I had in them remained.

"My wife ran away with my son. You need to find them. His life depends on it," I said.

They laughed hard. It was disdainful. Yet, I knew I sounded delusional. I knew I sounded like…Elizabeth.

"His life depends on it? That's a first." The officer mocked.

"I'm serious."

"Okay, um. How long has your wife been missing?"

"At least since 9 a.m., when I woke up."

"It's 9:20 now."

IN THE BACK OF MY HEAD

"Listen, I know how this sounds but she's psychotic. She's killed several kids."

He laughed again. "Okay, we have more grave matters to deal with than a housewife leaving her husband."

"No wait—"

The line disconnected, and with it, the minuscule trust I had left in the police.

I'm not going to say Grace died because of that cop, but if he took this even a bit more serious, he may have stopped what happened next.

An hour later I was frantic; I didn't know how I ended up in the predicament I was in. It was unfathomable. Have you ever just stopped, and wondered, how the hell did I end up here? What went wrong in my life to bring me to where I am now?

I gazed at the blood dripping from the kitchen knife. I didn't think it was going to be sharp enough. Regardless, I pressed into the skin and blood oozed out. I was trying not getting it on me but that was challenging, it was everywhere. The deeper I'd cut, the harder it became, which made sense because beyond the tender flesh was rigid bone.

That being said, I wished the leg had no bones it. That's actually what I was trying to do: remove all evidence of bones.

This stainless-steel knife wasn't strong enough. I saw an advertisement for this knife; it said it could cut through anything, yet right there it felt like it was going to snap.

I tossed the knife aside and with nothing but bare hands, ripped the bones out of the flesh. It was easier but disgusting. I didn't like seeing that stuff raw. It was unnatural, a leg without bones.

But I knew Cole only ate his chicken legs boneless. And last night I promised him I'd make him chicken legs for dinner. I know, I should've been out searching that snobby town, but I didn't know where to begin. I hadn't the faintest idea where they'd be. Still, it may seem odd that I was cooking chicken at a time like that, but when I'm in a panic state, I do the simplest of tasks to calm myself.

I also knew my wife was coming back and when she would, I'd convince her to give me Cole. She had been glued to her phone the entire week and after I called the police, I found her phone in the kitchen. She received a dozen messages from a man named Otis.

Where is my daughter?
Where is my car?
You're demented.
The sex wasn't even that good.

I wanted the hotel table to appear elegant so she wouldn't assume I had any ulterior motives. I poured red wine in my glass and Bartenura in my wife's, then set it on the table, making sure to differentiate between our two glasses. Her glass was poisonous. If I drank it, it would kill me. The flavor of Bartenura is extremely off-putting and rancid. It's not even real wine. It's basically Sprite. I fail to comprehend how a person drinks it and doesn't kill themselves.

Elizabeth loved surprises and I was going to use that to my advantage. When she'd come in, she wouldn't know what hit her. I planned everything more than meticulous, but that all went out the door as she opened it. A fight or flight response overtook me.

I couldn't think straight. All I knew was I needed to hold her. I sneaked up from behind and hugged her tight enough to confine her movements. I hoped it was also tight enough to suppress her breathing. Next, I took out my surprise and held it against her throat. Blood started dripping from neck. With the knife against her throat, I said, "I'll kill you."

The Defeatist

I had her in my arms, knife against her throat. Any sane person would be scared straight, but not Liz. She laughed, maniacally.

"You're going to drop the knife, and I'm going to walk out that door in just a few moments," she said.

"You really are insane, why would I ever do that?"

"Cole's going to suffer if you don't."

"You think I'm stupid? I know what you are, who you are."

She chuckled. "You have no *idea* who I am."

"If I let you go, you'll kill him regardless."

"True. He is going to die one way or another, but the way I kill these children is painless; pentobarbital doesn't hurt. It's painless. But starvation, well, that's true suffering. And if he does die that way, that won't be on me, it'll be on you."

I clenched my jaws. The knife was practically piercing her vein. I wanted to slit it. Just a little more pressure. It would take just a second, then all of this would be over. But Cole. The image of my eight-year-old son starving, because of me. That's not something I could bare.

The knife started trembling, blood started dripping from her neck. I couldn't do it. I couldn't kill her. I couldn't knowingly let my son suffer. I dropped the knife and fell backward.

Sitting on the floor, eyes transfixed on the wall, I asked, "Why are you doing this?"

She laughed once more. "I'm freeing him; I'm ending his affliction. Your abuse, your neglect."

"You're…you're psychotic."

"When's Cole's birthday?"

"What?" I ask.

"Answer me this and I'll let him go. When is Cole's birthday?"

My mouth hung ajar. "I-I-I…"

"That's what I figured."

She sauntered to the countertop, grabbed her phone and left. I didn't stop her. I couldn't. Cole would starve to death if I did.

I remained on the hotel room floor until my legs were numb, like my mind. Cole was gone because of my *abuse*. Was I really abusive? I didn't want to believe her, that I was abusive. No abuser ever does. But deep down, I knew the last few months had shown me how little I cared for Cole. How little I knew about him. He was my son and I didn't know his birthday. That stings me beyond words. I was forced to take a self-inventory and when I did, I came to the single conclusion: I was a horrible father.

I looked up at the ceiling. I'm not a religious man, never was. But that day I made a promise to God and to myself. That if I get a second chance with Cole, that if I could somehow find him, I'd save him at any cost. And after I'd save him, I'd be the greatest father I could be.

After a while I regained the courage to stand. To move. To live. I noticed an address written on the white board attached to the fridge. I thought—she slipped up, she assumed I was heedless enough to miss it.

I grabbed the keys from the counter which confused me. I had a car, but how did Elizabeth get around? How did she kidnap Cole and drag him to that address? She could've bussed there, but I doubted that.

The address led me to some construction site, where there was no parking so I turned left, parking on the side. A wide alleyway between two opposite facing buildings split the block like the Nile. A few fenced backyards and a few spray-painted dumpsters inhabited the place.

I anxiously walked back to the construction site and saw an animation of a high-rise fixed to a green wooden fence.

The grunts of workers and the buzzing of mechanical tools made me aware this place wasn't vacant. A few surveillance cameras were fixed above the fence, too. She couldn't be here. But why did she write down this address?

Standing in place, I leaned back, mentally scanning the buildings down the block—which all stood cheek by jowl. These red brick buildings seemed poverty stricken. Most didn't even have addresses posted on them.

I was about to head back when I saw her. Elizabeth. Her eyes met mine and she froze for a moment, then she sprinted like I've never seen before. I followed her to an abandoned building, the same one she took interest in earlier. I walked toward it and saw that the building had no posted address. That's why she wrote down the address to the construction site, it was one of the closest buildings.

I pulled out my phone and begun dialing *9-1-1*. Then stopped. I already called them and they refused to believe me. They were of no use to me and I was short on time. Cole was short on time. The door to the abandoned building was unlocked. I didn't understand why, though I was about to. To my better judgment, I entered. Glass cracked under my feet, startling me. I raised my foot and looked down, finding a syringe. I gazed ahead, seeing many of them spread throughout the floor. I examined one. Pentobarbital. I've heard that word twice that day which was more than I've ever heard it before.

I prowled throughout the stark rooms, until I heard movement. Peeking from behind a foyer, I saw them. Cole tied up, unconscious and branded. Elizabeth wearing an incongruous sundress, resembling a housewife from the sixties. She was facing a wall, and I heard the beep of three digits being dialed. To the left of her was a back door.

When I saw the girl from the restaurant, Grace, my body went limp. She was branded and blanched, making it difficult to dictate whether she was alive or dead.

I glanced back at Elizabeth, who was now holding a kitchen knife. The same knife I once held against her throat. I hadn't even realized she took it after I dropped it.

I couldn't breathe. Grace appeared dead, and Cole looked like he was going to follow.

Elizabeth, gripping the knife, turned to Cole. Like many of my options, waiting was taken from me. I looked behind me before creeping up behind her. I grappled her, then slammed her onto the ground. Looking down at her with anger, I hammered my fists into her deceivingly amiable face over and over. I can't begin to describe how wounded she appeared. There was just as much blood on her face as there was on me. Standing solemnly over her, I glanced at the knife beside her. I snatched it off the floor before she got the chance.

She was big boned for a woman but I was heavier built. I thought that was why she didn't put up a fight. I turned to Grace whose mouth was concealed by tape. Her eyes were wide open. I didn't know how much she saw.

Elizabeth began whimpering, "Please, please don't kill me." She coughed blood.

I was bewildered.

"Please, I'm carrying a child."

Fed up with Elizabeth's deception, I ignored her and trudged to Grace, who was shivering. Though she was seventeen, her eyes said she witnessed more than any adult. I placed my hand on her cheek trying to remove the tape, but she flinched. She began screaming as if I was The Cauterizing Killer, then I understood. She thought I was. That I was the one behind this. Elizabeth set this up.

She left the address on the whiteboard for me to find, the door open for me to enter, and she wore 'motherly' clothing and let me hurt her for Grace to see.

I needed to think. I needed to convince Grace that I wasn't the killer, but before I could, I heard sirens. That's who she was dialing on her phone. The police. Elizabeth's blood from earlier was still on the knife. So were my fingerprints. I was arrested once before on suspicion of being The Cauterizing Killer. If they came here, to find this scene, they wouldn't believe my story. The *real* story. There was too much evidence against me. It was over. Grace would say what she saw here today and I'd be put in prison or on death row. I'd never get the chance to be the father Cole deserves. I dropped to my knees and glimpsed at Cole. His eyes were closed. At least, they seemed closed. I thought he didn't see any of this. And if he did, maybe, just maybe I could convince him he didn't. That all of this was some hallucination.

I looked back at Grace. The only way I'd get out of this, is if she was dead. It was me or her.

Her life would be the cost of my freedom. A second chance with Cole. This is the time to do things right. I wouldn't just be his father; I'd be his dad.

Me or her.

Grace was the one thing in my way. I squeezed the knife.

Me or her.

I stood up, with heavy steps and slogged toward Grace. My hands, trembling. My eyes, teary.

Me or her.

Self-preservation surged through my veins. This was for my son. For my freedom. A survival instinct I didn't know I had consumed me. Panic clouded my vision. My sanity.

I shut my eyes and whispered a painful, "I'm sorry."

Then…I slit her throat.

The Defeatist

I was going to kill Elizabeth, too, but Cole's eyes started opening and the sirens stopped outside. There was no time, I grabbed Cole and ran through the back. The backyard was mostly concealed by a broken-down wooden fence, except for one part where three boards were missing; my exit.

With Cole on my back, I shimmied between them, leading me to the alleyway. I glanced left, then right. Now was not the time to forget where I parked. Right, I parked on the right side.

I galloped to my car, kicking alcohol containers in my way.

Driving away, I saw a cop car outside the construction site. Why weren't they outside the derelict building? The sirens were still flashing but the noise was mute. Two police officers shut their doors and set foot behind the green fence.

Adrenaline-filled, I drove back to the hotel. Cole sat in the shot gun seat, forehead furrowed, wriggling unconscious. He had his first nightmare in that car beside me.

When we reached the hotel, Cole was awake, but dazed. I placed my arm around him and kept my head down as we walked through the lobby. The doorman greeted us with an artificially elated, "Welcome back."

I ignored him, beelining for the elevator. Once in it, with the doors sliding shut, I eyeballed the lobby. To my surprise, there wasn't an officer in sight. I soon learned why.

Back in the hotel room, I sat on the bed, tensely watching TV, waiting for the 'Breaking News.' At first, I hoped they didn't find Grace. But as the hours passed, that hope turned to dread. A stomach-turning realization hit me.

The derelict building, it had no address. Where did Elizabeth tell the police to go to? Then I remembered, they were outside the construction site. The same address she wrote down on the whiteboard. In haste, she must've gotten confused or forgotten. She schemed everything so perfectly, accounting for my every move, but she messed up her own. You can only go right for so long…

Two days after killing Grace, polluted with grief, I went back to the derelict building. Stupid, I know, but I needed to see her, assuming she was still there.

When I opened the door, a revolting odor nauseated me. It was so thick I could almost taste it, making me choke a little. With my mouth and nose covered, I continued in the building until finding Grace, right where I left her.

Her skin was inhumanly pale. The blood, once dripping from her neck, was now dried. It should've given me chills, but instead it made me more heavy-hearted. Days ago, she was a person, a daughter, a student, and now she was nothing. No one would know she died; no one would get closure; no one would know what happened.

Untying her, I noticed the rope left rings around her wrists. They seemed familiar, but I couldn't place from where.

I carried her to the backyard—if you could call it that—where the concrete ground was cracked. I dug a grave for Grace there, telling myself I'd visit several times a year.

Our stay at the hotel drew to an end, and I still I didn't know where Elizabeth ran off to, though I had theories. I half expected her to be home, counting the seconds for me to walk through the front door so she could leap at me from the ceiling, like something in a bad 70s movie.

When we returned to Greenville, I pulled into the driveway and told Cole to wait for me in the car. He initially complied, like the good kid he is. I snuck around the house, prowling on the narrow, paved pathway. Peeking through the side windows, I saw the lights off. The house seemed just as I left it, at least I thought that's how I left it. I wasn't a perceptive person, if you haven't already learned.

I made my way to the backyard, which was large but unkempt. We didn't have a patio or anything special; it was mostly dead grass and a small slab of pavement. Leaning forward against the sliding doors, I surveyed the house before opening it. The fireplace was unlit. No glasses sat on the wooden coffee table. My flat screen was off.

Setting foot in the house, the distinct odor of burning feces mixed with rotten meat hit me like a truck. There was no mistaking that revolting smell. Though I didn't know where, somewhere in here was a dead body. And, I had to have been the most unlucky man to experience this stench twice in one week.

A light tug on my arm scared me shitless. Thinking Cole was Elizabeth, I shoved him off me.

Now on the floor, wiping his runny nose, Cole said. "I needed to go to the bathroom."

Jesus, barely two days since I swore to be a better father; yet here I was shoving my son. I helped him up, apologizing, before saying, "Go to the bathroom, and afterwards we'll go get ice cream."

His face brightened, even after being pushed by his father.

Moments later, I heard a shriek coming from the bathroom. Cole. Sprinting there in what felt like a flash, I found him frozen, staring at Elizabeth with wide eyes. Dried puddles of blood around her wrist stained the white tiled floors. I wasn't a morgue practitioner, but she appeared and smelled dead much longer than Grace had. Meaning she died while we were in Franklin.

But how could that be?

I saw her, Cole saw her…and Grace, she saw her.

I peered at her open wrists, recalling something from months earlier. We were arguing, I grabbed Elizabeth's arm, finding red circles on her wrists. Grace had them, too.

Then I remembered how Elizabeth wholeheartedly believed someone was kidnapping her, keeping her hostage. But I saw her all those times, was I hallucinating?

I gazed at my reflection in the oval mirror, above the mounted sink. Though it was rusty edged and grungy, I still saw the face of a defeated man looking back at me.

Cole was breathing short and rapidly. "M-m-m…mom."

My poor son. A boy fighting so many demons, he was practically an eight-year-old exorcist.

Though I didn't trust the police, I knew I needed to report this ASAP, or somehow, I'd be arrested for this.

A day later, the police confirmed my suspicions; she killed herself while we were in Franklin. I didn't understand it. Was I going crazy? Was I hallucinating?

And the branding I saw, the letters O.M. What did they mean? Before I could figure it out, it was time to go to Elizabeth's funeral. I was taken aback when I found out she already bought herself a grave, considering she never thought ahead. I guess death was on her mind more than I knew, which haunts me all the more.

Not many people showed up, seeing as we didn't have many friends, which is very stereotypical for psychopaths, if Elizabeth was one. The few that did show up I didn't recognize, other than Mrs. Miller, who observed me curiously.

The sun was blinding, and in the black suit I was wearing, also fatiguing. Even as Elizabeth's casket was descending, I stood more perplexed than lamented.

I glimpsed at all the other graves, standing shoulder to shoulder with Elizabeth's. It felt almost disrespectful how thronging this cemetery was. Someone had to have been standing on someone's grave...crap! I was. It was the one neighboring Elizabeth's.

I was going to leap off it, but when I saw the name written on the tombstone, I couldn't move.

Ophelia Monroe beloved sister.
09/21/75

I glanced at the date of birth on Elizabeth's tombstone.

Elizabeth Monroe
Beloved wife and mother.
09/21/75

"Don't worry," a pastor murmured. He was elderly, with as many wrinkles on his face as years he was alive. "You're not stepping on any grave, it's a cenotaph. The body was never found."

And just like that, everything clicked.

The puzzle piece you're looking for Olivia, I gave it to you earlier:

There were two sisters.
That's what I failed to realize that night.
Two seemingly indistinguishable sisters.
One is now dead.
The other is alive.
One I killed.
The other I could've killed.
If only I had known.

Cole has confused these sisters, too.
It's understandable.
Cole loves one of these sisters.
The other sister, he's had a few conversations with.
He assumed she was a product of his imagination.
She wasn't.

It was almost comical, like a dark, twisted freaky Friday scenario. And I realized Elizabeth wasn't schizophrenic. Or maybe she was but she never lied, about being kidnapped, disappearing, or abandoning Cole. This was all the work of her sister, Ophelia Monroe, The Cauterizing Killer.

How many times did I think Ophelia was Elizabeth? How many times was she in the house? How many times did she talk to Cole?

And the scariest part of all this is, she's still alive...out there, searching for us. I was fighting a ghost, a person that didn't exist. A hallucination.

Tired and tormented, defeated and out of my depth, I ran. We were gone before the dirt settled on Elizabeth's coffin.

Cole had schizophrenia before he was kidnapped, which while extremely rare at his age, was mild. But after he was kidnapped, when we first moved here, it was like a whole different disorder. His nightmares and insomnia were beyond extreme. The doctors, along with myself, didn't understand it at first, but eventually, after thorough research, I came to understand. Though, I didn't tell the doctors, I knew It was the all the pentobarbital Ophelia injected him with.

All the same, no medications worked...until they suggested that same drug: pentobarbital. I was against it from the get go. Until, one day he disappeared and I found him in the woods shivering. He was talking to someone he called 'mom' but there was no one there. It was a voice in his head. It's odd, hallucinating your dead mother. If I had to guess, it's because somehow, subconsciously, he knows or thinks she kidnapped him.

Either way, his insomnia was making his schizophrenia worse, and I knew I could no longer ignore it. So, I came around, and it worked. The thing that exacerbated his schizophrenia was the thing easing it. I didn't know what to make of that but I was more than uncomfortable. Luckily, the doctors only allowed him take it for a short while because of all the negative side effects.

A while ago, I tapped his phone and added mics and cameras outside and inside the house. I figured Ophelia may try reaching out to Cole, messing with his head, pretending to be his hallucination. That's how I discovered Mr. Haynes. I heard you guys' conversations, and listened to Blake threaten Cole over the phone call.

Though I wanted to kill Blake for what he said, I can promise you this, I didn't touch Finn.

The Defeatist

Do you know what death sounds like? The inhale of a final breath. The last beat of a heart. Seeing a kid's eyes shut and knowing they'll never open again. To see their body shiver one second and go limp the next.

You can't fathom what that does to a person. You're aware of Cole's nightmares but aren't aware of mine. How often I see Grace. How I wish I would've done things differently.

Or how Elizabeth wasn't Elizabeth for months, maybe even years and I never realized. I didn't just kill Grace. I killed Elizabeth. She was my wife and I drove her to taking her own life. There was a killer abducting her and the one person she confided in, didn't believe her. I was the one who proclaimed to protect her and I failed.

You know, she was a very distant woman, but there was a time, just once, when she was drunk and really opened up to me about her past. Her childhood. The abusive parents she had. How horrible the foster care system is.

"Kids are suffering and no one does anything. They just act like they don't exist because it makes life easier."

I was also drunk and distracted by her rancid breath. I pinched my nose waiting for her to finish talking. Once she noticed, she did.

Looking back, I want to kill the man I was and hug the woman Elizabeth was. I should've been there for her. She needed me. She needed someone.

As you can see, I deserve to be here for my sins. No one else but me. Time after time, I had a chance to stop this and I never did. I mean, I saw the branding iron in her tent and ignored it.

And, maybe I could do something to stop all of this now. But I'm scared. I'm shaken to my core. I don't know what she's capable of.

I can't fight her. The only thing I have the courage to do is pay penance.

I know Cole thinks he has to protect you, but Olivia...protect him. You are the only one that can.

Part 4

All these voices in my head get loud.
I wish that I could shut them out.
I'm sorry that I let you down.
L-l-let you down...

-NF

The Stoic

Two police officers stood beside me while Mr. Torsney gave his tell-all. I'm not a cop, but that had to have been the most pessimistic, slightly condescending, if not patronizing confessions ever given.

One officer hands me my crutches and the other hands me back my phone. Then they eagerly escort me out of the investigation room. In the adjoining room, there are at least ten officers staring through the one-way glass. They all glance at me, speechless.

While balancing with the crutches, I power on my phone then head to the lobby. I have two missed messages and one missed call, all from Cole. He also left a voicemail.

One message is actually an image with an abundance of drawings that look like Green Point Lake.

The other message reads: was at Mr. Haynes house, come to green point lake ASAP.

These messages seem panic-stricken.

I call Cole, no answer.

"So was the meeting eventful?" Johnny asks.

"Yes."

"Great, what will he be—"

"I hate to interrupt but I think Cole's in trouble."

"What do you mean?"

"Ok, what I'm about to tell you isn't so legal, so we should go outside for this."

"As if rules don't apply outside a police station."

"I'm serious, Johnny."

"Ok, let's go outside."

I begin maneuvering myself to the front door, but stop, noticing Johnny walking in a different direction. I follow him through a short, gray, lighted corridor, leading me to the back.

"The press is still camped on the lawn."

"Oh, okay."

The cold air envelops me like a slap, even with my coat on. Johnny shoves his hands into his pants pockets, I assume because he doesn't have gloves.

"Cole has a key to Mr. Haynes' house," I say. "Mr. Haynes gave it to him, so I don't think it's breaking and entering. Still, he told me half an hour ago that he was there, and now he isn't answering."

"Jesus." He rakes his pinkish hands through his hair. "Is this what teenagers do nowadays? Just put themselves in life threatening situations for the hell of it?"

"He told me to come to Green Point Lake."

Johnny raises an eyebrow. "Why would he tell a girl on crutches to come to a lake?"

"I don't know, Johnny, and I don't have time for this." I limp around the building to the front, where Mom's car is.

"Olivia, you shouldn't be driving while you have a broken leg!" Johnny shouts.

There's a lot of things I shouldn't be doing, but this, I feel, is the one thing I should be.

The Existentialist

The drive to Green Point Lake was deadly. It began snowing. I didn't check the forecast today, but I remember two days ago they mentioned something about a snow storm this week. And, judging from the heavy snowfall, I have to assume this is what the newscasters were referring too.

"Why did I drive us here?" I ask.

"You know why, Cole."

"Right, Finn may be here."

That's not me, Cole.

"What?"

Mom looks at me. *"What?"*

"Nothing."

With gloves on her hands, she starts patting her oversized jacket.

"What are you looking for?"

"Cole, you're losing focus. We must find Finn."

I scratch my head which stings my frostbitten fingers. "Why is it you seem most real when I'm here?"

"I don't know what you're talking about, Cole."

I chafe my hands together.

"This forest is enormous; we aren't going to find him here."

"There's a knife." She points at the ground.

"It looks like the same type Robert uses."

It does. If I didn't know any better, I'd think I was hallucinating. But I do know better.

"How did that get there?"

"You brought it."

"No, I didn't."

"You were supposed to kill yourself months ago. We talked about it. Why didn't you go through with it?"

"Because Olivia was there."

"She's not here now."

No. She isn't.

"Pick up the knife."

"I'd never leave Olivia."

"She can't understand you, Cole. Nobody can." I can see Mom's warm breath in the air. *"Not even Robert. He lied to you for years. It's only a matter of time before Olivia does too."*

I gaze at the knife. It looks like it's from the old knife set we had in Greenville, and I begin to wonder if that's because it is.

"Do it, Cole."

She lifts the knife and extends it in my direction. I think she may be right. Death…it's the only way this ends.

The Stoic

With a shove, I unlatch the car door and leap out.

"Ah!"

I put too much pressure on my fractured leg, my whole body goes limp and I collapse on the rutted ground.

Clasping onto the car door, I stand up. Then in a rush, I grab the crutches from the passenger seat.

Shit!

They slipped out of my twitchy hands.

Propped against the car, my legs quiver with trepidation. There's only devastation waiting for me by that lake. I bend down, pick up the crutches, then slam the door.

Ophelia could be killing Cole right now. He could already be dead. Just like Grace. My heart flutters.

First Grace, now Cole.

She may even have Finn.

No. No one else will die.

I hobble along the undefined dirt path. I've mastered the art of walking with crutches on smooth ground, I can conquer the gritty dirt.

I *need* to conquer the gritty dirt.

Cole may not even be here. It's extremely optimistic, thinking he's here. Yet if he is, he may be with Ophelia. He might not even know she's not a hallucination. She could kill him without him even realizing she's a threat. At least, not until it's too late.

I should've believed him.

The last time we talked, I told him he was reaching. Our last discussion together will be of me, not believing him.

"Nooooo!"

My crutches soar as I stumble over a gnarled tree root, plummeting head first onto the ground.

Everything's spinning. Lifting my head, I spit the vexing soot out of my mouth.

I can't save Cole.

I can't even save myself.

Sitting up, I look at my grazed hands, then at my broken leg.

Cole saved me. He was hurt protecting me the night Ophelia attacked.

Now, I need to protect him.

I'm going to protect him.

I crawl toward my antagonistic crutches. Like my leg, one of them is now broken. That's fine. One will suffice.

Limping toward the lake, a burned-out fire beside a tent materializes. I've seen that tent every time I've been here.

Ophelia used a tent in Greenville.

There's no way.

I tentatively glance forward, then back at the tent. Hobbling toward the tent, a greater sense of dread consumes me.

I slowly unzip the latch....

"Mocha," I breathe. "No."

She's lying there, dead and branded, with several lacerations. My legs, now weaker than before, make me want to drop to the ground, but I can't. I know if I do, I won't be able to rise back up. I need to get moving, yet my eyes are glued to Mocha. *My Mocha.*

Beside her is a rope, guns, a branding iron, journals, and pictures. Pictures of Cole, Finn, Tyler, and me.

Scrutinizing the shotgun, I contemplate taking it. I'm seventeen. I've never fired a gun. I'm not even sure how it works. I'll probably do more harm to myself than Ophelia. However, thinking about my situation, a crippled seventeen-year-old fighting a retired serial killer, I know I wouldn't stand a chance.

I grab the heavy shotgun with one hand, and with the other clutching a crutch, I limp toward our spot by the lake. Struggling to balance with each step I take is aggravating, but I won't fall, not again.

I'm going to save Cole.

I need to save Cole.

Peering ahead, I hobble and it stings.

I hobble and it burns.

I hobble and it swells.

I hobble and start hearing ringing.

I hobble, and trying to subdue the pain, I shriek, causing birds to flap off the trees.

My legs feel like someone firmly tied a rope around it cutting off circulation, then poured gasoline on it and burned it.

The pain is unbearable, the ground is enticing, but I don't stop.

Because if I do…Cole's going to die.

The Existentialist

"You keep calling me Cole."

"That's your name."

She isn't wrong, but only when I'm here does she refer to me by my actual name. Everywhere else, she refers to me by *sweetie*. The same is true for how she only refers to Dad as Robert over here. I start to think about the fact that the only time I can actually see her—not just hear her—is when I'm here. And now I understand. For the first time in my life, I fear I'm *not* hallucinating.

This woman that shares the same appearance as my mom and the same voice as my hallucinations, is not my mom or a hallucination. How she managed to deceive me for all this time is beyond me, and it's as unrealistic as my delusions.

"Cole, what are you waiting for?"

I fail to speak. This woman is the same person that took me ten years ago, the woman that dad battered.

As I assimilate this revelation, I fear she's assimilating a revelation of her own. Her motherly eyes fill with malice causing a lump to form in my throat. My hand vibrates as I reach for the knife.

She pulls it back.

My eyes widen.

She tsks. "Oh, Cole."

My body feels as light as the snow falling on my hair.

"You're not my mom or a hallucination."

"Afraid not."

"I'm...not...going...to...kill...myself." The nippy weather along with my apprehension create an ill-timed shiver.

"No, you won't kill yourself," she says. "At least not until you kill Finn and Olivia." She reaches into her pocket, drawing out a phone. My phone. "Olivia is on her way."

"And Finn?"

"Finn, come out."

A newly snow-covered bush rustles before Finn emerges, hugging himself, without a coat. His eyes are dry with red splotches under them. He makes his way to the disturbed woman. "Mommy, I'm cold." His lips are a smooth purple.

"Don't worry Finn, you won't be cold for much longer."

My untimely shivers die out. "Finn," I say, "I'm going to give you my coat."

"Don't." She snatches Finn and holds the knife to his throat. "Headlines read, schizophrenic son following in father's footsteps. Kills victim's sister, then abused boy, then himself."

My muscles stiffen. I look at Finn, seeing myself in him. A boy too perplexed to be scared. He doesn't have a grip on his current reality. He doesn't understand one wrong move and he could die.

"No one's dying."

"Everyone's dying," she says, "And these kids, they died long before I ever killed them."

"You're crazy."

"Am I? You want to know what the initial response to all these kids dying is?"

I don't respond.

"They say they're in a better place, and the horrible reality is, that's true whether you believe in heaven or hell."

312

I notice she's gripping a small silver gun. I'm not sure when or where she got it from. Her coat is big so I'd have to assume it was in there.

"You know, I've been taking Finn here for over a year," she says. "Blake never once realized."

Ophelia glances at Olivia who's just emerged, face sweat-soaked, hands clutching a gun. She's here to save me. Ophelia pushes Finn on the ground, aiming the gun in my direction.

Not Finn's, not Olivia's, but mine.

A blast deafens me and Ophelia's bullet pierces through me. I blink and I'm on the icy ground, watching Olivia ricocheting backward after firing her gun at Ophelia. Tilting my head down, I glimpse at my aching chest. Blood spewing out. I look at Ophelia. Pieces of her head lay across the blood-painted snow.

Olivia, using her arms, drags the rest of her limp body closer to me.

"Cole, stay awake, please, stay awa…"

Drifting off, I hear a different voice, Grace's voice. "Cole, stay awake," she wails, "stay awake."

"Shut up!" A masked figure yells.

Pain shoots up from my lower abdomen. I glimpse down, disturbed by a fresh branding seared onto my skin.

O.M.

Grace's screams unnerve me. The horrid fumes of her burning flesh make my nose crinkle. Her bellows grow louder, drowning out the hissing of the branding iron. A figure dressed in thick black clothes, gloves, and a ski mask stands in front of her.

I'm exhausted and the intense burn in my stomach promises a near death.

"Protect her," Grace quivers. "Protect Olivia."

"Why…why me?"

"Because," she coughs, "The Cauterizing Killer…is your mother."

The masked figure injects me with something. My vision blurs fading back to the outside. Back to Green Point Lake.

Olivia's on her knees, palms on my chest, crying.

"What's going on?" Lying on the ground, I place my hands on my stomach. A puddle of blood alarms me. "Is this," I shudder, "my blood?"

Olivia sniffles before nodding. I can feel her tears drip onto my face. I want to make them stop, but I can't. Not this time.

"My dad…"

"He loves you, Cole. He always has."

I clench my jaws in pain and let out a small groan. I look at Olivia's hands, she's wearing the mittens I gave her.

"Take my beanie," I say.

"What?"

"Your ears, they're red."

She giggles over her cries. It's heartwarming, knowing one of the last sounds I'll hear is her giggle.

"I wanted to protect you," I mutter.

"You did."

She's shaking with sobs and I feel bad, because this is all my fault. "I'm sorry."

"Y-y-you have nothing to be sorry for."

I observe my surroundings. Where am I? I'm in my safe place. The place the nightmares don't follow.

I feel Olivia's frail hands holding mine. She says something that's hard to make out because of what sounds like a layer of water between us. "Cole, please, don't leave me."

Everything goes silent. The voices come to a halt.

As my reality comes to an end, so do the hallucinations and I realize something.

It doesn't matter what your reality is. If all you have is hope, you have more than most.

If all you have is the promise of tomorrow… you have more than me.

The Cynic

When I first met my wife, she wasn't crazy. Or at least I hadn't realized it. Kind of funny how that works. She was pregnant, with whose child I'll never know. I assume that's why she stopped killing kids, because she had one of her own. Regardless, I treated Finn like he was my son.

Ophelia and I never legally got married. I never met any of her friends or family members. All I knew was her name. Ophelia Monroe. And that was probably the only piece of truth she every willingly gave me.

I didn't know about the foster home burning down, or her sister, or even about her nephew. She was a mystery. And I didn't care. Because if the sex was good, that's all I needed. And trust me, the sex was *good*. She was a passionate woman who never feared initiative. But I guess she was too passionate and too initiative.

Our relationship was all love, until one day, when I was searching for something in the basement and stumbled across vile pictures of teenagers, children, infants. All with brandings. Some dead.

I knew about The Cauterizing Killer. Who didn't? But when I saw the branding on those pictures. Cole. The letters O.M.

Ophelia Monroe.

I knew. She was The Cauterizing Killer.

When I brought it up to her, she didn't deny it. I told her I was going to call the police and she told me we'd both burn. She told me she'd hurt Finn and when the police come, she'd blame me. Who would they believe? The house wife or the socially inept dad?

Even if Finn was hurt by his mother, he'd vouch for her. They always had a better relationship. Which is what makes this all the more sickening.

It's almost ironic, when it came to saving herself, the woman fighting abusers would become one.

I couldn't have her arrested, but I did kick her out. And that's what reinvigorated this all. She may say this is all justice but it's not. Not really. She was bored and wanted to correct all her shortcomings. Cole, Olivia, and Finn.

She is egotistical. I mean she burns her initials onto kids. There's no justification for that.

Now you may be wondering, how did an abuser marry someone that kills victims of abuse? You'd think it was paradoxical. It's not. Everyone hates abusers, yet everyday more and more people are ignorantly marrying them. And besides for that, I didn't always abuse Finn. It was only after she left that it started. When I had to care for him all alone. Being a parent is hard. I wouldn't wish it on my worst enemy. Which also happens to be my ex-wife.

Cole's pictures were time-stamped, like the rest of them. I didn't know it was Cole in the picture at first, but the more I saw him at school, the more I noticed the resemblance.

I googled Ophelia Monroe and there was only one result with her name; the burned down foster building. But below it was another article.

Elizabeth Monroe kills herself while family's out of town.

I was shocked when I saw the picture of Cole, his father, and Ophelia. Except it wasn't Ophelia. The article said it was her sister, Elizabeth. Cole's mom. And then I understood why she lived like a hermit. She couldn't risk Robert or Cole recognizing her in public.

I studied Ophelia's other pictures. The time stamps made evident Grace was with Cole when she died in Franklin. They were together there and somehow, unlike Grace, he managed to escape. To live.

I didn't understand it, but I knew his father did. Because he must've been in Franklin, too. What was really damning was that there was never a police report with Cole.

Mr. Torsney was hiding it. Because just like me, she found a way to keep him quiet. I didn't know if it was blackmail or pure fear. But one thing I knew: don't mess with Ophelia Monroe, she always gets her way...

The Stoic

The temperature keeps dropping; my breath becomes all the more discernible while Cole's has ceased entirely. His youthful body is lifeless. He's gone. In this glacial weather, if I don't start moving, I'll be, too. But I can't take my hands off of him. I can't stop staring at him. Someone taps my shoulder and I flinch.

"I-I-I'm cold."

Finn. I take my coat off and hand it to him. His discolored skin is almost indistinguishable from the snowflake-filled winds.

"I can't move." I've lost all feeling in my legs which are now buried.

"Where are my crutches?"

He doesn't speak. I can't make out if he's vibrating or if I am. I try hoisting myself up but fail. The sun begins to fade and the gray air is so thick that even if I could stand, I doubt I'd be able to find Mom's car.

I conclude either the pain from my legs will kill me or the snow will. All the same, I'm joining Cole. I lie down beside him, just like he did, the night he protected me from Jack. Finn's watching me, horror stricken. I figure only now he understands; we are both going to die.

Looking upward at Cole, I say, "I love you."

Then I close my eyes.

The Stoic

I open my eyes, softly. The familiar sound of monitors beeping and distant gurney wheels swiveling don't comfort me. I trace wires running from my hand into the sleeves of the hospital gown I'm wearing. I didn't make it to heaven, quite the opposite. I've made it to hell. Back in this confining hospital room. Gazing at the thin blanket covering my feet, I realize I can't feel my legs. And after all the pain they brought me, I can't tell if I'm relieved or concerned.

"The doctors said you won't be able to walk for a while."

I know that egotistical voice. I turn my head right. Dad sits on the chair beside me, wearing a navy parka with his zipper down. His t-shirt is dingy, like usual.

"What are you doing here, Dad?"

"What do you mean? You're my daughter, I wanted to check on you."

I roll my eyes. "Right, right."

This is something Dad often does. He acts like everything's fine when it's not. Like he's a caring father, when he's not.

There's only one thing I want to find out before I kick him out. "Where were you when Grace was taken?"

He looks away. "I don't remember. I was drunk."

I chuckle, "Right, I'm sure you don't."

He raises an eyebrow.

"Do you regret fucking her?" I ask.

He rises from the chair and turns away from me. He utters a dismissive, "You're insane."

Truth is, I probably am insane, but in the world we live in, being insane, is the only way to stay sane. Still, it doesn't diminish what I've discovered.

Dad's note: I hope we can do it again.

The texts he sent Ophelia.

The twenty five minutes they spent together in the bathroom.

And his car ending up in some random motel.

"Even after all this time, you still can't admit it," I say. "You don't have to. I already know the answer."

He turns back to me. Sweat along with denial clogs his pores. "What do you want me to admit, that I fucked the person that took my daughter's life? That I'm to blame for that kid's father going to jail? For Grace dying? For your legs? Well guess what, I'm not. That's on you. She wouldn't have come for us if you weren't fighting with Grace at the restaurant."

This is pointless, I know. Trying to show someone like him his errors is like trying to convince an astronaut the earth is flat. But the fire inside me won't stay silent.

"All of this," I say. "It's all on you." I was looking for Grace's killer, without understanding what that meant. You'd think, either the person that slit her throat killed her. Or the person that kidnapped her. But it's neither of their faults. You can't blame a fire for burning you. Who you can blame is the man that lit the match. The one who set things in motion. Cole's dad was forced to take Grace's life, only because Ophelia was targeting victims of abuse. But Dad, you were the abuser. If you were just a better father, a better man—no, if you were just a half decent human being—none of this would've happened."

Dad's parka creates a squishy sound as he crosses his arms. "I didn't kill anyone. I didn't end anyone's life."

"No, you did far worse. You gave her a life someone could perceive as not worth living. A life so bad someone felt obligated to take it from her."

He shakes his head, refusing to accept my words.

"Cole's dad was wrong for doing what he did, and so was Ophelia. But they both ended up with what they deserved. Yet, the one person that remains unpunished and unmoved, is you."

Dad storms to the door. It opens before he reaches it. Mom's there and he shimmies past her.

"I'm sorry honey; he wanted to see you."

I start sniffling.

Mom wraps her arm around me then catches me up.

Apparently, I've been asleep for four long days. I've missed Cole's funeral, which makes me all the more downcast.

When I passed out in the snow, Finn found my phone and after several attempts, unlocked it using my finger. He called my emergency contact: Johnny. He was already on his way. After I ran off the way I did at the police station, he called Mom, who gave him the password to Find My iPhone and tracked my precise location.

Snow kept falling and Finn kept using his hands as a shovel, preventing it from burying me. Johnny found us twenty minutes after Finn called. He's also been in the hospital these last four days, and Johnny hasn't left his side the entire time.

Mr. Torsney's trial is predicted to be a lengthy, convoluted one. I wouldn't be surprised if a book is made from this. Not that it would be any good, I mean all this stuff is highly implausible.

Mom hands me my phone after laying all this on me. It's cracked, but fully charged.

"I'm going to get that fixed for you," she assures.

"Mom, please don't worry about it."

I unlock it, spotting an unopened voicemail from four days ago. It's from Cole. I tap play.

"Hey Olivia, I wanted to tell you at the police station. The person I saw outside your house, that asked me to unlock the door was my mom. Or at least the hallucination of her. I saw her die and her body being buried. Yet, it seemed like it was her. I hallucinate her voice on a daily basis, so I'm sure I'm making this up, especially now that my father confessed. Anyways, the reason I'm telling you this is because I never want you to think I'm lying to you. All I've ever really wanted was someone to trust me. To rely on me. I'm a schizophrenic after all, I can't rely on myself. But you did. You trusted me. Put your faith in me. I let you down and I'm sorry. For all of this. I'm going to Mr. Haynes' house now. I hope you see this message and meet me there. I don't know what's real, but with you by my side you can tell me. We're good together. After all this is done, I look forward to sitting on your couch with Mocha on my lap. And when your mom tells me to get my arm off your shoulder, I won't listen, because life is short, and we have to make the most out of whatever time we have left."

The Stoic

Driving to Johnny's house, here in Fairview, I replay the nightmare that woke me up last night. The same one that's been waking me up the last three months.

Ophelia was holding Finn with a knife pressed against his throat. Cole was there, fretful until he saw me, then he turned hopeful, grateful. His foggy breath switching from heavy to relaxed. His eyebrows raising with glee.

I should've focused on Ophelia, I should've shot her right when I saw her, but seeing Cole, still alive...I just wanted to hug him.

But the bullet met him before I could. Then I woke up, relieved it was just a nightmare. Except it wasn't *just* a nightmare.

Cole's dead; Ophelia killed him. And what's crazier is, she could've saved herself by shooting me.

But her vendetta against Robert, it was more crucial than anything else. And when push came to shove, she wanted him in pain above all else.

In a way, it illustrates how all of this came from a place of anger. She was angry at Mr. Tornsey for how he treated her sister and Cole. This was all vengeance, not righteousness. And she got what she wanted. Robert is in pain, and in jail, reeling over Cole's death.

Though, she was wrong; the cycle of abuse, it can be broken. It has been broken. Finn is safe, healthy, and happy.

I'm safe, healthy and…I'm healthy.

I park on the curb outside Johnny's house. He moved here shortly after Finn was released from the hospital, getting a great deal on a split level.

The scent of freshly mown grass flourishes in the air as I step up to his mahogany door. I push the copper circular doorbell. No one answers. I push it once more. Through the oval fiberglass, a blurred figure is dashing nearer. The door swings open. Finn stands there with a disconcertingly white face.

I find it odd that Johnny allows Finn to open the door by himself. Especially after everything's that's occurred.

"Where's J—"

Finn grabs my hands in a haste, dragging me to his room. His small palms are moist with sweat. Upon reaching his rear first floor bedroom, he slams the door shut. The pacing in my heart is strong.

"What's going on?" I ask.

"Shh." Finn says, while pressing his index finger to his dry lips. He's panting. "This was a mistake. I saw his gun. It's not the type the police use; he's going to shoot me."

There must be some type of mistake. Johnny would never. He's a good g—

The whisky-colored door bursts open. Finn shrieks, rupturing my eardrums. Johnny emerges clasping a gun. The same one Finn mentioned. Johnny's eyes are filled with conviction. He's going to shoot Finn. He may even shoot me.

"Say hello to my little friend," Johnny says, in a horrible Arnold Schwarzenegger voice.

Finn leaps behind his ready-made bed. Then reappears holding a bigger dart gun and shoots Johnny multiple times. Johnny plays along, waggling his body to the beat of the foam bullets hitting him. Then he thuds onto the gray oak floor.

Finns jumps up and down on his bed. "Ha-ha, I got you."

Johnny rises. "You sure did, kiddo."

Finn descends from the bed. "Can we play again? Can we? Can we?"

"I'd love to play again," Johnny says. "But Olivia doesn't have a gun."

"Oh, oh, she can have mine," Finn says. "She'll protect me, just like Cole."

Johnny throws a ponderous look my way. "What do you say?"

"I say you better get running, because me and my little friend are a force to be reckoned with."

Johnny chuckles. "Quick, look behind you." He points to the shuttered window.

"Don't, it's a trick," Finn stresses.

I look behind me and Johnny rushes off.

"Olivia! He's getting away." Finn tosses me his dart gun and we chase after Johnny.

After the intense game and dinner, Finn's in the high-ceilinged living room, making imaginary snow angels in the extravagantly thick rug. I watch him from behind the pony wall in the kitchen. His eyes are glued to the large flat screen playing *Boy Meets World*.

I turn to Johnny who's washing dishes. "Finn really loves that rug."

Johnny shakes his frowning face. "That rug cost more than the down payment for this house."

He twists the faucet knob and tugs off his rubber gloves. White bubbles brimming from the sink follow his gloves as he tosses them on the counter. "I begged him to sit on the couch, but he refused. His dad would not allow it, said it was," Johnny used air quotes, "disrespectful."

Johnny pulls out a chair and sits on it. "I got a call from his school. He was in a fight, some older kid sucker punched him saying his mom was a loony. Finn then beat the crap out of him."

"He's been through a lot."

Johnny slowly nods.

I make my way to the couch, thinking about Cole. When he first told me Finn was abused, I didn't believe him. I knew Mr. Haynes. He couldn't hurt a fly if he tried, or so I thought. I flattered myself, thinking I knew what those kind of people acted like. I guess no matter how well you think you know a person, you never really do.

Finn lying on the rug, waves his feet in the air. His shark t-shirt isn't fully covering him. I catch a glimpse of a red bruise on his stomach. He rolls over and I notice there are a few more on his back. Were these from Blake or that kid Johnny told me about?

"Finn," I say.

He turns to me with a smile. The type of smile that makes you want to wrap your arms around him, trying to absorb his innocence.

"How does Johnny treat you?" I ask.

Finn's face turns ashen. "He treats me better than Mr. Haynes."

I look back at the flat screen. A moment passes before I realize that doesn't mean anything.

"But he doesn't... you know..."

His smile turns brittle. "He loves me."

Acknowledgements

Thank you to all the kind readers who read this book, and supported a young, 18-year-author. I honestly wrote this novel thinking only my family would read it, so you could imagine my shock when I sold more than 100 copies! Anyways, thank you again and if you enjoyed *In The Back Of My Head* please leave a review sharing your thoughts on Amazon.

Thank you, Mom, for never giving in. I wouldn't be here if it wasn't for your incredible willpower, endless sacrifices, and tremendous heart.

Thank you, Shimi, for being the **only** person in this world that has heard me out and not just supported me, but believed in me (and trust me, there's a difference). You've always been the first person I tell my future plans to and every time I do, you push me. And every time I get closer, I thank you. You are an innocent soul and as long as I live, I'll keep it that way.

Thank you, Tali, for being the light-hearted angel in my life. Before I left, you'd want me to tell you bedtime stories (that I'd create from the back of my head) and while you may be too young to read this now, I thank you for being one of the things that kept my imagination alive.

Thank you, Huvi, my highly esteemed editor, role model, and friend. This book would not be half of what it is without you. I don't confide in many people (I didn't tell anyone I was even writing this), but I knew I needed help: someone that had a pulse for stories, someone who could distinguish between paint on a canvas and true art, someone intelligent enough to read, not only books, but people. I needed an empathetic artist that I could respect enough to give me feedback, and that was you.

I don't think saying thank you is adequate, so I want you to know, when my book turns into a movie starring Jake Gyllenhaal, I'll make him hand-gift you the scarf.

Thank you, Hindy, for being someone who didn't have to say you cared about me, to let me know *you care about me*. You are one of the only people that I genuinely respect. I hope I grow to be at least a fraction of the person you are, because just that is a thousand times better than most.

Thank you, Leah. You've made my life (and my Shabbosim) easier. Thank you for being a positive Jewish influence in my life. I respect you in a way I could never put into words (which may be shocking considering I write). All I know is, the world would be a much better place if people were as giving, supporting, and understanding as you.

Thank you, Johanna, for taking time out of your day to answer and explain all my medical questions (no matter how odd they were). If I'm ever (God forbid) injected with pentobarbital, I'll make sure to call you...or an ambulance. (;

IN THE BACK OF MY HEAD

Made in the USA
Monee, IL
08 April 2022

94382282R00194